CW01084427

A GHOSTS OF SHADY LY NOVEL

Long before we Lingered...

A little human child called Hapwyne stood on the knoll with her pets: a white cat, a red dog, a black horse, and a pale bird. The animals could not see her enemy, but they all shared her fear as a cold wind rustled the leaves on the surrounding trees.

'Where do we go now?' Asked Uimywim, the cat.
'We hide in the caves below the knoll,' said Hapwyne.
They all agreed and followed her into the darkness.

'And what do we do now,' asked Arlyweh, the dog.
'You sit close to me and make your promises.'
They all agreed and moved closer to her.

'And after we promise?' asked Niyuwki the horse.
'You must protect me and save my humans.'
They all agreed and prepared to fight for her.

'Will *you* make a promise?' asked Tiyoawe, the bird.

Hapwyne nodded.

And the animals made their promises...

'Cats will save you from disease,' promised Uimywim.
'Dogs will protect your home,' promised Arlyweh.
'Horses will carry you far,' promised Niyuwki.
'Birds will guide you,' promised Tiyoawe.

Cat, dog, horse, and bird looked at Hapwyne.
She opened her hand.
They looked at the thing in her hand.

'What is that?' asked Uimywim.
'The Atorwitt fruit,' she said, 'I stole it from my enemy.'

'What does it do?' asked Arlyweh.
'You eat it, and it takes you where you need to go.'

'Who will eat it?' asked Niyuwki.
'We will.' Hapwyne split the fruit into five equal pieces.

'Only when you have made your *own* promise, will any of
us eat that,' said Tiyoawe.

Hapwyne agreed. And as she gave each of her pets a piece
of the Atorwitt fruit, she said,

'I promise that humans will always care for you.'

Satisfied with Hapwyne's promise, the animals ate up their
pieces of fruit.

But Hapwyne had not told them the true nature of the Atorwitt fruit. They barely felt the pain of the poison before death took them all. And as their bodies returned to the ground, the five pieces of fruit grew as branches from their stomachs, entwined, and bound their souls to linger as eternal ghosts.

Then the tangled branches grew out of the ground, to stand forever as, the Twisted Tree on the Knoll.

Some believe that the promise forever binds the souls of cats, dogs, horses, birds, and humans. Others reason that the promise has already broken, and now the pet begets the master's demise.

And so, we linger, until ashes and broken hearts, bear a cat so bent on revenge, that no human will ever sleep soundly again...

RATTERS

to Jordan,
hope you Enjoy it

This book is dedicated to Trouble, the teacher I once raised. The one who showed me where to find everything I needed to write this story.

Cats have protected humans from the Ills of Rodents so diligently, and for so long, it's almost as if they once promised to do so.

Anna Twist, CEO Ratevict.

All good things are wild and free.

Henry David Thoreau.

RATEVICT RATTERS | FAO C. Frost. Quote 10-08-2032-PMD – Perfect Mountain Depot Ltd. Shadleigh Industrial Estate, Mercehampton, MC12 1SL

	Registered Ratevict Name	Gen.	M/F	Mother	Father	Description	Tattoo	C	S	M	R	P	Total	Hire cost
1	Nipanholt Wild Rose	1	Female	Nipanholt Wildberry	Wrangland Steppingstone	LH. Solid Red E. Green	0000 0001 0001 (17)	5	3	2	4	5	19	£950.00
2	Nipanholt Free Violet	1	Female	Nipanholt Wildberry	Wrangland Steppingstone	LH. Solid Blue E. Green	0000 0001 0010 (18)	5	4	5	4	4	22	£1,100.00
3	Grenfider Gloworm	1	Male	Snawdun Icicle	Grenfider Glitterbug	LH. White E. Blue	0000 0001 0101 (21)	3	5	4	3	4	19	£950.00
4	Aldorholt Dream Dust	1	Male	Dellmere Dawn Breeze	Aldorholt Barkchip	LH. Brown Tabby E. Yellow	0000 0001 1000 (24)	5	5	5	5	5	25	£1,250.00
5	Doxianren Edge Briar	1	Male	Daelbeorg Dewfrost	Doxianren Dark Cloud	SH. Brown Tabby E. Yellow	0000 0001 1100 (28)	5	3	4	4	5	21	£1,050.00
6	Faestburn Hill Fern	1	Female	Faestburn Fair Flurry	Aigreot Hot Ash	SH. Tortoiseshell E. Yellow	0000 0010 0010 (34)	4	4	5	3	3	19	£950.00
7	Graesdun Tor Spinney	1	Male	Haedaleaf Setting Sun	Graesdun Great Stem	SH. White & Red E. Green	0000 0010 0101 (37)	4	5	4	5	4	22	£1,100.00
8	Eascraef Blue Onyx	1	Female	Beorhtstan Bangle	Eascraef Rock Hawk	SH. Solid Black E. Blue	0000 0010 1010 (42)	5	4	5	4	5	23	£1,150.00
9	Brauntreo Black Conker	1	Male	Hwitsol High Brook	Brauntreo Redthorn	LH. Solid Black E. yellow	0000 0010 1110 (46)	5	4	4	3	4	20	£1,000.00
												Total Annual Hire Cost		£9,500.00

Hire charged @ £50.00** per score point* up to a maximum of 25 points; £1,250.00 per year

*Score points are a guide only and cannot guarantee performance of Ratter over time.

**Price correct as of 01.01.2032. subject to change.

C	Constitution
S	Sociability
M	Manageability
R	Readiness
P	Predacity

The Boxes (PMD warehouse and Office)

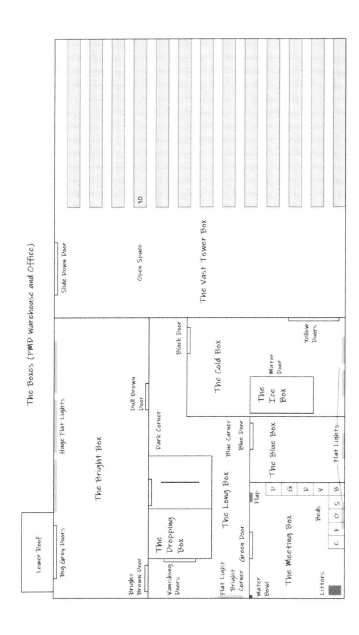

Basement One

The Vanishing Doors

The Dropping Box

The Under Box

The Nook

White Door

Red Door

The Healing Box

Basement Two

The Vanishing Doors

The Dropping Box

The Orange Door

The Water Box

The Channel

Contents

Prologue: Welcome to PMD 1

Chapter 1 – The Meeting Box 9

Chapter 2 – A Little Bit More 17

Chapter 3 – The Game 25

Chapter 4 – The Long Box 35

Chapter 5 – Know Your Territory 41

Chapter 6 – Ratbots 45

Chapter 7 – Food 51

Chapter 8 – Scouting 61

Chapter 9 – The Blue Box 69

Chapter 10 – The Hunt 77

Chapter 11 – Leaders 89

Chapter 12 – Know Your Cats 99

Chapter 13 – The Healing Box 103

Chapter 14 – The Code 113

Chapter 15 – Icicle 121

Chapter 16 – Boirey 131

Chapter 17 – The Bright Box 143

Chapter 18 – The Moving Box 153

Chapter 19 – The Only Way 161

Chapter 20 – The Only Cat 171

Chapter 21 – The Engel's Tale 179

Chapter 22 – Lullaby 189

Chapter 23 – Watch Lights 201

Chapter 24 – The Water Box 213

Chapter 25 – When Your Territory Goes bad 221

Chapter 26 – Chances 225

Chapter 27 – Light Bumps 235

Chapter 28 – The Roof 243

Chapter 29 – When Your Cats Go Bad 251

Chapter 30 – Up 255
Chapter 31 – Lament 261
Chapter 32 – Holes 275
Chapter 33 – Doors 285
Chapter 34 – The Ice Box 295
Chapter 35 – Shadow White 303
Chapter 36 – What She found 311
Chapter 37 – A Twisted Tree 321

Bonus Scene – Onyx 333
Bonus Scene – Conker 335
Bonus Scene – Fern 337
Bonus Scene – Violet 341
Bonus Scene – Spinney 343
Bonus Scene – Briar 345
Bonus Scene – Gloworm 347
Bonus Scene – Rose 349

Prologue
Welcome to PMD

THE BRIGHT MORNING SUN SAT LOW in the clear blue sky. Three crows circled high on the breeze above Fiona as she waited on the grass verge by the reservoir, her back to the warehouse car park. She watched the sunlight dance on the water as she listened to the muffled meows rumbling around inside the Ratevict van behind her. There was one cage left, secured in the back of the van, and covered in a heavy blanket. She glanced at her watch, sighed, and let her eyes wander back across the glistening surface of the water...

'Oy! Miss ... er ...Whatever.'

Fiona looked up to see a gaunt, icy eyed youth of around nineteen frowning at her from the warehouse foyer. She straightened her curly red hair and green tunic, but she couldn't stop her shoulders sagging as she recognised her supervisor. He was wearing the same white lab coat and ripped jeans he'd worn at her interview, and it didn't look as though he'd washed his greasy black hair or shaved his stubbly chin since. She didn't know how he'd become a supervisor of anything, but her first day was not the time for questions like that, so she greeted him with a polite smile and said, 'Good morning, Mr Frost. It's Ms Best, Fiona Best.'

1

Mr Frost curled his upper lip and replied. 'Well, now you're here, you can bring that last Ratter inside.'

The forlorn meows of the last cat quietened as Fiona hurried over to the Ratevict van and pulled the back doors open, and as the sunlight reflected off the windows, she was reminded of her instructions...

14. Ratters must be shrouded when transported outside.

14.1.   *Never expose a Ratter to external light or stimuli, including scents, sights, and sounds. Doing so will cause distress to the animal...*

Leaning into the van, she checked over the heavy blanket. It was damp and smelt of bleach, but it was okay, the cat was completely covered. Fiona wasn't sure that shrouding any cat from the outside world was okay, but those were her orders.

'Come on then...' she read the label, 'Aldorholt Dream Dust. R24. Male. Long haired brown tabby.' Carefully she slid the large cage towards her and lifted it from the back of the van. The cat was heavy, and as she put the cage down on the ground, claws scraped its bare metal floor.

'Quickly!' Mr Frost was holding the foyer door open.

Fiona closed the van doors, picked up the cage and hurried toward the warehouse. As she walked, she stared up at the huge dreary box, nonchalantly crafted in cold grey metal and slumped on top of an office of uniform red bricks. Through the large dusty windows at the front, two ladies in flowery blouses smiled at her, and a young woman in a red uniform shirt, waved. Fiona returned their smiles and waves, and quietly wondered how anyone could be so excited by the arrival of the unfortunate cats who'd try to make this soulless place their home.

Mr Frost drummed his fingers on the door, then let it go.

Fiona hurried after him and made a desperate grab for it, almost trapping her fingers as she struggled to pull it open again with the heavy cage in her hands.

'Oh! is this the last one, Craig?' asked a flowery-bloused lady from behind the reception desk.

Mr Frost ignored her and picked up a clip board.

Fiona struggled through the door and hurried to the desk. Her hand was beginning to sting from the cage's narrow metal handle, so she put it down at her feet as she caught her breath.

Claws scraped metal.

'Hello, you must be Fiona, said the lady, 'I'm Janice, and that's Helen, and that's Steph from the warehouse,' Janice waved her hand around the office. Fiona smiled and nodded to everyone, and Janice went on, 'Welcome to PMD...' she lowered her voice and whispered with a conspirative glance at Mr Frost, '...what's this kitty called?'

'Dream Dust,' Fiona told her.

'Oh, how sweet, they all have such—'

'Aldorholt Dream Dust is the Registered Ratevict name for this animal,' Mr Frost looked up from his clipboard and glared at Fiona. 'You can read their tattoo's, right?'

23. Understanding Ratter ear tattoos.

23.1.   All Ratters have a binary ear tattoo for ease of marking and identification.

23.2.   All Ratevict employees must learn to read the tattoos, see appendix 7.3...

Fiona had been ready for sleep by the time she'd read to directive twenty-three. She understood the idea behind the tattoos, but as she'd only be caring for nine cats, she wasn't worried. She'd get to know them all by sight quickly enough. 'Of course,' she told Mr Frost.

'Good. Now follow me.'

Fiona smiled apologetically to Janice, picked up the cage and followed Mr Frost towards a brown door in the back corner of the office. This time, under the watchful gaze of the other staff, he held it open for her. She followed him into a dimly lit corridor. The door swung closed behind them.

'Right,' Mr Frost mumbled as he turned over a sheet on his clipboard.

Fiona gripped the cage handle in both hands. There wasn't enough room in the cluttered corridor to put it down, and she didn't want to lean any closer to Mr Frost and his overpowering odour of damp ponds, so she leant back against the door. The cat shifted below the blanket. She silently thanked his frightened little soul for being so patient.

'Okay,' Mr Frost looked up, 'This is simple, so you should understand.'

Fiona raised an eyebrow ... and nodded.

Mr Frost frowned, 'I was hoping for someone younger,' he leant back and looked Fiona up and down, 'aren't vet techs supposed to be young? Will you be able to cope?'

The cat in the cage hissed.

Fiona tightened her grip on the handle and silently told the cat not to worry, she may be old enough to be Mr Frost's mother, but she was not too old to care for cats. Then she smiled and said, 'I'll be fine, I'm a registered veterinary nurse with an advanced diploma in small animal—'

'Ratters are big.'

Fiona took a deep breath. She didn't want to get on the wrong side of him, but she knew her job. 'Mr Frost,' she said politely, 'these cats are cross bred from large domestic breeds, but they are mostly hand reared and handled since birth, so, pliant. And the largest cat here is only seven and a half kilograms, so—'

'Ratters are not cats. Crazy old women have cats. Warehouses with rat problems have Ratters. Try not to get ... emotionally confused.'

Fiona took another deep breath.

Mr Frost went on, 'Ratters are a business asset. An investment for companies, like these people, who want to protect their stuff from rodent damage. They are scientifically bred from some special bloodlines then intensively trained for six-months to track and hunt rodents in industrial places like this. They don't care about fuss, or laps, or catnip. Or you. And before you ask, no — they can't escape. They won't even try. These animals don't even know the outside world exists. And I have CCTV in case anyone gets any stupid ideas. A Ratter's only purpose is exterminating vermin. A Ratter is not a cat, do you understand?'

2. What is a Ratevict Ratter?

2.1.   A Ratter is a large breed of cat...

Fiona nodded.

'Good. Now, these first-generation Ratters all excelled at killing Ratbots—'

'Ratbots?' Fiona asked.

'It means, Remote-control Attention Training Battle Offensive Targets, didn't you—'

'Like those cute little mousy cat toys?' she chanced a smile.

'No.' Mr Frost sneered, 'Ratbots are designed to simulate vicious wild rodents, not for having fun with little pets. These Ratters are the best predators in their generation, and I have been given the job of studying their effectiveness against real rats. So, I will decide how these animals are managed, and you will follow my orders. Do you understand?'

Fiona nodded again.

The cat in the cage growled.

'Good. Let's get it to its cupboard.'

Cupboard...? Fiona didn't like the sound of that, and she didn't like the look of the cluttered corridor either. Too many cardboard boxes, stuffed full of paper and precariously stacked against the walls, didn't make this a safe environment for any animals, cats, or rats... 'So,' she asked, 'are there really any rats here? It's a paper document storage warehouse, isn't it?'

'Of course, there's rats here. Why do you think PMD agreed to the Ratevict Ratters trial?'

'But why would there be rats here? They infest food storage warehouses not—'

'Because of the ancient underground tunnels,' Mr Frost smirked.

Fiona doubted that any modern warehouse would have ancient underground tunnels, but she didn't want to ask any more questions. She followed him through the cluttered corridor, past a small lift and around a corner to where an elderly black man with frizzy white hair and blue overalls stood waiting patiently in front of a tatty green door.

'Get ready to open it,' Mr Frost demanded.

The elderly man gave him a curt nod and gripped the door handle.

Mr Frost turned to Fiona, 'Put the cage on the floor, remove the blanket, open the cage door and back away. knock when you are ready to come out. Do you understand?'

'Yes.'

'When you're done, take the lift to Basement One. Our lab is the white door. You can't miss it.' And without waiting for her to reply, he turned and walked back towards the lift.

Fiona waited for him to go, then said to the elderly man, 'Hi, I'm Fiona. This is the last cat, I think.'

'John. John Bonner, or slow old John,' he chuckled, 'It should be the last one, I fetched all the others in. Poor little lad. Is it a lad?'

Fiona smiled, 'Hey, John ... er, yes, he is a lad, his name is Dream Dust.'

John nodded.

The cat in the box shifted.

'Be careful,' John whispered as he opened the green door, 'That young Craig Frost ... watch out for him. I just does the mopping down 'ere, but if I missed a spot ... well, he'd tell his dad and I'd lose my job.'

'Thank you,' Fiona whispered.

John's warning made her feel uneasy, but not uncomfortable as she felt carrying the last Ratter into his new home. She put the cage down gently behind the other eight in the middle of the cold damp floor. The cupboard, as Mr Frost had called it, was a room no bigger than her own living room. A cat flap had been hastily installed in one wall. Battered cardboard boxes lined the outer walls around the far corner, bulging with paper and strewn with dirty, threadbare towels.

John pulled the door closed.

On the wall above the cardboard boxes, a small, frosted window let in just enough light to bathe the room in a soft blue glow. A dusty and long ago blown light bulb hung from the middle of the yellowing ceiling tiles on frayed cables. Too unsafe to be used. The air was stuffy and reeked of bleach and musty paper.

Fiona felt a pang of guilt as she knelt and carefully peeled the blanket off the cage. When she opened it, Aldorholt Dream Dust licked his lips and shuffled backwards. And as she stood again and looked around, her eyes caught flashes of colourful fur and flickers of sadness in bright frightened eyes. She picked up the blanket and knocked lightly on the door. Glancing back at the cages on her way out, she whispered, 'Good luck'.

1

The Meeting Box

'GOODLUCK...'

The gentle voice of the female human lingered in his ears even after her footsteps had faded away. Dust curled himself up in the back of his trap. He felt alone. He'd never felt so alone. But as he closed his eyes, his exhausted senses tore at him, screaming that his feelings were wrong. He lifted his head and parted his jaws to taste the air, searching for whatever they were trying to tell him. Yearning for that one familiar scent in the fetid amalgam of smells around him.

There.

His skin tingled. His fur rose along his spine.

Cats.

He was surrounded by cats.

Dust opened his eyes and peered out of his trap. He was inside a large box. There were other traps around his, softly illuminated by the blue glow of a small flat light. They were silent at first, but as he manoeuvred his ears, he heard breathing. He crept forward. Nearby, claws scraped against metal.

Dust stopped and listened. His ears found more sounds. Panting, scratching, shuffling. He counted eight more traps scattered around his own, and there was a cat in each one. He took another step forward and opened his jaws to

9

decipher their scents. The closest cat was a tom. His fear scent was strong and his breathing shallow. *Frightened tom...*

Dust stepped out of his trap, stretched his neck, and sniffed. The frightened tom shuffled back and licked his lips. He tried to think of a word of comfort, but his thoughts were interrupted by a deep voice that came from behind him.

'Who are you?'

Dust raised his tail and curled its tip in a friendly gesture. When he turned his head, he saw two cats watching him from the far side of the box. A brown tabby tom, much like himself, but with shorter fur, broader shoulders, and inquisitive deep yellow eyes. Behind the tom sat a small silver tabby she-cat, blinking slowly at him with curious bright grey eyes.

Frightened tom. Brown tabby tom. Silver tabby she-cat... Dust memorised the cats as he dipped his head, ready to greet them.

The brown tabby tom sniffed the air and without waiting for Dust's reply, meowed, 'All of you. Who are all of you?'

Dust sat down and looked around at the other traps.

A heartbeat later, a bold sweet voice replied, 'I'm Violet,' and a tall and elegant she-cat stepped out of her trap and looked around. Her long grey fur shone silver in the blue glow of the flat light, and her gentle eyes were deep green.

Frightened tom. Brown tabby tom. Silver tabby she-cat. Violet, grey she-cat...

'Thank you, Violet,' meowed the brown tabby tom, 'I'm—'

'VIOLET!'

Claws scrabbled on metal as a red she-cat, as tall and elegant as Violet, with eyes of brilliant green, thrashed her way out of her trap and gazed around, panting. 'Violet! It's Rose, Violet, where are you?'

Frightened tom. Brown tabby tom. Silver tabby she-cat. Violet, grey she-cat. Rose, red she-cat...

'Rose?' Violet curled her tail up and padded forward slowly, her green eyes widened as she scanned the box, 'Rose? Is that you, I'm here, I'm over here.'

Rose leapt forward, her fluffy red tail streaming out behind her as she shoved traps aside in her rush to get to Violet. Dust felt a shudder of warmth wash through him as he watched the she-cats entwine their tails and greet each other with happy purrs and delighted chirps.

'Violet, it's you!'

'Oh, my goodness, Rose. Yes, it's me. I didn't think I'd ever see you again. I was so scared when they took me ... I ... I thought I'd ...'

'I won't let them take you again,' Rose growled.

'And you are?' the brown tabby tom meowed as he flicked his tail towards the red she-cat.

Rose lifted her head from Violet's neck, her brilliant green eyes went wide as she turned to glare at the tom, and holding his gaze unflinchingly, she growled, 'I am Rose, and Violet is my sister.'

The brown tabby tom held Rose's gaze, 'Sisters, good, I'm happy for you.'

Rose hissed and swished her tail.

'Rose,' Violet mewed softly, 'I've missed you. We have much to catch up on, come with me.'

Rose looked back at her sister and nodded.

Dust let out his breath as Violet draped her tail over Rose's back and led her to the end of a stack of full boxes.

Other cats shifted in their traps.

The brown tabby tom watched the sisters move away, then flicked his tail again, 'Okay, so who are the rest of you?'

'Who wants to know?' a she-cat mewed tartly from the far corner.

Dust watched as a smooth furred black she-cat with curled ears, deep blue eyes, and a long thick tail stepped gracefully between the traps. He dipped his head as she passed him, and she flicked an ear in reply.

The brown tabby tom twitched his whiskers and waited for the black she-cat to sit down in front of him and shuffle herself comfortable. Then he mewed, 'I am Briar.'

The black she-cat dipped her head, 'I am Onyx, it's lovely to meet you, Briar. Are you in charge?'

Frightened tom. Briar, brown tabby tom. Silver tabby she-cat. Violet, grey she-cat. Rose, red she-cat. Onyx, black she-cat...

Briar sniffed, 'I was the first to arrive and I've already explored this box.'

'And what did you find?' Onyx purred.

Briar lifted his head and flicked his ears around the box, 'There's a door where the humans come in, and a flap over there. There's water, but no food, and litters, and those full boxes.'

Dust sat down and let his eyes follow Briar's ears around the box. The transparent flap near the grubby green door looked clean and new. The row of stacked full boxes that clustered around a corner looked old and dirty, they were strewn with equally old and tatty covers. Above them, a rectangular flat light glowed bright blue. In the opposite corner, a fresh and full water bowl sat on the floor, and above it, high up on the wall, a little red light flickered from inside a small black box. There was no food by the water bowl yet, but that didn't surprise him. The litters at the end of the full boxes were familiar and unused. The floor was hard and cold, covered in human footprints and it seeped the same sour damp smell as the trap covers. The roof was made of yellowish-white squares, set into tarnished grey lines. A large drip light hung from its centre, like the ones in the Old Place, except this this one was crusted with dirt. Dust looked at Briar and twitched his whiskers, *He hasn't explored... he hasn't been out of his trap...*

'Anything else?' Onyx mewed.

'The female human with red head fur and green covers said "Goodluck",' Briar hung his head and shook it sorrowfully, 'It means goodbye. I don't think they'll be coming back.'

'Well, it's a good job that you're in charge then, Briar,' Onyx flicked him playfully with her tail, 'I never listen to human words ... I only watch their eyes.'

Briar snorted, 'Well, I'm not—'

'They'll bring food when we catch the Ratbots.' A deep friendly meow interrupted Briar.

Dust looked around to see a large tom with long black fur, a thick mane, tufted ears, and bright amber eyes stride boldly across the floor. He sat down next to Onyx and dipped his head to Briar.

Briar nodded, 'I haven't seen a Ratbot yet, and I've been here a while now.'

'So, who are you?' Onyx curled her tail as she looked the black tom up and down, 'Briar wants to know.'

The black tom purred, 'Tell Briar that I am Conker, and ask him why he *needs* to know.'

Onyx nodded to Conker, then looked at Briar.

Frightened tom. Briar, brown tabby tom. Silver tabby she-cat. Violet, grey she-cat. Rose, red she-cat. Onyx, black she-cat. Conker, black tom...

Briar raised his head, 'I was put in a trap and bought to this box. It's different to the other boxes I've known, and it's strange that we are all here together. But we don't need to be strangers.'

'We're not strangers, we are sisters,' Rose hissed.

Violet purred reassuringly to calm her.

'You are,' Briar continued, 'but I don't see my littermates. And maybe no other cat here will either. My point is that, as we are all in this ... Meeting Box together, it's in our best interests to get along.'

'He's right,' Onyx mewed, 'let's all be friends.'

Dust felt the cats around him relax, their fear scent began to soften, and as he looked from Briar to Onyx to Conker and then over to Rose and Violet beside the full boxes, he saw fur flatten and tails curl as curiosity replaced anxiety.

'I agree,' Conker sat up tall and looked around, 'So who's left that we haven't met yet?'

Dust rose to his paws, ready to step forward and introduce himself, but he hesitated as the frightened tom sniffed. He peered through the small holes in the side of the trap and saw a tuft of trembling white fur.

'Hi! I'm Spinney.' A slender orange and white tom with green eyes and a stripy tail leapt over a trap and slid to a halt just before he barrelled into Conker.

Frightened white tom. Briar, brown tabby tom. Silver tabby she-cat. Violet, grey she-cat. Rose, red she-cat. Onyx, black she-cat. Conker, black tom. Spinney, orange and white tom...

'Sorry, I was asleep, did I miss anything?' Spinney purred as he dipped his head to Onyx, ignoring the toms sat either side of her.

'Everything, Spinney,' purred Onyx, 'I'll fill you in later, we still have cats to meet.

Dust padded slowly to the front of the white tom's trap and mewed quietly, 'Come on out, no cat here will hurt you.'

The tom shivered and backed away.

'I'm Fern, pleased to meet you all,' a sweet voice mewed from the other side of the box.

Dust watched as a sleek tortoiseshell she-cat with pale yellow eyes and a long thin tail stepped daintily towards the group of cats.

Frightened white tom. Briar, brown tabby tom. Violet, grey she-cat. Rose, red she-cat. Onyx, black she-cat. Conker, black tom. Spinney, orange and white tom. Fern, tortoiseshell she-cat...

'Pleased to meet you, Fern,' Conker dipped his head.

'Good to meet you too,' purred Onyx.

'Hi, Fern,' Spinney greeted her with a friendly nod.

'So, who's left?' Briar looked at Dust.

Dust caught Briar's eye and nodded, then he flicked an ear to the trap beside him. 'I'm Dust, but this tom here, he's very scared ... and I think he's injured, I can smell blood.'

'Blood?' Briar meowed loudly.

'Can he get out of his trap?' Conker mewed.

'Let me help, I've helped injured cats before,' Violet padded towards the tom's trap. Rose followed but stopped a few paces back and sat down in front of the full boxes, her head low and her eyes trained on her sister.

Dust moved to let Violet see into the trap.

'Hey there,' Violet purred, 'don't be afraid, we are all friends now, but we can't all get in your trap to meet you, so you will have to come out.'

The white tom sighed, 'Yes, you're right.' And with a grunt, he shuffled to his paws and stepped towards Violet. As he emerged from the trap, Dust could see that his gait was stiff and unsteady, and dried blood matted the long white fur on his hind leg. His big blue eyes were full of pain.

'Come and sit with me and my sister. You need to stay warm if you're injured, and I'll look at your wound,' Violet gave the tom's ear a reassuring lick.

'Thank you,' the tom lifted his head, 'My injury is my own fault. I tried to escape, and a human caught me by my leg ... it hurts, but I should introduce myself first. My name is Gloworm, and my Mother Name is Maer'sik Kiru.

Gloworm, white tom. Briar, brown tabby tom. Violet, grey she-cat. Rose, red she-cat. Onyx, black she-cat. Conker, black tom. Spinney, orange and white tom. Fern, tortoiseshell she-cat... Dust shook his head as he looked around the cats. He went through their names again, trying to remember, *Gloworm, white. Briar, brown tabby. Violet, grey. Rose, red. Onyx, black. Conker, black. Spinney, orange and white. Fern, tortoiseshell.* That was all of them, but he was sure there'd been another cat in the Meeting Box.

2

A Little Bit More

'YOU HAVE A MOTHER NAME?' BRIAR padded after Gloworm.

'I knew her well,' Gloworm stopped and turned to Briar, 'Her name is Icicle. She told me my father's name is Glitterbug, and she told me many stories ... some I remember, some not. But I'll always remember the name she gave me, and its meaning. Maer'sik Kiru, means, "*Seek Dreams in the Trees*". I don't know why she gave me that name, or how she expected me to find my dreams. I don't even know what trees are... But this new place is not like any of the places in her stories.'

An uneasy shiver ran along Dust's spine, from the base of his neck to the tip of his tail as Gloworm spoke. *Did this cat really remember his mother...?*

Violet rested her tail lightly over Gloworm's shoulder and turned him back towards Rose, 'Come on, you can rest while you talk.'

Dust saw the sadness in Gloworm's eyes as he slumped down beside Violet. Conker and Onyx exchanged confused glances with Fern and Spinney. Briar remained where he stood, studying the injured tom with suspicious eyes. Dust felt compelled to speak up, even though his own memories were hazy. He stepped forward and dipped his head to Gloworm, 'I also remember my mother.'

Rose growled.

Briar flicked his tail, 'You too?'

Dust nodded, 'Her name is Breeze ... I don't remember her giving me a Mother Name, or much about her, but every time I think of her, I get the feeling that I need to escape. It's as if she wants me to get out.'

'Out? Out where?' Spinney mewed.

Dust shook his head, 'I don't know...'

'Out of The Boxes? Onyx tipped her head to one side.

'Why would any cat want to go out?' Conker mewed. 'we're safe enough here.'

'My mother, Icicle...' Gloworm mewed, 'she believed in The Outside. An endless place—'

Briar interrupted Gloworm. 'My mother's name is Dewfrost, and my father is Dark Cloud. Dewfrost named me Skar'esi Risi. I don't know what it means, and I don't care. And the only useful thing she ever said was "*Never forget you're a cat.*"'

'Icicle believed—'

'I believe,' Briar interrupted Gloworm again, 'that our mothers named us all, and spoke kind words to give us hope. Maybe we remember our mothers, maybe we don't, but they are gone now, so their words are worthless.'

'You knew your mother,' Rose growled, 'yet you think her words are worthless?'

Dust cringed at the anger in Rose's voice, and at the sorrow in Violet's eyes. He wondered if they had known their mother too. His own hazy memories of Breeze were important to him, even if he couldn't recall anything about her. *Maybe I will someday...*

'I'm just saying that we'd be better off concentrating on where we are now, not worrying about where we came from,' Briar glared at Rose.

Conker got to his paws and flicked his tail to get every cat's attention. 'How about we treasure our memories and concentrate on winning some food.'

'But ... I don't see any Ratbots, Fern mewed, padding to Conker's side.

'They'll be here,' Onyx got to her paws. 'Let's look. There's always Ratbots in new boxes.'

'So, let's find them,' Spinney jumped up and followed Onyx as she began padding slowly around the walls.

Dust hopped up onto a full box and watched the cats as they moved around the Meeting Box. *Gloworm white, Briar brown tabby, Violet grey, Rose red, Onyx black, Conker black, Spinney orange and white, Fern tortoiseshell. Eight cats, not nine...* He lowered his head onto his paws and listened to their curious mewings. All the Ratbot boxes in the Old Place had been bright, quiet, and big enough for a cat to get into a good run. This box was small, just two good leaps from side to side. And it was noisy, the sound of paw steps barely audible over the reverberating background hum. Muffled bangs and thuds loitered around the edges of Dust's hearing, sliding in and out of existence on the muted murmurs of human utterings. *Many humans...*

'They'll come soon,' Spinney mewed, 'there's always fresh water in Ratbot boxes. I liked to drop them in it.'

'I like your thinking,' Onyx purred.

'I kept away from them,' Fern mewed softly, 'I hid under the ledges and curled up until the humans got bored of bashing their hideous Ratbots into me...'

Conker stepped towards Fern, 'Your scent, I thought it was familiar, I remember it now from the Turn Box.'

'You must have been taken there after they'd dragged me out,' Fern dipped her head to the black tom.

'I wondered if I'd ever get to meet you. Your scent was so full of fear...'

Dust remembered the Turn Box, where Ratbots would scoot around corners and come back out from under the ledges behind you. He had smelt cat scent in those old boxes too, but not the scent of any cat here now.

'Did we all come from the same Old Place?' Briar asked.

'I did. I remember the Turn Box,' Spinney mewed, 'It was fun catching the Ratbots in there.'

'Fun?' Onyx snorted, 'I don't remember anything about Ratbots being fun.'

Gloworm winced as Violet helped him to his paws and led him to the water bowl. He slumped down on his side as the grey she-cat began cleaning the dried blood from his matted fur.

Briar joined them, 'Where did you learn to heal wounds?' he asked Violet.

'In the Old Place. Rose was not careful catching the Ratbots. She got hurt sometimes, and she'd never let any human look at her wounds.'

'So, you healed her?' Briar mewed.

'The best I could. I don't remember the Turn Box as I was alone in the Grey Box most of the time, but when I met other cats, I would help them too.'

'Thank you, Violet,' Gloworm mewed, 'my wound feels better already.'

'It's the best I can do, Gloworm. Your leg is still sore and swollen, and it will need a lot of rest and warmth and time to heal.'

'You *are* good at this,' Briar purred.

Rose circled behind Violet and hissed, 'Of course she's good.'

Violet flicked her sister's ear with the tip of her tail, 'You gave me lots of practice.'

Dust flattened his ears and parted his jaws, concentrating on the scents around him. Briar's fear scent strengthened as Rose circled, and so did Violet's, but the collective cat scent in the Meeting Box had lost its fearful tang. The only other familiar scent was the sour damp that clung to the floor. But here, it had a staleness to it that he'd not noticed in the Old Place. Here, a thick frowsty stench clung to the walls and the full boxes, making all other scents harder to decipher.

'Dust?' Gloworm's claws tore into the full box as he scrambled awkwardly up beside him.

'Gloworm,' Dust shifted to give the injured tom more room, 'how's your leg?'

'I don't think I'll be chasing Ratbots for a while, but it will be okay, thanks to Violet.'

Dust nodded, 'I'll help you with the Ratbots, and we are lucky to have a cat like her.'

'Yes, Rose must have been ruthless for her sister to have gained such well-practiced skills. For littermates, they couldn't be more different.' Gloworm purred, 'What about you, do you have littermates?'

'No,' Dust shook his head, 'I was alone. I didn't meet any other cat until I was big enough to climb onto ledges.'

Gloworm rested his tail lightly on Dust's back, 'But your mother, you said you remember her?'

'I remember her, but I remember nothing about her. I don't even know what she looks like.' Dust shivered as bright grey eyes blinked in his mind. 'Gloworm,' he mewed, 'I saw another cat in here, a silver tabby she-cat. She was sitting behind Briar when we came out of the traps, but she isn't here now. Was I imagining my mother?'

'Remembering, maybe,' Gloworm took a deep breath before he went on, 'sometimes I see Icicle ... often after something has frightened me. And new places are frightening. They can feel so unreal that even our most distorted memories become a comforting reality in comparison.'

'I think I understand,' Dust mewed, 'but every time I try to remember her, the memories just fade away ... like the scent of water on my tongue.'

'That used to happen to me,' Gloworm purred, 'until I learned how to find my memories. Even the ones that didn't want to be found.'

'How?' Dust turned to see Gloworm's eyes glaze over.

'Close your eyes and concentrate on the noises around you ... then separate them. Stretch your mind and push the noises apart, just enough to let in a little bit more ... and more of your memories will slip through the gaps in the noise.'

Dust nodded, 'That sounds hard,' he wasn't sure what Gloworm meant, but he wanted to try. He closed his eyes and listened.

Gloworm purred and shifted beside him, wincing as he moved his injured leg, 'It's difficult at first, it took me a long time to get it right...'

Onyx and Spinney scratched at the litter box, 'These are the same...' they muttered quietly together.

Fern and Conker groomed each other in the corner behind the water bowl, their quiet purrs content and comforting, 'Don't worry, I will help you catch them...'

Briar padded around the door, sniffing at the gap below it, 'It's lighter behind this door...'

Rose and Violet dozed at the other end of the full boxes, Violet's breathing deep and steady, Rose's rapid and anxious like a cat cornered. She sniffed. She wasn't asleep.

Dust listened to their noises ... then he pushed them apart. Away from each other. Right out to the edges of his mind.

Breeze...

More noises flooded into his mind. Human voices, hectic and distant. Humming... clanging... thumping... He listened to them ... then slid them aside.

Breeze ... I need to remember you...

'Dust...'

His skin prickled. A cold touch ruffled his fur. Silent paw steps padded around him.

Breeze? Do you want me to get out of The Boxes...? How...? How can I get out...?

Faint noises scratched at the edges of his hearing. His ear twitched, then burned with a squirming heat that burrowed deep into his mind. Dust jerked his head around and opened his eyes. He was staring at the flap. Behind it, a shadow twitched, then skittered away.

23

3

The Game

THE TATTY COVERS BARELY KEPT THE chill from his bones. His back ached where he'd leant against the wall. His claws were sore from gripping the top of the full box, and despite the warm blue glow of the flat light above him, his fur felt damp and cold. Shivering, Dust raised his head.

Every cat had climbed onto the full boxes to sleep. Gloworm dozed soundly next to Violet, who, with one eye open, rested her head on Rose's shoulder. Rose faced the wall, the rise and fall of her flanks suggested she was asleep, but Dust couldn't be sure. Behind them, Briar snored with his tail arched over his head. Onyx's curly black ears stuck up above Spinney's orange and white rump, and the paler patches of Fern's tortoiseshell coat shone silvery against Conker's thick black fur. The Meeting Box smelt calm, and except for the occasional flicker of an ear or twitch of a whisker, nothing moved. They had rested well, despite their hunger. But there were still no Ratbots.

Dust stretched out his hind legs and retracted his claws, giving them a soothing lick before he hopped down onto the cold floor and padded towards the flap. The shadow had played in his dreams, not enough to wake him, but enough to lay in wait for his attention as he woke.

Cats began to stir, and as Dust reached out a paw to touch the flap, the Meeting Box began to fill with the sounds of yawning, stretching, and scratching.

Conker slid off his full box and padded over to Dust, 'I remember in the Old Place, there was a flap between two boxes, and I was given food for going through it.'

Dust nodded, 'I remember that too.'

'Me too, I was small then and it was hard to push open,' Spinney leapt from his full box, bounded across the floor, and slammed both front paws into the flap. It didn't move, and he crashed sideways into the wall. 'It must be sealed,' he growled, shaking himself, 'that worked last time.'

'Let's wait for a human to open it,' Onyx purred as she padded over to give Spinney's bumped shoulder a lick.

'They will open it for us, won't they?' Fern padded to Conker's side, a worried expression on her face.

'I'm sure they will,' Conker reassured her.

'Soon, I hope,' mewed Onyx, 'I'm starving.

Dust could feel the gnawing pangs of hunger grip his belly. He hadn't eaten since he'd arrived, so he wasn't surprised when the other cats agreed. He could hear their bellies rumbling as clearly as he could see the pain in their eyes.

Conker nudged Spinney over to let Briar join them. Gloworm half stepped, half fell awkwardly off his full box and crouched stiffly on the floor. Rose and Violet sat either side of him as they joined the group. Violet sniffed Gloworm's leg while Rose peered curiously through the clear flap.

'We need to find food,' Briar mewed.

Onyx flicked him with her tail, 'So are you going to go and find some, Briar? or wait here with us until the humans bring it?'

Briar swished his tail, 'We should wait, both ways out of this box are sealed.'

Onyx twitched her whiskers.

Shadow... Dust sat up and raised his tail, 'I saw a shadow behind it,' he glanced at the flap, 'before we slept, I was tired, so I didn't think much about it, but it looked familiar. Small and quick like a Ratbot.'

'So, they are through there,' Conker mewed.

Dust shook his head, 'I'm not certain, but that's what it reminded me of.'

'Well, Ratbots mean food,' Spinney meowed, 'so if they are through there, that's where I'm going!'

'Same here,' agreed Onyx, 'never saw the point in them, except to get food.'

'My mother told me that the Ratbots are just a human game,' Gloworm shuffled forward and peered through the flap, 'they could just give us food, but they like to watch us hunt.'

'Awful little things though, aren't they,' Violet shuddered, 'they hurt my teeth when I bit them, and those whizzy round things on their bellies ... they grazed my pads. Rose was the best at catching them.'

Rose growled.

'I hate the things,' Onyx purred, 'But if you swipe them hard enough, you can get them stuck under ledges. Then the humans can hurt themselves trying to retrieve them.'

'That must be them now, listen,' Spinney mewed.

'The Ratbots or the humans?' asked Onyx.

Dust flicked his ears. He heard a click and a scrinching sound and snapped his head around to see the lever on the green door move down. Then the door opened and a female human with long orange head fur and green covers stepped into the Meeting Box carrying a bubble of water and a black shiny cover. She closed the door quickly behind her. Dust sniffed the air. *No food...*

'I can't smell food or Ratbots,' Spinney complained as he also sniffed the air.

'Heyguys, wanttogetout,' the Green Female uttered, *'dontworrywontbelong, justwaitingforhometime.'*

The cats exchanged glances and watched as she poured the water from the bubble into the water bowl. Then she inspected the litters and removed the dirt in the black shiny cover. Her footsteps scuffed the floor as she walked around the Meeting Box.

Dust turned his ears back to the flap. He could hear more footsteps. Another human was approaching.

'Shh!' Briar flicked his ears.

'I hear it too,' Dust peered through the flap again. He saw nothing, but he could hear the other footsteps getting closer.

'*Okaywellbegoodandillseeyouallinthemorning,*' uttered the Green Female as she quickly slipped out of the Meeting Box and closed the door gently behind her with a little click.

Dust pushed at the bottom of the flap, first one side and then the other. It still didn't move, but as he moved his paw away, a new shadow appeared and wavered around the edge of the clear pane.

Briar took a sharp breath and stepped back.

The shadow grew, longer at first and then broader, until it was a circular mass that darkened the whole of the flap.

Dust glanced at Briar.

'Is that what you saw?' Briar mewed, 'it's not like any Ratbot I've ever seen.'

The other cats closed in, curiously watching the shadow.

'What is that?' Fern shuddered.

Dust parted his jaws and stepped forward. The shadow moved like ripples on a water bowl, to and fro, but with no discernible shape. He stepped closer and sniffed.

With a click and a bang, the flap jerked inwards. Dust leapt back and crashed into Spinney. As they scrambled back onto their paws, fur raised, and backs arched, the flap began to move again, and human scent drifted into the Meeting Box. Briar arched his back and growled but Dust stood his ground. Then the flap closed again with a soft bump and the shadow receded.

'What was that?' Briar sniffed the air.

'A human,' Dust mewed with a sigh of relief, 'A human just opened the flap.'

'No Ratbots then?' Spinney sat down heavily and began licking his belly fur.

'Are there any other scents?' Conker mewed, 'what about food?'

'I'll check,' Dust raised his paw and pushed the flap. It lifted easily, so he pressed his muzzle to the clear pane and pushed it upward. And winced, as a distant clattering din and hollering human voices pounded his ears. Human scent hung in the air, hearty and mature, and fading as fast as its owners' footsteps. When Dust was certain there was no danger, he pushed his head through.

The next box was long and stretched away from the flap in both directions. More full boxes had been stacked along the grubby walls leaving a narrow walkway through the middle. The dark floor stank of the same sour damp as the Meeting Box. Dust tipped his head up and saw that the roof was also made of white squares, but in this box, a long grey strip of yellowish light ran down the middle of them. One end of the Long Box was illuminated by a deep blue flat light. Dust sniffed the air. The human's scent was stronger in that direction. He took another breath, closing his eyes to let the stale air graze his tongue. There *was* something else. He licked his nose and tasted the air again. There. Faint and stale and coming from the darker end of the Long Box, was the unmistakably fleshy scent of food.

Dust pulled his head back through the flap. 'It's another box. like this, but much longer. I heard humans and strange noises, and I smelt food,' Dust gave the cats around him a heartbeat longer to sigh with relief before he went on, 'But the scent is faint and stale.'

'Then we need to find it quickly,' Onyx mewed, 'I'm not going to sit here and starve.'

'I agree,' Conker nodded.

'I can go through and have a proper look around,' Dust offered, 'I will try and find where the scent is coming from.'

'That's brave of you,' Briar got to his paws and nudged Dust away from the flap, 'but I don't think any cat should go anywhere alone, not until we know more about this next box. So, I will join you, and ... er ... Conker, and Spinney too if you don't mind.'

'Fine with me,' Spinney bounced to his paws.

Onyx put her paw on Spinney's rump, forcing him to sit back down.

'I'm happy to go,' Conker dipped his head to Briar, 'but what if the human came back and locked the flap again while we're gone? How would the cats who stay here get food?'

'Good point, Conker, 'Gloworm mewed, 'we don't know what the new game is yet. We should be careful.'

'Then we all go,' Onyx mewed, 'there's no reason for any cat to stay here.'

'Except for the water ... maybe...' Fern mewed quietly.

'She's right,' Violet rested her tail lightly on Fern's back, 'there's water here, and we don't know if there's any elsewhere,'

'That's' true,' agreed Onyx, 'we should stay near the water.'

'So, we drink first, then go,' Spinney meowed.

Briar waved his tail to get every cat's attention, 'Okay. We drink first and then all go together. And stay together. I will lead ... with Violet. Spinney and Rose next, then the others ... and Dust, I would like you to stay at the back and make sure no cat gets left behind.'

'Wait,' Onyx mewed, 'I think I should be up front with Spinney. So, I can keep an eye on him.'

Spinney flicked Onyx's ear with his tail.

'I would like to walk with Fern,' mewed Conker, 'she's smart and can watch my back.'

'Yes, I can do that,' Fern raised her head. Dust noticed the glimmer in her eyes.

Briar nodded, 'Okay, Violet and I will go first, then Spinney and Onyx ... then Conker and—'

31

'You, then Violet *and* Rose,' Onyx nodded to the sisters, 'They will walk together anyway.'

Briar sighed. 'Fine, I will go first. Then all of you, with Dust and Gloworm at the back.'

The cats all nodded their agreement.

Dust padded to Gloworm and leant close, 'Just keep your eyes and ears open, Gloworm, you're observant too and I'll watch your back while you listen out for us.'

'You don't need to protect me,' Gloworm twitched his whiskers.

Dust saw resilience flicker across the white tom's gaze, despite the pain of his injured leg, but he reassured him anyway, 'I'll be right behind you, just tell me if you sense anything ... strange.'

Briar flicked his tail impatiently, 'Okay, drink and get ready to go,'

Dust hung back as Briar, Onyx and Spinney padded to the water bowl, Conker followed, giving Fern a nudge.

'...And a boorish leader...' Rose growled as she pushed past Dust.

'Oh, I don't think he is, Rose,' Violet mewed quietly as she followed, 'He doesn't know us yet, he's being sensible that's all.'

Rose glanced at Violet and flicked her ears. Her eyes were sharp and angry, her thick red tail swished as she extended her claws and let them scrape on the floor. Violet saw it too, and gently leant into her shoulder.

Dust caught Violet's eye. He agreed that Briar was *trying* to be sensible. But it was Onyx who'd been smart enough to organise the cats in a way that pleased everyone. 'Briar's a good cat,' he told her, 'Sticking together *is* the sensible thing to do.'

Rose sniffed, then padded away towards the water bowl.

'She'll be okay, Dust,' Violet mewed as she watched her sister go, 'she just needs time.'

Dust dipped his head to the grey she-cat. He hoped she was right.

'Let's go and drink,' Gloworm mewed.

Dust nodded and padded after him. He waited for the others to finish before he drank his fill and joined them back at the flap. Gloworm's fur bristled as Briar slipped through first. Spinney dived through after him, his eyes bright and his ears pricked. Onyx ducked through after Spinney with an agitated flick of her tail. Conker let Fern go ahead of him and followed calmly a heartbeat later. Rose walked ahead of Violet and flicked an ear. Violet nodded, and let Rose slip through first, then followed without hesitation.

Dust padded to Gloworm's side, 'You go ahead.'

Gloworm closed his eyes, then raised a fore paw, licked it, ran it over his ear and mewed quietly, 'Wash for Shadow White...'

'Are you okay?' Dust asked.

Gloworm opened his eyes, nodded, then climbed awkwardly through the flap.

Dust couldn't begin to imagine what white tom's mumbled words meant, but as he pushed through the flap after him and stepped onto the cold damp floor of the Long Box, he found them oddly comforting.

4

The Long Box

DUST HOPPED UP ONTO THE NEAREST full box. The clattering and hollering noises were rapidly fading away, but the sour damp stench from the floor still lingered and clung to his paws.

Briar hopped up beside him, 'Where did you smell the food?'

Dust parted his jaws. Human scent hung in the air where the bright end of the Long Box turned a corner. A red glow had appeared along the bottom edge of the deep blue flat light on the end wall, and above it, another little red light flickered inside a small black box.

He turned to Briar, 'The food scent is coming from the darker end, but it's stale. Shouldn't we follow the human scent the other way to find the Ratbots?'

'Yes,' Briar agreed, 'The humans will give us fresh food when we catch them.'

Every cat nodded.

Briar hopped down from the full box and flicked his tail twice, signalling for the cats to follow him up the middle of the Long Box towards the Bright Corner. Onyx and Spinney kept close behind him, eagerly sniffing at the walls, the floor, and every full box they passed. Conker and Fern followed, Rose and Violet padding after them. Dust waited for Gloworm, who fell in silently by his side.

As they neared the end wall, Spinney trotted ahead of Briar and disappeared around the Bright Corner. Onyx hurried after him. When Dust had caught up, he peered around the Bright Corner to see them sniffing at the bottom of a silver door. He padded closer and saw that halfway up the wall, to the right of the door was a raised bump with a pale light that seemed to glow from behind it. Beyond the silver door, at the far end of the Long Box, was a bright brown door.

Spinney turned away from the silver door and wove back and forth across the floor, sniffing his way towards the bright brown door, 'The human went through this one,' he mewed, sniffing along the bottom of it.

'Thank you, Spinney,' Briar flicked his tail impatiently, 'The human has gone now, so we'll go the other way and follow the food scent.'

Briar led them back down the Long Box and past the flap to the next corner, where the flickering glow from the grey stripe on the roof illuminated a blue door and bathed the full boxes around it in a soft blue glow.

As they walked, Dust thought about Gloworm's words. He wanted to ask the white tom what *Shadow White* meant, but he decided to wait until they were alone before he asked. Gloworm caught his eye and slowed his pace. Dust didn't want to avoid talking to him, so he changed the subject of his thoughts, 'I hope we find food, then we can all relax a little. It would be nice to get to know each other without growling bellies making every cat feel uneasy.'

Gloworm nodded, 'I agree, hunger's no good for any cat. But this food scent is ... odd.'

'What do you mean by odd?'

'It changes, like the scent of a cat or a human ... it's different every time you smell it.'

Dust relaxed his jaw and let the scents drift over his tongue. The sour damp smell of the floor made all other scents hard to decipher, but even so, he couldn't pick out anything particularly odd in the faint scent of stale food. It was stronger in places, and sharper in others.

'Can you feel it?' Gloworm asked.

'Feel it?' Dust moved his head from side to side, trying to gather more of the scent.

'Where the scent is strongest ... I keep detecting that awful smell of fear,' Gloworm glanced at Dust, 'it's as if the food is afraid.'

'The food scent is different, that's true ... but afraid?' Dust glanced at Gloworm, 'Maybe it's getting muddled with our own fear scent...'

'Some of it is, but this is not the fear scent of cats, or humans ... but something like it.'

'We are in a new place, Gloworm,' Dust reassured him, 'Maybe the food here is different. Maybe hunger has upset our senses. I don't think my stomach cares what my nose thinks anymore.'

Gloworm purred. 'Let's just hope it's safe.

The cats stopped as they came to the Blue Corner, where the Long Box turned left and carried on into darkness. Dust looked up at the blue door. It was on the same wall as the flap, just a few fast strides away, and it had a silver lever, identical to the one on the green door. Unfamiliar scents wafted out from the gap below the door and drifted on the still air around him. Briar had noticed them too and was twitching his whiskers in confusion.

'Do you smell that?' Onyx asked.

One by one, every cat opened their jaws to taste the new scents. Dust sniffed along the gap. They seemed to be moving around in the air. Some scents were dimly familiar, but they were entwined in sharp fresh smells he'd never encountered before. He raised his paw and pressed it to the blue door's cold shiny surface and pushed. It didn't move.

'What is it?' Onyx sniffed at the bottom of the door.

'I don't know,' Dust took a deep breath and felt the uplifting air fill his lungs and quicken his heart,' I've never smelt anything like it.'

'Is it safe?' Violet peered around Rose's shoulder. Rose parted her jaws as she rested her tail on Violet's back.

'I think so,' Dust mewed, 'It doesn't smell dangerous.'

'We need to get in there,' Spinney joined Onyx and slid his paw into the gap, 'There's something good in there.'

'Later,' Conker purred, 'after we've found food.'

'Okay, let's see what's at this end then. Come on, Onyx,' Spinney spun around and trotted towards the Dark Corner.

'Hold on,' Onyx mewed as she padded after him.

Briar flicked his tail in annoyance and followed.

Dust watched them walk into the gloom. He could barely see the end wall where the Long Box turned right again.

'More doors,' Spinney mewed over his shoulder, 'a dull brown one and I can just see a black one at the end.'

Dust padded to Spinney's side and peered around the Dark Corner. More full boxes were pushed against the featureless walls, and another little red light flickered high on the wall above the black door.

As the other cats caught up and began to investigate, Dust closed his eyes and tried to imagine the confusing Long Box in his mind. As he faced the Dark Corner, both brown doors were in front of him. The black door, the green door and the blue door were behind him. The silver doors were on his left side, and as they had turned two corners, whatever lay behind them must end behind the wall beside him. The brown doors could both lead into a box beyond the wall in front of him, and he was sure there'd be more boxes beyond the blue and black doors.

'The food scent has almost gone,' Onyx grumbled.

'I can still smell it,' Spinney sniffed the air.

'Shouldn't we go back to the Meeting Box?' Fern mewed from beside Conker

'Perhaps,' Conker licked her ear, 'What do you think, Briar?'

Briar shook his head. 'If we go back to the Meeting Box, we could miss the Ratbots.'

Dust opened his eyes again and looked around. The Long Box wasn't much different from the Meeting Box, 'We could wait here,' he mewed, 'and rest on these full boxes.'

'Then we wait,' Rose sat down by the wall in the Blue Corner. Violet curled up close beside her.

'Come on,' Onyx nudged Spinney towards the opposite wall, 'let's rest for a bit.'

'Good idea,' Conker hopped onto a full box and beckoned Fern up beside him.

Dust curled up at the side of the blue door with his nose close to the gap. Gloworm squeezed into the corner behind him, and Briar flopped down against the full box opposite.

As Dust let the uplifting scents flow over his tongue, he closed his eyes and tried to shape them into images. But when none came to mind, he closed his mouth and listened to the chatter of the cats around him.

'Did you ever catch a Ratbot, Fern?' Conker's mew was gentle.

'No,' Fern replied, 'I couldn't bring myself to touch them...'

'Just flip them onto their backs, so they can't move...' Onyx mewed.

'Just don't bite the spinning legs,' Spinney purred, 'I hurt my teeth doing that...'

'Pin them between your paws, then if you bite the top hard enough, it will pop off,' Violet purred, 'I remember Rose dismantling all the Ratbots before ... before they took me away...'

'And I'll do it again...' Rose growled.

'If we find them before we starve...' Onyx purred, 'we know nothing about this place...'

Dust's eyes grew heavy as he listened, he was sleepy, and soon, he felt himself falling...

5

Know Your Territory

DUST ROLLED OVER ON THE COLD hard floor. His first breath shuddered with her scent. A dark shadow loomed above, spiralling, and spreading out over the Long Box, smothering the sleeping cats around him. He flicked his ears. Not a breath. Not a rustle of fur. Only the faint sound of paw steps padding steadily behind him, never getting closer, never fading away. He raised his head and watched as the shadow above him twisted and wove into the blurry outline of a cat. He sat up, and waited as the cat padded past him, hopped up onto a full box and turned to face him. Their eyes met. She extended a foreleg and bowed. Dust blinked, but he couldn't break the bright grey stare of the silver tabby she-cat.

'Hello, Dust...' she mewed.

'I saw you ... in the Meeting Box...' Dust took a step closer to the she-cat.

She nodded.

'Are you....?' Dust shivered, 'are you, my mother? Breeze...? Yes. Yes, you are. Of course, you are.'

She twitched her whiskers.

'Gloworm told me to push the noise away ... let in a little bit more. Is that why I can see you now?'

'He's a smart cat...' Breeze purred.

'I ... I try to remember you ... your words...'

'Forget the past...' her bright grey eyes glimmered as she mewed, 'There's something much more important for you to remember now...'

'Tell me, Breeze,' Dust took another step forward, not daring to take his eyes off her, 'what do I need to remember?'

'Look behind you...'

Dust turned to see the Long Box brighten as the dark shadow lifted and faded away. He could see the other cats again, sleeping soundly, their flanks rising and falling as they breathed deeply, motionless in their peaceful sleep.

But they *were* moving. He felt his skin prickle as their shadows began to slip out from beneath them and slide onto the floor. Then the shadows shook themselves into the images of their cats and padded around him. Dust got to his paws and turned around and around, watching the Shadow Cats as they halted in a circle and sat down, dipped their heads, and stared at him with their bright grey eyes.

He took a deep breath, 'How...?'

'Watch...' Breeze stepped aside.

An uplifting shimmer whirled around the Blue Corner.

Shadow Gloworm swirled through the blue door and returned with a long twisting tail. He shivered as he sat and licked a paw, and the glimmer in his grey eyes grew pale.

A silhouette lifted and danced along a bright gap.

Shadow Briar drifted with the darkness for cover, this way and that, undecided on his paws. Through one brown door and out through the other, he followed himself on a spiralling course.

A square uncaged from its lines and fell away.

Shadow Rose enraged the air all around as she gave Shadow Violet a protective shove. Then she led the darkness away from the ground with an incredible leap into the roof above.

A glow soothed the air as it broke from the gloom.

Shadow Violet moved and made herself small and swirled out of Shadow Rose's way. Then she padded to the flat light high on the wall and watched as it faded from red to grey.

A loud purr mithered the hum of the tranquil mood.

Shadow Conker hovered near the black door before he ebbed and flickered out of sight. Then he was back on the Meeting Box floor shivering and soaked in a curious light.

A sensation sunk as the ground faltered and bobbed.

Shadow Fern shrunk from the illuminated bump as it flickered so suddenly bright. And shrill rising sounds made her jump and reel and flatten to the floor with fright.

A damp moted mist roared above and rolled down.

Shadow Onyx floated before the silver door with nothing in her eyes to show but a glow as she circled and clawed at the floor, then sunk down into the darkness below.

A click stopped the glimpse as it melded into the wall.

Shadow Spinney hopped as he bounded and gripped the silver door lever in his paws. It stuck fast, so he landed and ran and rounded a corner and tried the next one with his claws.

'Wait,' Dust hurried forward as the Shadow Cats began to fade, but as he lifted his paws, his own shadow slipped from under them, twisted into an image of himself and turned to face him.

Then Shadow Dust took himself by his gaze and led him through the wall to the water bowl. And as he looked up through his mind, a haze drifted around a little red eye below a bitten hole.

'The cats ... their shadows ... what are they trying to show me?'

Breeze laid her silver tabby tail over Dust's shoulder and guided him back through the wall, 'Know your territory...' she mewed as they walked, 'it's the most important thing...'

6
Ratbots

DUST THREW OUT A PAW TO steady himself as he lurched awake. Shivering, he looked around. The Long Box was dark. The flat light in the Bright Corner was black, visible only as a glimmering rectangle in the gloom, it barely illuminated the cats on the full boxes around him as they began to stir. Gloworm was already on his paws, ears twitching and tail quivering, staring into the Dark Corner.

Dust parted his jaws and found the scent immediately. The growls from the other cats told him that they had too.

'Over there,' Spinney padded forward and dropped into a crouch, swishing his tail slowly from side to side, 'Ratbot.'

Creeping slowly along the wall towards the Dark Corner was a small domed shadow, so much like the outline of a Ratbot, yet... Dust sniffed the air again. *Something ... Odd...*

'Careful, that's moving weirdly,' Conker stepped lightly to Spinney's side.

'Don't worry, I've got this,' Spinney raised his rump, dropped his chest to the floor and padded the ground with is hind paws. Then he leapt forward, bounded into the Dark Corner, and landed on the Ratbot. He flipped it over and threw it into the air behind him, whirled around, caught it again, and slammed it hard into the floor with a dull thud.

Dust flinched as the Ratbot let out an ear-piercing squeal. Around him fur bristled, and claws scrabbled on the floor as every cat trained their senses on the prone Ratbot.

Spinney hissed and jumped backwards, fur rose along his spine, 'Legs! It's got legs,' he yowled. With eyes wide, he extended a paw and prodded the Ratbot. It twitched and slumped onto its side.

Movement in the shadows caught Dust's eye.

'Watch out,' growled Onyx, 'there's another one.'

A dark shape slid from the shadows and scurried towards Spinney. The orange and white tom hissed as it slid under his belly. He stepped back and trod on the first Ratbot. It twitched, then squealed, then it rolled over onto its paws and lunged upwards. Spinney yowled in pain as the first Ratbot clamped its teeth into his shoulder. Then the second one slid from beneath his belly and sunk its teeth into his hind leg. With a gasp, Spinney stumbled and fell to the floor.

A flash of red fur shoved Dust aside.

'Rose!' Violet meowed.

Rose leapt at the second Ratbot, dug her teeth into its back and dragged it from Spinney's hind leg. He yelped as the Ratbot squealed and thrashed, but it quickly let go of his leg to twist its head around and attack Rose. She strengthened her grip on its neck and shook it hard. A heartbeat later it went limp, and quiet.

'Watch out, behind—' Onyx hurled herself between Spinney and Rose as more domed shadows slithered along the wall towards the Dark Corner. Two more Ratbots scurried out of the gloom.

'Flip them over,' Briar yowled.

'Not these!' Rose hissed, 'Bite them. Hard.'

Dust raced after Onyx. Briar and Conker fell in either side of him. He leapt for the Ratbot on Spinney's shoulder and sunk his teeth into its back. Into warm wet flesh. *What...?* Shocked, he clamped his jaws harder into its neck and shook it, tearing it away from Spinney.

Dust stumbled back, dropped the Ratbot and stared down at it. It twitched and fell still, blood spilling from its neck and mouth. A metallic tang filled the air as warm fresh blood pooled out across the floor around his paws.

'Ratbots don't have ... blood!' Violet mewed.

Dust licked his lips.

'These do,' Rose growled from somewhere nearby.

Dust sniffed at the motionless Ratbot on the floor. They always smelt of food. Cold stale food had always clung to their backs, as if the humans had rolled them in it. But these smelt of food all over. Warm and fresh. His stomach growled, and as he sniffed it again, his head began to swim with a dizzying, crippling hunger. 'These Ratbots have food *inside* them,' he mewed as he looked around at the other cats.

Spinney lay slumped against the wall, panting. Blood dripped from his shoulder, and he held his hind leg out awkwardly. Violet crouched at his side, carefully sniffing his wounds. Briar and Onyx stood side by side a few strides away, their ears flicking nervously as they peered down the Long Box toward the black door. Blood dripped from Rose's chin as she stared down at the Ratbot in her paws. Fern cowered behind Conker, panting, her eyes wide and ears flat with fear. The black tom rested his tail over her back as he sniffed at a tuft of bloody fur in his claws.

'They're not Ratbots,' Gloworm's mew was muffled. Dust could barely hear his words above the sound of his heart pounding in his ears. He turned to see the white tom standing behind him, head low with the weight of a third Ratbot in his jaws.

'Then what are they,' Rose licked her chin.

Gloworm dropped his catch, 'I think ... they *are* food.'

Dust felt his fur prickle. He licked his lips again. The blood in his mouth tasted and smelt so familiar. He knew it was food. *But is the food inside them? Or...?* He looked back down at the sodden furry mass at his paws. *Gloworm's a smart cat, he could be right...!*

'We need to get Spinney back to the Meeting Box,' Violet mewed urgently, 'he's hurt, that ... whatever it is, cut him. The wounds are deep,'

'I can walk, it's not that bad,' Spinney groaned as he pressed his back against the wall and tried to push himself up onto his two steady legs. But his wounds were too painful, and he wobbled and fell against the wall, then slid back down to the floor.

'Take it slowly, Spinney,' Violet pressed against his side, 'You could be in shock. Shock can stop your legs from working properly.'

'Just slow down and let us help,' Onyx purred as she pushed her nose under Spinney's hind leg and slid in between him and the wall. Violet pressed close to his other side and took his weight as Onyx pushed him up onto his paws.

Spinney took a deep breath and puffed his chest out. 'Right, I'm good,' he mewed, and supported by the she-cats, he lifted his bleeding bitten legs and moved steadily forwards on his other two.

'Conker and I will head to the flap,' Briar raised his head, 'Fern ... go with Conker. Rose, Dust, Gloworm, bring your Ratbot ... things.'

Dust nodded and waited as Onyx and Violet lead Spinney away. Rose and Gloworm picked up their catches and followed the others back down the Long Box towards the flap. They had caught three. He had seen four. But he was sure there had been many more of them. He picked up his own catch and listened. Somewhere ... beyond the Dark Corner, beyond the black door, an eerie discourse of squeaks and squeals tugged at the edges of his hearing.

7

Food

BRIAR SLIPPED THROUGH THE FLAP AS Dust dropped his catch to help Violet and Onyx support Spinney.

A heartbeat later, Briar reappeared, 'Humans have been here, things have changed. Wait while I check it out.'

'I'll help,' Conker dived through the flap after him.

Fur rippled and tails swished as the cats waited in the quiet Long Box. The air felt heavy around them. Dust parted his jaws to taste it. The strongest scent was the metallic tang of blood, but it was only slightly heavier than the prickly scent of fear. The stench of sour damp had faded and the uplifting scents that drifted out from under the blue door had been overwhelmed.

'It's safe,' Briar mewed as he reappeared, 'the human's brought fresh water and bed boxes. Come on!'

Dust hung back as the other cats filed through the flap. Fern went first, helping to steady Spinney's shoulder as Violet and Onyx stayed on either side of him to keep him from falling. Slowly, he pulled himself through, wincing whenever his bitten legs took any weight. Rose picked up her catch and pushed through after them.

Gloworm hesitated, pawing at his catch on the floor, and when only he and Dust remained in the Long Box, he mewed, 'I remember once, I was with my brother, Hopper,

51

and my sister, Moth. We'd just caught a Ratbot, and Icicle warned us, "*Be careful it doesn't bite you.*"," he looked up at Dust, 'Is this what she meant? These ... things?'

Dust sniffed the furry mound at his paws, 'Maybe. They certainly bite.'

'Yes, they do,' Gloworm went on, 'and if they are food, it means that our food is alive.'

'Alive?'

'Like us... So, we have to kill it before we can eat it.'

'Kill it?' Dust asked, 'you mean...?'

'Stop it living. Send its soul to ... to *their* Shadow White.' Gloworm's eyes glazed with sadness as he gazed at the body between his paws, 'Like my other sister, Butterfly.'

Dust took a step towards the white tom and rested his tail on his shoulder, but Gloworm shook himself and picked up the body, 'Let's go,' he mewed.

Dust waited until Gloworm had climbed back through the flap before he picked up his own catch. Blood oozed over his chin as he carried it, and despite the troubling thought of this food being alive, his stomach growled with hunger.

'Put it there,' Rose flicked her tail to catches beside the water bowl.

Dust dropped his catch on the pile and began licking the blood from his fur as he looked around.

The flat light glowed a pale yellowish blue, illuminating the new bed boxes that had been placed on the full boxes below it. They were like the ones from the Old Place, smaller and shallower than the full boxes, and lined with soft covers. Briar hopped up and rubbed his chin along the bed in the corner, claiming it as his own.

Violet and Onyx helped Spinney haul himself up into the bed next to Briar's. Onyx took the bed on the other side of him. Conker stepped into the end bed, the one opposite the door, and motioned to Fern to take the one between him and Onyx.

When he'd finished grooming, Dust took the bed nearest the flap. Gloworm stepped into the one beside him, leaving two side by side for Rose and Violet.

The soft bedding inside the bed was more satisfying than Dust had expected, and as he lay down and made himself comfortable, he felt a breath of relief. He closed his eyes and allowed himself to doze. He was close to falling asleep when the door lever scrinched and clicked.

The Green Female slipped into the Meeting Box and closed the door behind her. '*Right letslookatyoulot, nowyourallback,*' she uttered as she glanced at the cats curled up in their new beds. Then she looked at the litters, and the water bowl in the corner. '*Rats!*' she gasped.

Dust had heard that sound before.

'*Youcaught rats, ididntthinkyoudfindthemthisquickly.*'

The Green Female slid one hand into her covers as she inspected the catches and pulled it out again full of little brown nuggets. She sprinkled them onto the floor in front of the water bowl. Then she stood and stepped towards the beds. Her eyes went wide when she saw Spinney.

Briar flattened his ears and Onyx backed away as the Green Female reached out a hand to Spinney. She gently lifted his hind leg and ran her other hand over the blood matted fur on his shoulder.

'*Ohdearokay,*' she uttered as she lowered his leg and took hold of his ear, bent it inside out and peered inside.

Then with one swift movement, she scooped Spinney up, pinned him to her chest with one arm and carried him out of the Meeting Box.

*

The flat light was grey. Onyx crouched by the door, worry clouding her blue eyes. Spinney had been gone a while but without the flat light's colours, it was hard to tell how long, or when the humans would return. Hunger gnawed at Dust's belly, the smell of blood hung in the air, and the cats were still deciding what to do with their catches.

'This is food. So, we eat it.' Rose dragged a body off the pile.

'They smell like food,' Violet mewed, 'but ... are they safe? And what are those things that the Green Female left ... they smell a bit like food too.'

'Leave them,' Rose growled.

'We should wait for Spinney,' Onyx meowed.

Rose flicked her tail, 'We should eat before it spoils.'

'I agree,' Violet sniffed the body in Rose's paws, 'they are soft and warm. Not solid cold like in the Old Place. They won't be good for long.'

'Ice...' Gloworm muttered, 'Icicle ... she told me that the food had ice ... a wet so cold it turned into floor...'

Conker glanced at Gloworm, then padded to Onyx's side, 'The humans in the Old Place healed us quickly. I'm sure Spinney will be fine and back soon, but they're right. Those things are starting to smell ... odd.'

Onyx flicked an ear to the pile of catches, 'You think he'll be fine? Have you ever been bitten by those ... things?'

Those things... Dust sat up as he remembered the Green Female's words. 'Rats,' he mewed, 'The Green Female, she said "*rats*". I've heard that sound before. They must be called rats.'

Briar looked up at him, 'I've heard that before too, like Ratbots, but not Ratbots.'

'So, we call them rats,' Rose mewed, 'and now we take them apart and share them out,' she nodded to Onyx, 'we'll save some for Spinney.'

'I've never thought about taking food apart before,' Violet flicked Rose's side with her tail as she sniffed the catches, 'How do we do it?'

'Here,' Rose tipped her head, 'hold them down, sink your teeth in, and pull.'

Violet pressed her muzzle into Rose's shoulder as she extended her claws and dug them into the nearest rat, pinning it down as Rose sunk her teeth deep into its flesh and began tearing away its fur.

'I just can't see how they get from being those ... hideous noisy things that attacked Spinney, to a pile of ... food?' Fern padded to Conker's side and stared wide eyes as the sisters tore the rat apart.

'They die.' Gloworm mewed from his bed.

Every cat raised their head and looked around at Gloworm with curious expressions.

Gloworm's fur rippled, and he shivered. Dust remembered what he'd told him about Butterfly.

'They do what?' Onyx mewed.

Gloworm's jaw quivered as he lifted his head, 'Those rats are alive ... like us. They must have a soul ... maybe a bit like ours. So, we must force their souls from their bodies before we can turn them into food.'

A heavy silence fell over the Meeting Box as the cats looked at each other in confusion.

Onyx stared at Gloworm, 'Then we can become food too?'

'I ... I don't' think so,' Gloworm flicked his ears nervously.

Dust stepped out of his bed and gave Gloworm's ear a lick. 'I think what he's trying to say is that we have to turn the rats into food ourselves now. The humans did this before, but here ... in The Boxes, we must do it.'

'Makes sense,' Rose held Dust's gaze with an intense, searching, stare.

'Which means we have to find them.' Briar hopped down onto the floor.

'Find them?' Fern gasped, 'they found us.'

'And we killed them, so they might not want to find us again,' Briar mewed, 'Which means we need to organise our hunts.'

'Organise?' Conker twitched his whiskers.

'These rats are dangerous,' Briar went on, 'We all saw what they did to Spinney. If we get injured, we get taken away by the humans and then there will be fewer of us to catch them.'

'He'll be back...' Onyx mewed.

'I'm sure he will,' Briar flicked his tail, 'but we need to organise our hunts properly. Find out where these rats live. If we keep running about aimlessly, we'll just get attacked again.'

Dust flinched. He didn't think any cat had done anything wrong. He stood and flicked his tail twice to get every cat's attention, 'Spinney was injured *only* because the rats surprised us. We were expecting Ratbots. We didn't even know these rats existed. But we still won. At the end of the fight there were dead rats, not dead cats,' Dust nodded to the growing pile of shredded rat at Rose's paws, and went on, 'But I do agree with you, Briar. We know the game now. We know what we must do to get food, so, we must organise ourselves according to what we know now. That way, we won't be surprised again.'

'I agree,' Conker looked from Dust to Briar, 'What do you suggest?'

'I suggest we go out in pairs,' Briar interrupted, 'then no cat will be alone to deal with a rat ... if a rat were to sneak up on one of us, then the other will be able to catch it. We can send out two cats when we need to find more food, and when they return, send out another two if we still need more food.'

'Two isn't enough,' Rose mewed around a mouthful of rat fur.

'Why?' Briar swished his tail.

Rose dropped the rat, 'If a cat is hurt, what does the other do? Stay, or get help?'

'Well, they should—' Briar began.

'Three,' Rose went on, 'one to stay, one to run.'

Briar took a deep breath, 'Four. Four cats! if one is injured, one stays to protect and help them, and two go and fetch help. This place is strange, and these rats are dangerous. No cat should be alone.'

'We've all been alone,' Rose sunk her teeth back into the rat. Bones crunched.

Territory... Dust flicked his tail again. 'This is our territory now. Not theirs. We should explore it and learn about it. Find out where the rats live, and where the dangers are. We need to know our territory, that's the most important thing.'

'Go on,' Rose dropped the rat again and looked at Dust with interest.

'Well,' Dust glanced at Briar apologetically, 'I think we should send scouts out ahead of the hunting groups. To look around and sniff out the rats.'

'Good idea,' Briar glanced at Rose, 'Two cats can scout ahead.'

'We could scout the other boxes too,' Onyx added.

'Scouts should go to one place only, then come straight back,' Briar went on, 'so we know where to find them if they run into danger.'

'Will two cats be enough? Fern mewed, 'What if Rose is right, what if one cat is hurt?'

'Two can scout, but not hunt,' Rose mewed.

'Yes,' Conker nodded, 'the scouts should be quick, find the rat scent and run straight back to tell the hunters where to go.'

Briar nodded, 'Then it's agreed. We send two scouts to find scents, and when they return, four hunters go out.'

'Three,' Rose growled.

'Let's try three,' Dust nodded to Rose, 'and if they struggle, we can send four.'

Rose nodded and clawed the next rat towards her.

Gloworm sighed and flopped back down into his bed. He ruffled the fur along his spine, then let it lay flat as he closed his eyes.

Briar caught Dust's eye, 'We can start now. Dust, if it's okay with you, I think you and I should scout first.'

Dust nodded, 'Sure.'

'Good, then this is what we'll do,' Briar waived his tail to get every cat's attention. Rose growled dropped the rat again as Briar let his gaze linger on her a heartbeat longer. Gloworm half opened his eyes to watch as Briar began speaking. 'We will scout to the Dark Corner and come straight back. If we find rats, a hunting group can go out. But if we don't see any rats, two more cats should scout to the black door, as that's where the rats we didn't catch went.'

'So, a hunting group needs to be ready for when you return?' Conker asked.

Briar nodded, 'Yes. You, Onyx, and Fern.'

'But what about Spinney, what if he comes back?' Onyx complained.

'Violet, Rose and Gloworm will be here, he won't return to an empty box. You won't be long.'

'What if we're injured?' Fern mewed nervously. Dust could see the fear in her eyes. 'How do we know which cat should stay and who should get help?'

Conker padded to her side and purred, 'Don't worry, it's easy, the fastest cat runs to get help, and the strongest stays.'

Fern nodded.

'Then are we agreed?' Briar asked.

Every cat nodded.

Dust looked up at the flat light. The grey had brightened into a soft blue. He hopped down to the floor and stretched out his front legs, arched his back, and yawned, 'Come on then,' he flicked an ear to the flap, 'let's see what's out there now.'

8

Scouting

DUST BLINKED IN THE BRIGHT LIGHT as he pushed through the flap after Briar. Squinting, he looked up. The long grey stripe that ran down the middle of the roof was glowing a bright yellowish white.

Briar flicked his tail, telling Dust to stay quiet.

Padding softly to Briar's side, Dust listened. The clattering noises were back, mingled with human shouts and hollers. 'The noises are only here when the humans are.'

Briar nodded, 'Do you think the humans are hunting the rats?'

Dust shook his head. 'I don't think so, I'm sure we have to do that ourselves now.'

'We could go and look, find out what they *are* doing.'

'Didn't you only want to scout to the Dark Corner?'

'Yes. And if we find nothing, we carry on to the black door. Just so we know what's there.'

'Lead the way,' Dust twitched his whiskers, *he breaks his own rules...*

The uplifting scents ebbed from beneath the blue door. Dust paused to try and decipher them, but the powerful smell of sour damp coming from the Dark Corner was too fresh and overpowering for him to fix his senses on any one scent, so he padded on to the wall where they'd been attacked. There was no sign of the struggle now, and no scent of blood or rat.

Briar sniffed along the wall. 'It's like we were never here. All the scents have gone.'

'There must be something...' Dust began to sniff the bottom of the wall but stopped at the sound of a click and scrinch. He raised his head to see the dull brown door opening. Soft bluish light spilled from the box behind it. Briar shifted back into the Dark Corner behind Dust, and they watched as a female human with brown head fur and red covers stepped out into the Long Box and closed the door behind her.

Dust shifted back a step.

The Red Female stopped, looked down at him and uttered, '*Ohofcoursethe Ratters, 'youshouldrun, beforehelenseesyou.'* she smiled, then turned away and walked towards the black door.

Dust followed her, and as she opened the black door, he caught a glimpse inside the box behind it. Many humans in red covers scurried about, pushing, and pulling huge traps that seemed to roll around in every direction. The clattering noise intensified as the humans shouted and bashed their rolling traps into each other. There were so many of them, and so much noise, fading only as the black door crept closed again.

Briar caught up to Dust and stiffened.

'A box full of humans and noise...' Dust mewed.

Briar nodded, 'And traps. Big ones. The box behind that door looks huge, far bigger than any box I've seen before.'

Dust took a step forward and sniffed the air, 'But no scent of rats.'

'No.' Briar agreed.

Dust flicked his tail, 'Let's go. The humans weren't there when we met the rats. So, I think the rats will return when the humans go, and their noise stops.'

Side by Side the toms turned and padded back around the Dark Corner, past the blue door and back to the flap.

'We could have another look that way,' Briar flicked an ear to the Bright Corner.

'We could,' Dust looked up at the blue grey flat light at the end of the Long Box, 'but didn't you make it clear that a scout group should check one place only, and return.'

Briar twitched his whiskers. 'You're right, Dust. If we report anything other than what we're supposed to, Rose will add my ears to the food pile.'

Dust purred, 'Yes, she will.'

'What do you think of her,' Briar narrowed his eyes, 'do you think she can be trusted?'

Dust considered Briar's question about the red she-cat. 'Well,' he began, 'I think she's afraid of losing Violet again, and that's making her defensive. And maybe she's angry about them being separated in the Old Place. But I think she's a good cat, we should give her a chance.'

'A chance maybe, but I'm not sure I can trust her.'

Dust went on, 'We haven't been here long. Violet's a good cat, and I'm sure Rose will settle with her help.'

'Yes ... Violet I can trust, but not Rose. There's something perilous about that she-cat,' Briar took a deep breath, 'What about Gloworm? Does he seem strange to you?'

Dust purred, 'A little. He and his littermates were raised with their mother, and it seems he can remember everything

63

she taught him. If what he says sounds strange, it's only because we didn't know our own mothers.'

'*"Never forget you're a cat",* that's all my mother said to me. All I can remember anyway. Gloworm shouldn't worry too much about his memories. He should worry more about finding food.'

Dust nodded, 'He should, but there may be some truth in his beliefs. What if there really is a place outside The Boxes? We came from the Old Place. That's not here, and the humans ... they go somewhere.'

'Like back to the Old Place? The last place I want to go.'

'You think this place is better?'

Briar sat down and took a deep breath, 'I was glad to leave.'

'Why?' Dust rested his tail lightly over Briar's back, 'Were you alone?'

Briar shifted away from Dust, 'Quite the opposite, there were too many of us. I'm from a big litter, six of us in total, and my sister, Bolete ... she was unbearable.'

'She bullied you?' Dust took a step back to give Briar room to talk, he could tell this tom wasn't one for affection.

'No!' Briar shook his head, 'She was weak. The first time we were taken to the Turn Box to hunt, Bolete flipped a Ratbot over, bit it, and broke her tooth. Then she refused to continue hunting. She called our other littermates back and told them that we should all refuse to catch the dangerous Ratbots and just wait for the humans to bring us food. But the humans bought nothing. The Ratbots carried on bumping into us. The humans laughed, and I was getting hungry.

'I tried to tell her she was wrong, but the others, my sister, Morel, and my brothers, Lichen and Reed believed Bolete was right. They didn't want to hurt their teeth. My other brother, Stalk, was undecided, but when I told them I'd catch the Ratbots myself, he reluctantly decided to help.

Stalk was a good cat. He listened and did everything I said, and we caught all the Ratbots. That's when I knew that I'd been born to lead.

'Every time we were taken to the Ratbot Boxes, Stalk and I would hunt, and before long, Reed and Morel joined us. But not Bolete and Lichen. They sat at the side of the Turn Box, watching the humans, and refusing to catch anything. They said they were too weak to hunt and that humans only wanted strong cats to catch Ratbots. Then they began to make friends with the humans.'

'Make friends?'

'That's right, Bolete grovelled to them, begging for scraps of food, and Lichen followed her.'

'And the humans gave them food?' Dust asked, 'even though they didn't hunt?'

'Only scraps. But I'm sure they were given more than scraps when the humans started taking them to the Soft Boxes to let them play with soft round toys. You see, she was right about one thing, the humans wanted strong cats to catch the Ratbots, not weak kittens afraid to lose their teeth. I lost many teeth, but I stayed strong, and I carried on hunting. Maybe that's what Dewfrost meant by "*Never forget you're a cat.*" Cats hunt. I loved to hunt, and I knew that I would reap the rewards. I led my littermates well and together we caught every Ratbots in those boxes. That was, until the humans put me in a trap and bought me here.'

65

'And this is a reward? The Boxes?' Dust twitched his whiskers. Briar was certainly a strong cat, but clearly not as smart as his sister.

'It's better than the Old Place. Rats taste better that than the cold flesh we were given for catching Ratbots, and strong cats don't get injured.'

'Then maybe The Outside could be an even greater reward for strong cats.'

Briar gave Dust a long look, 'You're smart, Dust. That's good. You understand why these cats need a strong leader. We will look for better places, for sure, but I don't want any cat being fooled by kittenhood tales and hazy memories. I think you should listen to the stories these cats are telling and tell me what you make of them.'

Dust nodded, 'Okay.'

'Good, then let's get back,' Briar flicked an ear to the flap, telling Dust to go first.

As Dust slid into the Meeting Box, he felt the excitement in the air. The cats were huddled around piles of shredded rat. Spinney crouched in the middle, eating heartily. Onyx sat beside him, purring. Only Rose watched them return.

Dust greeted her with a nod as he approached, then he looked at Spinney. The orange and white tom appeared to be in good spirits and his wounds had healed.

Spinney pushed a dry nugget towards Onyx, 'Try it!'

Onyx wrinkled her nose and sniffed the nugget.

'It's safe,' Spinney purred, 'and they don't tase too bad.'

Conker stepped forward and lapped up a nugget. His tail quivered as he crunched it. 'Not bad, but I can't tell what it is. It's like food, but not. Did the humans give you these?'

'After I'd woken up and my wounds were healed, the Green Female gave me some to eat,' he mewed as he crunched another nugget.

A small patch of fur was missing from Spinney's shoulder. Dust could see where the rat bite had healed into a sore bumpy line. There was also a patch of fur missing from around the wound on his hind leg too, and another from his front leg, but he couldn't remember him injuring his foreleg.

'I've eaten them before,' Spinney went on, 'When the Old Place went dark, the humans gave us these. My brother, Esker, hated them, but Thistle, Moss and Nettle, my sisters, they didn't mind.'

'I've never eaten anything other than ... that,' Onyx flicked her tail to the shredded rat flesh, 'even when the Old Place went dark.'

'I didn't know there was any other food, where ... what does it come from?' Fern added.

Spinney shrugged as he crunched another nugget.

'More importantly,' Onyx pushed the nugget away, 'where did the Green Female take you?'

'A Healing Box behind a white door. It was too bright to see much. I went through those big silver doors in the Long Box...' Spinney tipped his head, struggling to remember, 'they closed, and when it opened again—'

'Is this more important than the scouts' report?' Briar interrupted Spinney.

The cats stopped talking and turned to look at Dust and Briar.

'Then, report,' Rose mewed.

Briar looked at Conker, 'There's no point sending a hunting group out now,' he mewed, 'We went as far as the Dark Corner. A Red Female came out of the dull brown door and went through the black door. Whatever is in the box behind the black door is dangerous. We saw huge rolling traps and many humans in red covers. And there was no sign or scent of the rats anywhere.'

'So, what now?' Rose asked.

Briar glanced at the red she-cat, and went on, 'The humans weren't there when we met the rats. So, I think the rats will return when the humans go, and their noise stops.'

Rose held Briar's gaze.

'I think he's right, Violet padded to Rose's side. 'Perhaps we should eat now. We can scout again later.'

'Good idea, thank you Violet' Briar mewed, then he looked at Dust. 'I want you to scout the Long Box again after the noise has stopped, go as far as the black door, and take Gloworm with you.'

'If that's okay with Gloworm,' Dust mewed.

Gloworm's fur bristled a little as he glanced at Briar, 'fine with me,' he mewed as he took another small bite of rat flesh.

With that agreed, Dust sniffed at an untouched pile of shredded rat. It was cold and starting to smell stale, but his stomach growled as he lapped up and chewed his first mouthful. He couldn't remember when he'd last eaten.

9

The Blue Box

A DOOR SLAMMED SHUT.

Dust woke with a start. A male human with white covers and greasy black head fur was standing in the Meeting Box. His pale face frowned as he glared around with angry eyes.

Every cat ducked down in their beds, except Rose, who sat glaring up at him from beside the flap.

The White Male wrinkled his nose. Then he turned and stepped over to the corner, kicking the water bowl and spilling its contents as he crouched to examine the remains of the rats.

'*Thatallyoumanaged,*' He uttered as he pulled something white and crinkling from a fold in his covers. He scooped the rat remains into it and he was about to stand when he stopped, frowned, and stretched out a hand to the uneaten dry nuggets.

'*Howdidthesegethere, whosfeeding Ratters petfood.*'

The White Male picked up the dry nuggets and shoved them into his covers with the rat remains. Then he left the Meeting Box, slamming the door behind him.

'Are you okay?' Violet mewed as Rose hopped up beside her and climbed into her bed.

'I'm fine,' Rose mewed, 'He spooked me.'

Violet purred and laid her tail over Rose's back, 'He scared me too, he's ferocious, not kind like the Green Female who took Spinney.'

Dust looked over Gloworm's back and watched as Rose curled down into her bed. She began to purr as Violet licked her ears, but she kept her eyes open and glanced around the Meeting Box nervously. She looked anxious but had no fear scent. He shook away his thoughts. They were still strangers, and he shouldn't try to guess what might scare her. As he closed his eyes, he remembered being small and alone in the Old Place, where even the kindest new human had terrified him.

*

When dust opened his eyes again, a red glow had appeared along the bottom of the flat light, bathing the quiet Meeting Box in a soft pink light. Gloworm was snoring gently, and the sisters had fallen asleep with their tails entwined. Conker, Fern, and Onyx slept soundly while Spinney shuffled in a comfortable dream. They were relaxed and happy. The meal had done them good.

Only Briar was awake and when he saw Dust lift his head, he hopped lightly over the full boxes to his side, 'The noise has stopped,' he mewed, 'this is a good time to scout.'

Dust glanced up at the reddening flat light again, 'Sure,' he nodded.

Briar leant closer, 'But this time, when you return, I want you to go back out with the hunting group.'

Dust tipped his head to one side, 'Why?'

'I've had a thought,' Briar lowered his voice, 'If we can find the rat's scent, they can find ours too. But if a scout goes back out with the hunting group, then they will think it's the same cats and not be alarmed.'

Dust shook his head, 'I couldn't tell one rat's scent from another, maybe they can't decipher our scents either.'

Briar flicked his tail dismissively, 'It will be quicker for the hunters to get back to the rat's trail if a scout leads them. So, when you return, tell us what you found and head back out with Conker and Rose.'

'We will hunt better with rested cats,' Rose mewed.

Dust turned to see the red she-cat sit up in her bed. He nodded a greeting, and she blinked her brilliant green eyes at him.

Briar flicked his tail again, 'They won't be scouting far enough to get tired.'

'And if they get injured,' Rose glared at Briar.

'Then we won't send the injured scout back out,' Briar argued, holding Rose's stare.

'I agree with Briar,' Conker yawned as he shuffled around and scratched his chin, 'It's a good idea to send a scout back out with the hunters, just until we know this place better, it could stop cats getting lost.'

Dust nodded, 'That's true. Following a scout is quicker than explaining where to go.'

'Sorry, Rose,' Briar mewed tartly, 'But Conker and Dust are right. The scouts may find the rats but not be able to *describe* where to find them.'

'I can follow a scent,' Rose growled.

'Scents get washed away, Rose,' Conker added, 'Look, we don't know much about The Boxes yet, or the rats ...

scouts probably won't need to go back out with the hunters after we get to know this place.'

'Thank you, Conker,' Briar nodded, 'Dust and Gloworm will go to the black door and check for scents, if they find some, Dust will lead Conker and Rose back out to hunt.'

Rose shook her head and lay down again.

'So, when do we go?' Gloworm arched his back in a long stretch and yawned.

'When you're ready, if we wait too long, the noise might come back,' Dust greeted Gloworm with a friendly nod.

Gloworm glanced at the red flat fight, licked a paw, and mewed, 'Ready when you are.'

*

Shuffling human footsteps were the first thing Dust heard as he slid through the flap. He raised his head and listened. The footsteps were approaching from beyond the Blue Corner.

'Human,' Gloworm mewed as he climbed through after Dust, 'should we go back and wait?'

'No,' Dust rested his tail on Gloworm's back, 'let's see who's coming.'

'Okay...' Gloworm crouched behind the nearest full box and pricked his ears.

The footsteps slowly grew louder. Whoever was approaching was in no hurry and as he listened, Dust realised that they were the same footsteps he'd heard just before the flap had been opened. A heartbeat later, a hunched male human with brown skin, fluffy white head fur and baggy blue covers loped around the corner. He stopped in front of the blue door and took a bite from something in his hand. Dust sniffed the air. *Human food...*

As the Blue Male put his hand on the door lever, fragments of food tumbled from his mouth, down the front of his blue covers, and onto the floor. And as he pushed the blue door open, he turned to smile at Dust and Gloworm.

Dust purred. This human's scent was calm, like the Green Female, and his dark eyes lit up as he stretched out his hand and spoke softly, '*Heythereyou cats yougonnahelpoldjohn keepthe rats outofmycupboard.*'

Dust glanced at Gloworm, 'He seems friendly, let's find out where those uplifting scents are coming from,'

Gloworm's eyes widened, but he nodded, 'Will Briar mind if we scout other places.'

'We don't need to tell him,' Dust flicked his tail as he trotted towards the Blue Male. Hesitantly, Gloworm followed.

The Blue Box was almost identical to the Meeting Box. A flat light sat high on the wall, casting the same reddish glow across the stacks of full boxes that slumped against the wall below it. There were more of them here, and piles and clusters of other things; Soft covers, like bedding were strewn over the floor, and bowls of all different sizes lined another wall next to a haphazard jumble of long thin sweepers. Dust recognised them. Humans used them to cover the floors with the sour damp.

'*Comein cats, yousniffthemblightersout, dontwantno rats inhere,*' the Blue Male uttered.

The stench of sour damp was intense, but the uplifting scents were stronger inside the Blue Box. And they moved, evasively ebbing, and flowing from behind the stacked full boxes below the flat light. Gloworm padded to Dust's side and sniffed, he had found them too.

'Findanythinglad?' the Blue Male shifted a large silver bowl with his foot as he watched the cats with gentle eyes.

Dust looked up at him and blinked slowly, 'Where do these scents come from?' he asked.

The Blue Male laughed; a strange wheezing cackle that sounded painful. *'Cantfindany rats eh, wellgood, don't wanteminmycupboard.'*

'Dust, here!' in the corner opposite the door, Gloworm had wedged himself between a full box and a large white box with a dark reflective circle on its front. 'The scents are coming from a hole in the wall, over here.'

Dust padded to Gloworm's tail and tried to look over his back. A slip of light lit up the side of the white tom's face as he pushed his nose to the wall. Dust sniffed the air. A myriad of refreshing scents rolled over his tongue. He recognised none of them but savoured them all.

Gloworm squeezed further behind the full boxes, 'There's something ...'

The Blue Male stepped across the floor and gently nudged Dust's rump with his foot.

'Hey, John, saystimetogo, cats, theresno rats inhere, soyoudbestbeout.'

John...? The Blue Male is called John...

Gloworm's fur rippled along his back. His tail bushed. 'Cat, there's a cat in there!'

'A cat?' Dust tried to see past Gloworm's fluffed-up fur.

'I can smell a cat,' Gloworm's voice quavered, 'A tom! The scent is fresh.'

'*Theresno rats backthereyoujustsmellingfreedompoor soulsyou Ratters betyouneverevenseenthesky.*'

John's foot pressed into Dust's side again and steered him away from the full boxes.

'Come on, we need to get out.'

Gloworm wriggled backwards out of the gap, turned clumsily, and hurried for the door as fast as his sore leg would let him. Dust darted through the doorway behind him and followed him back up the Long Box.

They stopped halfway between the flap and the blue door. Dust helped Gloworm climb up onto a full box and hopped up beside him. John picked up his bowl and sweeper and closed the door, then with a smile, he walked towards them.

'*Gnightlads, hopeyoucatchsome rats tonight,*' he uttered with a nod as he shuffled on past, and away around the Bright Corner.

As John's footsteps faded, Gloworm mewed, 'Do we need to tell Briar and the others what we saw?'

'Yes ... but I don't think you should tell them about the other cat.'

'Why not?'

'Some cats might not believe you.' Dust hadn't smelt any cat scent except their own. And while he was certain Gloworm wouldn't lie, he still could have been mistaken. 'We should wait until we can get more evidence.'

Gloworm shook his head, 'That cat could be in trouble.'

'It could be another group like us. They could be fine. Did you smell fear?'

'No. No fear. His scent was calm. But we don't know when we'll get back into the Blue Box.'

'We will get back in there. We need to explore every part of this territory.'

'Know your territory. You're right, Dust, we do need to explore.'

'It was my mother, Breeze. She told me that. I did what you said, opened my mind a bit more and I saw her in a dream. But those are the only words I remember.'

Gloworm stepped closer, a delighted glint in his eyes, 'That's great! You must listen—'

A high-pitched squeal interrupted him.

'Get down,' Dust hopped off the full box and peered out from behind it, 'Rats!'

Gloworm followed and pressed himself against the wall behind Dust. 'Yes, I smell them.'

A shadow swelled across the wall, and a twitching nose appeared around the corner, followed by a head with a glinting black eye. Then a rat shot out and snatched up the crumbs of food that John had dropped. It rocked back onto its haunches and began to chew. Then it froze.

'Back. Now. Smell cat,' another rat peeped from around the corner.

Dust pricked his ears. Gloworm gasped.

The first rat turned its head slowly. It looked at the wall, and then at the blue door. Its little black eyes scanned the Long Box and its fur bristled as it spotted Dust peering out from behind a full box.

It dropped the crumbs and skittered around the corner, screeching, 'Cat! Swarm back! Skeeal. Call Skeeal!'

10

The Hunt

DUST SLID TO A HALT IN the middle of the Meeting Box floor, panting. Gloworm pushed through the flap and limped to his side. Every cat turned to stare in alarm.

'What happened?' Briar mewed as he hopped down from the full boxes.

Dust caught his breath, 'The rats can talk.'

'Talk?' Onyx nudged Spinney aside as she stepped forward, 'what do you mean?'

'They spoke,' Gloworm sat down, raised a paw, and licked it, 'they said ... cat swarm back, and ... Skeeal, call Skeeal.'

'Skeeal?' Rose got to her paws, 'A name?'

'I don't know,' Dust shook his head.

'If they speak like us then they could have names,' Onyx mewed.

'Then let's go find out,' Rose turned to the flap.

'Shouldn't we wait?' Violet padded to Rose's side, 'What if they've called more rats? What if there's a whole swarm of them out there now?'

'Yes, we could wait, they—' Briar began.

'We'll be fine,' Rose interrupted.

'If there are too many, we'll grab the closest and run back,' Conker padded over to join Rose.

'Then after we return, Rose and Conker can go back out with ... Onyx, maybe? And I can rest,' Dust dipped his head to Rose, 'So there are fresh cats hunting.'

Rose nodded.

'Sure,' Onyx mewed.

'Then go,' Briar flicked his tail to the flap, 'before their scent gets washed away.'

As Conker and Rose padded to the flap, Gloworm flicked his tail, beckoning Dust over.

'Are you okay?' Dust asked the white tom.

'Should I tell them about the Blue Box?'

Dust didn't want to hide what they'd discovered, but this wasn't the time to unsettle the other cats. He glanced at Fern. The tortoiseshell she-cat was curled in her bed, and she looked frightened enough. Fear scent already hung in the air. 'It can wait,' he told Gloworm, 'We can tell them later when we're all fed and rested.'

'Then I'll wait,' with a sigh, Gloworm turned away and scrambled awkwardly up onto the full boxes and slumped down into his bed. He looked tried and dejected.

As Dust followed Conker and Rose through the flap, he decided to keep his senses alert for signs of other cats.

*

The stench of rat was strong as Conker led the way down the middle of the Long Box, his attention trained on the Blue Corner. Rose went next, her head and tail high and her ears flicking impatiently. Dust trailed behind. Briar had wanted him to lead the hunt, but he was sure he could do that without telling these cats what to do.

As they passed the blue door, Dust hesitated to let the uplifting scents flood his nostrils.

Rose halted and turned to look at him, 'Are you coming?'

Dust flicked his tail, asking her to wait as he searched for any trace of cat scent. If he could find it, it would be easier to believe Gloworm.

'It does smell good, doesn't it,' Conker sniffed around the door, 'I wonder what's in there.'

'We saw inside, Gloworm and I...' Dust began, hesitating as Rose and Conker exchanged a glance, then he went on, 'A male human in blue covers opened the door. He was eating human food and dropping crumbs everywhere. That's what the rats came for.'

'What's in there?' Rose asked.

'Lots of full boxes...'

'Just boxes?' Conker pressed.

'And sweepers and bowls. And a hole in the wall. That's where the scents are coming from.'

'And you didn't tell Briar?' Rose twitched her whiskers.

'It would have taken too long and Gloworm wants to rest first ... he was a bit unnerved. We can talk about it after the hunt.'

'Briar doesn't need to know everything,' Conker mewed, 'but what unnerved Gloworm? Is he thinking of escaping through the hole?'

Dust shook his head, 'I don't know.'

'He's daft if he does,' Conker purred, 'it's safe enough here and there's plenty of food...'

'Not if we stand around talking,' Rose growled, 'Let's go.'

Rose took the lead around the Dark Corner. The dull brown door was closed, but the black door had been propped open with a full box.

'Is this where the Red Female went?' Conker glanced at Dust as he padded on to the black door.

'Yes. There were other humans in there. They had rolling traps and were making lots of noise.'

'What were they doing?' Conker asked.

'Does it matter,' Rose swished her tail.

'Probably not. I can smell rats, so let's go find them,' Conker hopped over the full box and through the gap in the door, flicking Rose with his tail as he went.

Rose hissed and leapt after him.

Dust followed, and almost collided with Conker as the black tom stopped suddenly to look around. Rose had stopped a pace in front of them, her head raised and tail twitching.

'I've never seen a box as big as this,' Conker mewed.

Rose nodded, 'Every box is bigger than the last.'

Dust padded ahead and looked around. Two deep blue flat lights sat high on the end wall and a small red light flickered above them. At the far end of the new box, a pair of yellow doors were propped open with a full box, like the black door behind them. The roof was made from the same yellowish white squares as the other boxes, and the white walls were patchy and dirty. His paws tingled with foreboding. *Rose is right... the boxes are getting bigger...*

'And it's cold,' Conker shuddered.

Dust hadn't noticed the cold. The air felt warm around his paws, but as he lifted his head, his ears felt a chill higher in the air, and a strange humming sound grew louder. 'What's making that noise?'

'That mirror,' Rose growled.

Dust stepped back as he spotted his reflection. The mirror was set into a huge Metal Box. Its top reached almost to the roof, and it spanned half of one wall. He padded closer. The mirror had a door lever and a set of light bumps to the side of it. They glowed bright green, not pale white like the one on the silver door in the Long Box. 'It's a door...' he mewed, 'This mirror is a door.'

'Are you sure?' Conker asked.

'It has a lever and light bumps...' Dust turned his ears to the large rolling traps that leant against the wall behind him, then to the yellow doors at the end of the Cold Box. They were quiet. The humming sound was coming from inside the Metal Box. He padded to the end of it and peered around the side. There was a gap at the back, 'This Metal Box is inside the Cold Box, you can get behind it and on top of it.'

'Boxes inside boxes?' Conker flicked his tail, 'I've never seen that before.'

Dust shook his head, 'I remember Two Door Box in the Old Place. But the walls went all the way up to the roof.'

'What about you, Rose, do you remember Two Door Box?' Conker's mew was friendly.

'Just a White Box.' Rose's fur rippled along her spine, 'I smell rats, so I'm going to hunt.'

Dust watched Rose as she padded forwards, her tail low and swishing across the damp floor as she headed for the yellow doors.

Conker glanced at Dust, 'White Box?'

81

Dust shook his head. 'I don't remember a White Box.'

'Wait here!' Rose hissed.

Dust glanced at Conker as she leapt up onto the full box that propped open the yellow doors and stared through the gap into the darkness beyond. Dust crept closer, Conker padding softly behind him, but Rose was not going to wait.

'Stay here, I see them,' she hopped off the full box and slid through the doors.

'We can't let her go in there on her own,' Dust flicked Conker's shoulder with the tip of his tail as he quickened his pace towards the yellow doors.

'Wait,' Conker held out a paw to hold Dust back, 'let her go, we'll get to her if anything happens.'

'What if we don't,' Dust glanced at the black tom, 'Things can happen very quickly with these rats.'

Conker lowered his paw, 'I don't want my ears clawed off for interrupting her hunt.'

'She won't do that...' Dust crept forward and peered through the yellow doors. The next box was even bigger than the Cold Box. In a darkness so vast Dust couldn't see the walls or the roof, rows of impossibly tall towers stood in a line along the edge of an endless open space. He watched Rose slip beneath the nearest tower, then turned back to Conker, '...she's just afraid of losing Violet again.'

'We were all separated from our littermates...'

'It's her way of coping...' Dust caught a flash of red fur in the corner of his eye. The tip of Rose's tail flicked around the end of the closest tower. As his eyes began to adjust to the gloom, he saw that the towers were like tall traps, stuffed full of full boxes.

I think she's trying to decide who her enemy is,' Conker purred, 'I hope it's not any cat here.'

Rose flicked the end of her tail twice. *Follow...*

'Then let's help her,' Dust hopped over the full box, dropped into a low crouch, and stalked after Rose.

Conker followed in a low crouch to the end of the first tower. Rose was just ahead, peering underneath the bottom ledge.

'Go for the same rat,' she hissed, 'the one with the white rump.'

Three rats shuffled around the floor between the first tower and the next one along. The one with the white rump was closest. Dust watched it pick up a crumb and sit back on its haunches to nibble it. He focused on its scent and was surprised to find it was sharper than that of its companions. *They do have their own scent...* He crouched lower.

'What's it eating?' Conker lowered his head to get a better look.

'Human food,' Dust hissed back, 'Like the crumbs John dropped.'

'John?' Rose mewed.

'The Blue Male, his name is John, I heard him say it.'

Rose nodded. 'Then the rats hunt human food,' She flicked her tail once, telling the toms to wait as she slipped further under the tower and positioned herself behind the rat. Dust understood what she was going to do. They would attack the rat from three different directions. But for it to work, they would have to attack with their bellies skimming the floor. There was no room to leap out from under the bottom ledges.

Rose glanced at Dust and flicked an ear towards the end of the tower, then motioned with her tail for him to move around it. Then she glanced at Conker and flicked her tail down.

'She wants you to attack from here, and me from over there,' Dust mewed.

Conker nodded and crouched lower, watching Rose as he waited for her signal. Dust slipped around the end of the tower and fixed his gaze on the white rumped rat.

'ATTACK!' Rose's screech filled the air.

'Cat! Up! Up!' squealed a rat as Rose and Conker lunged out from under the tower.

Two rats leapt for a full box on the bottom ledge, hauled themselves over it and scrambled up into the darkness.

The white rumped rat shot forward and raced away under the towers. Rose followed, stooping to slide under the bottom ledges as she tried to keep pace. Conker, too big to keep up, crawled out from under the ledge and followed her down the open space at the end.

Dust sped after Conker and raced ahead of him to try and intercept the rat before it could escape. But the rat swerved between two towers and hurtled towards the end wall. As Dust lunged after it, he glanced up to see human markings on the end of the towers. He almost didn't see the rat leap onto the side of a full box and push itself off backwards. It twisted in the air, leapt over Dust, and landed facing Conker. Then with a screech, it zigzagged across the floor towards the black tom.

Conker slid to a halt, swaying this way and that as the rat wove towards him.

Dust spun around and tried to follow the rat, but as he leapt forward, his hind paw slipped in a patch of water at the bottom of the tower, and he fell. Conker leapt for the rat, but he missed, and couldn't stop himself crashing into Dust.

Rose lunged from under the tower, but the rat was too fast. It sped past her before she could turn and snare it in her extend her claws. Then it circled and scurried back towards the open space. Dust scrambled to his paws and followed it. Conker got up bounded past Dust, trying to head the rat off, but it swerved and dived back under the towers. Conker plunged into the gloom after it.

Dust slowed to catch his breath. Red fur flashed under the ledges, and as he turned to follow Rose, something small and hard hit him in the ribs. He stumbled and fell onto his side, landing heavily against the bottom of a tower. Pain seared through his hip as a rat scurried over his hind legs and dug in its teeth.

A muffled voice squeaked, 'Cat go. Leave rat.'

Dust clawed at the rat, trying to dislodge it, but its fetid yellow teeth were clamped firmly into his flesh. He turned his head and snapped at it, but the more he struggled, the harder it bit.

'It's coming back!' Rose yowled.

As Dust hauled himself onto his paws and swung his rump to shake off one rat, another dropped from a ledge above and sunk its teeth into his foreleg. He winced, then extended his claws, and dug them into the white patch of fur on its rump.

'Hold it there,' Conker panted as he leapt from the shadows. But the white rumped rat twisted and rolled away and Conker's claws sunk into Dust's leg. He yowled in pain as his skin tore away from his bones. The black tom landed heavily beside him.

'Go slide down, trick, back-back,' squeaked the first rat as it let go of Dust's hip and leapt up onto a full box. Dust swiped for it, but it was too quick and had vanished into the darkness before his claws could connect with its twirling tail.

'Trick, what trick?' Rose mewed as she slid to a halt beside Conker.

The white rumped rat shot out from behind Dust and scampered down the open space. He watched it go, and as his eyes focused, he could see that it was heading towards two large dark squares set one above the other in a distant grey wall.

Conker started after it.

'Let it go!' Rose meowed.

Dust dragged himself onto his paws and limped into the open space.

Conker slowed and looked back, 'It's a dead end.'

Dust peered at the squares on the wall. One was high up, and the one below it looked like another stack of full boxes, 'Follow it,' he told Conker, 'You're right, there's nowhere left for it to go.'

Rose hissed, then bounded away between the towers.

As Conker set off again, the white rumped rat squeezed through the stack. The black tom kept his ears trained on it as he leapt onto the top full box and dropped down behind them.

Hot blood trickled down Dust's leg as he limped down the open space toward the stack of full boxes and peered into the gap. He could see more full boxes behind. It wasn't a stack of full boxes. It was a box *full* of full boxes.

A rhythmic clanking sound began echoing around the Vast Tower Box, and Dust looked up in time to see the top square start to slide down. His fur prickled along his spine, *slide down trick...*

Shuffling footsteps approached. A human sniffed.

'CONKER, GET OUT!' Dust yowled.

'Wait ... I can see it...' Conker's muffled mew came from somewhere within the full boxes.

The footsteps shuffled closer. Dust looked up to see a male human with a bright pink shiny head, wispy cheek fur and shabby grey covers approaching the slide down square. Their eyes met, and the Grey Male uttered, '*Dontyougetnearmytruck, cat, gohuntsomewhereelse.*'

Dust looked up at the square. It was sliding down over the box of full boxes, closing the box. *It's a door... a slide down door...* 'Conker, leave it! Get out of there!'

The Grey Male stepped closer and lifted his foot.

Dust ducked and stepped back as the Grey Male's foot sailed over his head, 'Watch me,' he mewed, 'That's right, human, keep your eyes on me...' Then he yowled, 'I'VE GOT HIS ATTENTION, CONKER, GET OUT!'

There was a thump from behind the full boxes, followed by a frustrated hiss. The clanking from the slide down door quickened.

'CONKER! HURRY!' Dust yowled as the Grey Male kicked out again.

'I lost it! I'm coming out...'

Dust watched in horror as the white rumped rat slid out from under the slide down door a heartbeat before it thumped heavily onto the floor. The rat scurried away along the wall.

'CONKER?' Dust yowled as the Grey Male swung his leg up again.

'Where's Conker?' Rose dropped a dead rat behind him.

'In that box. Behind that door.'

'Then we can't help him,' Rose picked up her rat again and slid under the nearest tower.

Dust's paw slipped in his own blood as he turned and crawled under the tower after Rose.

11
Leaders

DUST LEANT ON ROSE AS THEY padded back to the Meeting Box. She carried her head high, the dead rat swinging from her jaws. Tension rippled through her fur, but he couldn't be sure if it was helping him or losing Conker that fuelled it.

'Wait here,' Rose ducked through the flap.

Dust swayed on his paws. His shoulder burned and his bitten and scratched foreleg throbbed so deeply with pain it wouldn't bear any of his weight. As he leant against the wall and sat down slowly, more pain seared through his hip. He raised his blood-soaked foreleg and sniffed it. He didn't know where to begin licking it.

Violet's head appeared through the flap, 'Dust!' she glanced at the wound on his bloodied foreleg, 'can you get in?'

'I think so.'

'Okay, good, I will hold the flap open for you. Do you have other wounds?'

'My hip,' Dust flicked his tail to his right side, 'This one.'

'Right, well, take your time,' Violet moved to the side, 'Fern, I need your help.'

Dust eased himself onto his paws as Fern appeared and glanced anxiously past him.

'Get ready to support him,' Violet told her.

Dust clenched his teeth as he shifted his weight onto his wounded foreleg, lifted his good paw, and stepped through the flap. Fern pressed against his side as he manoeuvred his other legs through and sat down heavily. Through the dizzying haze of pain, he could barely see the other cats, but he could hear their anxious mewings.

'Where's Conker?' Fern pulled away from Dust's side and hopped through the flap.

'Fern,' Dust shook his head, '...he's not here.'

'He's Gone,' Rose's mewed.

Gasps of shock and frantic meowing filled the air.

'What?' Fern climbed back into the Meeting Box. The flap bang shut behind her.

'He's trapped.' Rose explained.

Fern glared at Rose, 'Where? How?'

Briar hopped down from his bed. 'Fern, we need to help Dust first, then we can look for him.'

Rose glanced at the flat light, 'When I've eaten, I will go.'

'We ... some cat should go now,' Fern wailed.

'The flat light ... is almost black...' Dust panted, 'The Grey Male could still be near the slide down door...'

'Slide down door?' Briar mewed.

Dust got to his paws again and leant on Violet. 'Rose is right ... there's plenty of time to search before the humans return.' Then, with Violet supporting him, he limped slowly across the floor and slumped down against the full boxes.

Fern followed them, her eyes wide with worry as she sat down next to him and parted her jaws to speak, but her words didn't come. Nervously she licked her chest fur, then tried again, 'Please, Dust, what happened to Conker?'

Dust stretched out his wounded foreleg as he told Fern about hunting the rats in the Vast Tower Box, 'I'm sorry, Fern, it was my fault. I told him to follow the white rumped rat. I didn't know the door would slide down. It was a trap. The rats knew it would close. Rose told him to get out, but we didn't listen to her.'

'Did the rat hurt him?' Fern asked.

'No, he wasn't injured,' Dust reassured her, 'The rat got out, and I'm sure he will too, as soon as the slide down door opens again.'

'I hope you're right.' Fern hung her head as she turned away, climbed up onto the full boxes and sunk down into her bed.

'She will be okay,' Violet sat down by Dust's side, 'Let me look at your wounds.'

Dust shuffled onto his side and laid his head on the floor. The cold was soothing. He felt weak and lightheaded, as if all his energy was draining away with the blood he was losing.

Violet sniffed at the wound on his foreleg, 'It's still bleeding. Did the rat do this?'

'No, Conker did. He leapt on the rat that was biting me, but it moved, and he caught my leg with his claw.'

Violet nodded, 'And your hip?'

'That was a rat.'

These rats are fast, vicious, and smart,' Briar peered over Violet's shoulder.

Rose looked up from shredding her catch, 'So are we.'

'But they are more organised than us,' Briar growled, 'If we can't be organised, we will keep getting hurt.'

'We were organised!'

Briar turned to Rose, 'Organised enough to lose one cat and have another so badly injured he can barely stand?'

'The rats are an enemy,' Rose growled, 'dangerous and unpredictable.'

'And cats get hurt every time we meet them,' Onyx added. 'They are not Ratbots.'

'Rats died, cats didn't,' Rose growled.

'We don't know that!' Fern raised her head and wailed, 'We don't know if Conker's still alive.'

'He's fine,' Rose hissed.

'Enough!' Briar hopped onto the full boxes and thrashed his tail to get every cat's attention. 'We need a leader. Those rats have leaders. They have tricks, signals, and orders. That's why we get injured. That's why Conker ran into a trap. That's why Dust is lying injured on the floor. We pull in our own directions when we need to pull together.'

'So ... are you going to lead us, Briar?' Onyx mewed.

'I'm going to ask you all to vote. Vote for the cat you want to follow.'

'If that's what you want,' Onyx purred, 'does everyone agree?'

'Why not?' Rose mewed.

Dust lifted his head to watch Briar,

'Stay still,' Violet pressed her paw over his wound, 'the bleeding won't stop if you keep moving.'

There was determination in Briar's eyes. Dust knew he was a strong cat, but he doubted the other cats would follow him for that alone. *He needs to follow his own rules first...*

Briar flicked his tail, 'Then let's start,' he turned to Rose, 'You can vote first. Who would you choose as leader?'

'Violet,' Rose mewed without hesitation.

Violet sighed and shook her head. She pulled her paw from Dust's wounded leg and tucked it under her chest, flicking her ears nervously.

Briar nodded to the red she-cat and turned to her sister, 'Violet, who do you vote for?'

Violet's fur rippled along her back as she slowly raised her head, 'I'm sorry, Briar, I know you want to lead, and I'm sure you will make a good leader. But I vote for Rose. She's hot headed, I know, and has a temper ... but I could never follow any other cat.'

Briar twitched his whiskers, 'Thank you, Violet, for being honest. But having a leader won't harm your loyalty to your sister. A leader will keep us organised and—'

'And make decisions that put our lives at risk,' Rose hissed, 'I will only ever trust Violet with my life.'

Violet relaxed, but she kept her head low and as she turned away from the other cats, Dust could see sorrow in her eyes.

Briar nodded. 'Dust, what about you? Who do you vote for?'

Dust wasn't ready for the question, and he wasn't sure he could answer it.

Briar noticed his hesitation, 'Take your time. I can see you're in pain.'

'And undecided ... it's not an easy decision.' He collected his thoughts and went on, 'Rose could be a great leader,' He dipped his head to the red-she cat, 'You took the lead against the rats in the Vast Tower Box, but when we didn't listen to you, you left us and went hunting alone. I'm sorry Rose, but I'm not sure I'd trust you to keep *every* cat safe.'

Rose nodded but remained silent.

Dust winced as he shifted onto his elbows, and went on, 'Violet would make an excellent leader, but she'd suffer if she was forced to go against her sister's wishes to help another cat.'

Violet closed her eyes and nodded.

'Gloworm and Fern would never want to lead, their skills lie elsewhere. Spinney, he'd support a good leader, but I don't think he'd ever want to take charge himself. And Onyx ... I don't know ... I think she'd make a great leader, but on her own terms. I'm sure that if she wanted to lead us, we'd already be following her.'

Onyx and Spinney looked at each other and purred.

'Conker,' Dust went on, 'He's strong and calm. But maybe a bit too relaxed. And he doesn't always listen ... which is why he's not here now.'

Briar flicked his tail.

'Briar, I vote for you,' Dust dipped his head, 'Now that I've thought it through. You want to lead but asked us to vote. You've risked cats voting against you to let them have what they want. Maybe you lack confidence in your decisions sometimes, but I'm sure you will grow more confident when cats start to support you.'

Briar dipped his head in return, 'Thank you, Dust,' he purred, then went on, 'Gloworm, who do you vote for?'

Gloworm shuffled in his bed, 'I vote for Dust, I'm sorry, Briar, but Dust is the smartest cat here. And he listened to me when we first arrived. He could have dismissed me as a silly frightened tom, but instead, he put me before himself...'

Dust closed his eyes and rested his head on his paws. *What if they all vote for different cats....?*

'Spinney, what about you? Who do you vote for?'

'I vote for you, Briar,' Spinney mewed without hesitation, 'You want to lead, so, you must know what you're doing...'

Dust sighed. *Perhaps it would work out after all...*

'Onyx? Who do you vote for?'

There was a pause as the black she-cat considered her answer, then she mewed slowly, 'Dust. I vote for Dust. He's smart, and I trust him.'

Rose one, Violet one, Briar two, and two for me...

'Fern?'

'I'd vote for Conker,' Fern mewed, 'I know he's not here, but he's still the cat I'd vote for.'

Rose one, Violet one, Briar two, Conker one and two for me...

'Why vote for him if he's not here?' Rose mewed.

'He'll be back soon,' Spinney mewed, 'I wasn't gone long.'

'Then shouldn't he have a vote too,' Onyx meowed. 'Who would Conker vote for?'

'He would have voted for Dust, I'm sure,' Fern mewed, 'He told me ... sorry Briar, he said Dust would be a better leader.'

'We can't guess his vote,' Briar mewed, 'We'll count it when he returns.'

'So, what about you, Briar?' Onyx purred, 'Who do you vote for?

Briar twitched his whiskers as he looked down at the blood dripping from Dust's wounded leg.

Dust felt his fur tingle along his spine. *Rose one, Violet one, Briar two, Conker one and two for me ... three if Conker was here...* He glanced at the tabby tom. Briar had the last vote and had been quick to dismiss a vote on

Conker's behalf. *He'll vote for himself...* With a sigh of relief, Dust rested his head on his paws.

Briar jumped down from the full boxes and padded to Dust.

Dust looked up at him and blinked congratulations, but Briar shook his head.

'I'm sorry, Dust, but I vote for you.'

Dust snapped his head up, wincing at the pain in his foreleg, 'Why?'

'If I voted for myself, I could win, but if Conker returned and voted for you, we would tie. And I wouldn't respect a cat who voted for themself. I want to lead, but more importantly, I want us to have a good leader ... and you are the only cat I'd follow.'

Dust sat up as straight as he could. His head swam with panic and pain. He didn't even know how to lead, 'I thought you would vote for yourself. I'm sorry, Briar, I misjudged you. Maybe I'm not as smart as you all think...'

Briar licked Dust's ear, 'I couldn't lead if you didn't trust me.'

'Congratulations, Dust,' Violet mewed, 'from both of us.'

Dust glanced at Rose.

The red she-cat nodded, 'I'll follow you... If I must.'

'I'm glad it's you,' Gloworm sat down opposite Violet and looked at Dust's wounds, 'we need to get back into the Blue Box. As soon as your leg is better.'

'And find Conker,' Fern padded to Violets side.

'Don't crowd the boss,' Spinney chirped as he leapt onto the full boxes, 'let him have a quick snooze first.'

'Snooze?' Onyx flicked Spinney's shoulder with her tail as she leapt up beside him, 'he needs to go to the Healing Box before he bleeds to death.'

'He won't bleed to death ... will he?' Fern gasped.

'No, he won't,' Briar took a step back and raised his head, 'He's our leader, he will be fine.'

'Thank you ...' Dust wanted to say something. What kind of a leader would he be if he couldn't even thank the cats for their trust in him? But as he tried to stand, dizziness washed over him, and he swayed.

Violet ducked under his shoulder to stop him falling. 'He should be his bed, he needs to stay warm, he shouldn't sleep on the floor.'

'I can't get up there...' Dust mewed, feeling helpless, 'Can you push my bed down here?'

'Of course!' Onyx mewed, 'come on, Spinney, help me push.'

A heartbeat later, Dust's bed crashed to the floor. Dust purred and rested his head on Violet's shoulder while the other cats milled around righting the bed and replacing the covers. Then they helped him to his paws and steadied him as he climbed into it and slumped down heavily. His head was swimming, his breathing shallow and he was shivering hot.

Violet stayed by his side and helped him raise his bleeding foreleg onto the side of the bed. His head dropped onto his good leg as he listened to the content mewings of the cats around him. They seemed happy that he'd been voted leader. Soon he would have to learn how to lead them, but now he needed to concentrate on breathing.

'Congratulations,' Briar mewed quietly as he rested his chin on the side of Dust's bed, 'Rather you than any other cat.'

Dust opened an eye, 'The humans will take me to the Healing Box...' he glanced at the flat light, the blackness was fading to pale grey, '...soon.'

'Do you want me to lead in your absence?'

'Yes...' Dust nodded, unsurprised at Briar's offer of support, '...just until I get back.'

Briar purred and gave Dust's ear another lick before he turned and padded to the water bowl.

Dust rested his head again and closed his eyes. As his ears hummed with the racing rhythm of his heart, he began to fall asleep, and he wondered; *How can I lead them? What can I possibly do for these cats?*

12

Know Your Cats

DUST ROLLED OVER IN HIS BED. His first breath shuddered with her scent. A dark shadow loomed above, spiralling, and spreading over the Meeting Box, smothering the sleeping cats around him. He flicked his ears. Not a breath. Not a rustle of fur. Only the faint sound of paw steps padding across the floor beside him. He raised his head and watched as the shadow above him wove into the blurry outline of a cat. The cat gently licked his ear before leaping away into the middle of the floor. Dust blinked as he sat up and caught the warm grey gaze of the silver tabby she-cat.

'Breeze...'

'Congratulations, Dust... You won the vote...'

'I... I didn't really want to.'

'But you did... You are their leader now...'

'I don't know how to lead.'

'That's the easy part... You listen to them... Get to know them... Walk with them until they become blind to you leading the way...'

'Yes... but?'

'Watch...' she lifted her tail and flicked it twice.

Movement caught his eye. Dust looked around and watched as the shadows of his cats rose from beneath their bellies and stepped out of their beds. Then as one, they hopped down as a silken wave from the full boxes and formed a circle around Breeze. When they had settled, she padded away from them and sat by the flap, where all but her eyes melded into the gloom.

The Shadow Cats looked up at Dust expectantly, and he saw the Meeting Box darken for a heartbeat as his own shadow rose from beneath his paws and leapt into the centre of the circle.

Shadow Dust swirled around every shadow cat and peered into each pensive grey eye. Then he nodded to Breeze before he sat and embraced all the knowledge he could Pry.

Shadow Briar swept forward right away, prowling to Shadow Dust with a curl of his lip. He waved his tail in a friendly way before the dark in his eyes, he let slip.

Shadow Rose drifted until Shadow Dust crept towards her and bowed his head. But her eyes resisted his patient trust and she shifted to where he dare not tread.

Shadow Violet closed her bright grey eyes and ebbed back as she bowed so low. All around her a bright light began to rise, surrounding her in a pale eerie glow.

Shadow Gloworm moved boldly on, and Shadow Dust met him on the way. They circled together, stepping as one, until he gently dulled and faded away.

Shadow Fern shifted back out of sight. Behind a wave of fear, she remained. Until showered in a curious light, she shook off her terror, and waned.

Shadow Onyx ebbed and flickered her tail as Shadow Dust padded to her flank. He stood with her until she grew pale and bowed as she twisted and sank.

Shadow Spinney eddied and leapt and landed before Shadow Dust's nose. Then all around him he eagerly stepped ready to follow wherever he goes.

Dust blinked as the Shadow Cats wavered and flowed back into their circle. Breeze padded back into the middle of them and held his gaze. Then he felt the floor turn around and around as the Shadow Cats dispersed into a hovering mist, leaving them alone.

'Are they telling me how to lead my cats?' Dust asked.

Breeze stepped forwards and stopped him spinning with the tip of her tail, 'Know your cats...' she mewed, 'It's the most important thing...'

13

The Healing Box

'*STAY STILL, DUST OR YOU'LL LOSE MORE BLOOD.*'

The Meeting Box spun as the Green Female lifted Dust up into her arms and carried him through the green door. The smell of dead rat was the only scent stronger than the metallic tang of blood that stained his bed and smeared the floor. He blinked rapidly as he hung his head over her arm, but his vision was too blurred to clearly see his cats staring after him. They looked like the hazy shadows from his dream. He was their leader now, but would they always follow him?

As the Green Female pulled the door closed, Dust let his eyes follow the movement of the silver lever in her hand. *Push down ... pull ... let up...* The door clicked closed on his cats and he was carried away, around the Bright Corner to the silver doors. Feeling comfortable with this human, Dust relaxed and watched as she tapped the light bump beside the door. It lit up orange, and there was a loud ding. Then, to Dust's surprise, the silver door parted in the middle and the two halves pulled away from each other and vanished into the walls, revealing an empty box behind them.

The Green Female stepped in and tapped another light bump on the inside wall. *Three in a column ... middle one...* The doors slid back out of the walls and closed again in the middle. Then the box lurched and began to move. Dust raised his head and pricked his ears. *Down...* It rocked as it dropped, and he felt his stomach tighten. He gripped the Green Female's arm with his claws to steady himself.

'*Ohcareful,*' she winced, and gently prised his claws out of her arm covers.

The Dropping Box stopped suddenly, and with another ding, the doors parted again.

The Green Female stepped back out into the Long Box and carried him around the Bright Corner. Dust blinked. *Is this the Long Box...?* The grey strip that ran down the centre of the roof glowed so brilliantly bright that he could not look at it. The flat light had gone, and there were no full boxes stacked against the walls. The Meeting Box door was red. He looked around for the flap, but it had gone. Dust closed his eyes and tried to orientate himself. He should be outside the Meeting Box, but the Dropping Box had gone down. *Down where?*

When Dust opened his eyes again, there was a bright white door in front of him where the wall adjacent to the blue door should have been. The Green Female stopped and grabbed the silver lever. *Down ... push ... up...* It moved silently and the door opened easily.

Healing Box....? The light inside was blinding. *Spinney said it was too bright to see...* The Green Female carried Dust to a bed that looked like the bottom half of a trap and laid him down carefully inside.

'*Youshouldcarrythemdowninacage,*' uttered a cold male voice.

Dust lifted his head to look around just as a figure in white covers stepped out of a hidden nook at the other side of the Healing Box.

'*Hesokayhessoft.*' The Green Female replied.

'*Tryitwith Ratter seventeen, haveyoureaditsfile?*'

'*Seventeen ... Rose ... thatwasanaccident.*'

Dust pricked an ear at Rose's name, but he couldn't decipher any more of their words.

The male grunted. '*Whatsitsnumber?*'

'*Hisnameisdream*   *Dust,*
hehasadeepscratchonhisleftforeleg   *anda*   *rat*
bitesonhisrighthip,' the Green Female stretched out Dust's injured foreleg.

Dust flicked his ears as he heard his own name.

'*Thecodeinhisearfiona, ordontyouunderstandit.*' As he came closer, Dust recognised the voice of the White Male who'd taken the dry nuggets from the Meeting Box.

'*Isaiditsdream Dust thelonghairedtabbytom,*' the Green Female   went   on,
'*Theresonlynineofthemtheyalllookdiffernt.*'

'*Hey Fiona*', the White Male growled, *readthecode.*

Fiona... Her name is Fiona... Dust looked up at her. Her red head fur, scraped back away from her pale face, reminded him of Rose's tail. Worry clouded her soft brown eyes, but her pink lips turned up in a creased smile as she gently took hold of his ear and turned it inside out. Fear tainted   her   fresh   scent.   '*Justconvertit,
itsnotharditsjustnumbers,*' the White Male sneered.

'*iknowwhothis cat is, canihavehisfileplease,*' Fiona said as she released Dust's ear and gave it a rub.

'*Ratters, Fiona, not cats.*'

The white male pushed Fiona aside, grabbed Dust by the scruff and forcibly bent his ear back. As his frowning face loomed closer, Dust watched the dark circles in his icy blue eyes shrink to pinpricks. He looked young, but unkempt, and his scent reminded Dust of forgotten water bowls that had started to turn green.

'*Hey craig, begentlehessweet.*'

Craig.... The White Male's name is Craig... Dust hissed as Craig pulled his ear closer to his icy blue eyes.

'*Justwritethecodedown.*'

Fiona took a something from under the ledge. Dust recognised it as a scratching stick and sheet, like the ones the humans had used in the Old Place.

'*Goon,*' Fiona said as she put the sheet on the ledge and clicked the scratching stick.

'*Generation, dotdotdot, dotdotone, idnumber, dotdotdot, dotdotdot, dotoneone, dotdotdot,*'

Fiona frowned as she scratched on the sheet.

Dust shook his ear as Craig let go.

'*Twentyfour,*' Fiona dropped the stick onto the sheet. Her voice was cold.

Craig opened another compartment and took out more sheets, '*Aldorholtdream Dust, longhaired tabbytom, mother, dellmeredawn, Breeze fatheraldorholtbarkchipageninemonths, noinjuries todate.*'

Breeze...? Dust flicked an ear.

'*Comeon Dust letshavealookatthesewoundsthen,*' Fiona lifted him out of the bed and laid him down on the ledge. She ran her hand down his shoulder and pulled out his foreleg. She was gentle, but fear clouded her scent whenever Craig spoke. *Is he her leader...?*

Fiona glanced at Craig, '*Deeplacerationtonearfore, twentymillimetresinlength, abovethewrist, willneeddissolvingsutures illdothem,*' *andsmallpuncturebelowit, nosutreneeded, butitwillneed antibioticspray.*

Craig sniffed.

She lowered Dust's foreleg, ran her hand along his back, and smoothed away the long fur around the wound on his hip. *'Subcutaneouslacerationtooffthigh, tenmillimeterslong, andtwo punctures, skininflamed, soiwillgivean antibioticbyinjection.'*

'Alldonebya rat?' Craig uttered.

Fiona shook her head, *'Thiswas, butthisonelookslikeitwas donebya cat's claw.'*

'Good, iftheyarefightingeachothertheyarehungry, andtheylldotheir jobbetter.'

Fiona took a deep breath as she lifted Dust back into the bed. He could feel her hands shaking, *'Iftheyre injuredtheycanthunt, theyreheretostop rats settling—'*

'Plentymore Ratters,' Craig interrupted with a sneer, *theydontcostmuch, keepthebest, burytherest.'* He glared at Fiona, *'Getthatonefixesandbackupstairs.'* Then he left the Healing Box and slammed the white door behind him.

Dust looked up at Fiona. Her eyes were weeping, a drop of water ran down a crease in her face. Her fear scent was strong. *Craig's a cruel leader...*

As she rolled him onto his side and raised his uninjured foreleg, he tried to watch her work, but the bright drip lights that hung from the roof cast her face into shadow and he could no longer read her expression. Dust looked up at the roof squares, then around the top of the Healing Box walls to where a little red light flickered inside a small black box in a corner. There were no flat lights.

'Thiswonthurtjustsomenoise.'

Fiona's hand tightened on his leg and a loud buzzing filled his ears. Dust flinched but didn't pull his leg away, even as something cold vibrated against his skin. Then the buzzing stopped. He looked at his leg. A little patch of fur had gone. Spinney had lost some fur too. *Spinney is fine... I'll be fine...*

'*Sorry Dust.*'

A sharp pain stabbed his leg where she'd taken his fur. He flinched then relaxed as he felt Fiona's hand rest lightly on his head.

'*Shhnowhaveasnoozeandiwillfixyouup.*'

She moved her face close to his and smiled. He took a deep breath, surprised at how tired he'd become. Then he leant on Fiona's hand and closed his eyes.

*

Human voices dragged Dust from a deep sleep. He struggled to open his eyes in the bright glaring light and his head felt fuzzy. He parted his jaws to taste the air. Fiona's scent. Then Craig's sneering voice.

'*The Ratter isawake, takeitbackupstairs.*'

Dust lifted his head as much as he could. Craig leant on a ledge, scratching on a sheet. Fiona was at the other side of the Healing Box, moving shiny objects around.

'*Heneedsrest, andfoodbeforehegoesback.*'

'*Feeditthen,*' Craig snapped.

Fiona took a deep breath as she crouched and took a colourful packet from under the ledge. Standing again, she tipped the contents into a small blue bowl. A familiar scent drifted across Dust's tongue. *Dry nuggets...*

'*Hereyougo,*' Fiona put the bowl down in Dust's bed and scratched his neck.

'*Howmuchofthathaveyoubeenfeedingthem?*'

Fiona's hand trembled as she pulled it away. *Notmuch, itstohelphimrecover.*'

'*Didyouputfoodinthe Ratter room.*'

'*Sorrywhat?*' Her fear scent strengthened.

'*Ifoundpetfoodonthefloorinthe Ratter room, Fiona.*'

'*Ihadsomeinmypocket...whenireturned Spinney... er Ratter numberthirtythree,*' Fiona spoke quickly but didn't look up. '*Theymusthavefallenout.*'

'*Welldontdropanymore.*'

Fiona shook her head and inspected Dust's foreleg. More fur was missing from around the scratch, which had healed into a thin, bumpy line. His hip throbbed, but the only pain he felt was his aching stomach. He shifted into a crouch and lapped up a mouthful of nuggets.

With his stomach soothed, Dust sat up and gave his fur a quick grooming, and when he'd done, Fiona gently lifted him from the bed and hoisted him over her shoulder. She carried him carefully through the dazzling box that must have been directly under the Long Box, past the red door and back to the silver doors that vanished into the wall. The Dropping Box swayed and juddered, upwards this time.

As Fiona opened the Meeting Box door, Dust heard muffled mews and claws scrabbling across the floor. He lifted his head to see wide eyes peering out from beds and behind full boxes. Briar stood in the middle of the floor, sniffing the air, his fur bristling along his back. As Fiona carried Dust inside and closed the door behind her, he could feel the tension in the air.

'Dust!' Briar meowed, 'How are you?'

Fiona lowered Dust to the floor. He shook himself and staggered slightly, then feeling a little lightheaded, he sat down. The other cats exchanged nervous glances.

'I'm fine,' Dust assured them.

Fiona gave him a little scratch on his head, '*Becarefulnexttimeokay*,' then she left the Meeting Box, closing the green door quietly behind her.

'Told you he'd be okay,' Spinney padded up to Dust and sniffed his fur, 'I was fine, they just fix your wounds.'

'I knew you'd be back soon,' Onyx purred.

'Conker isn't back, and neither is...' Fern's mew trembled, and she went quiet.

Dust looked around the cats in front of him. *My cats...* He should be leading them, but he was still too tired to make sense of their anxious expressions.

Briar nodded and flicked an ear to the beds, 'You look like you need more rest. We can talk later.'

'Talk?' Dust asked as Briar helped him climb up onto the full boxes. He was glad to find that his old, bloodied bed been replaced, but as he stepped into the fresh new covers, his skin tingled. *Something's wrong...* He stopped and looked back at Briar.

'It's okay, Dust, I've got you,' Briar mewed.

Dust saw a flicker of unease cross Briar's yellow eyes. He looked at the other cats and saw the same worry in their eyes too. Fern and Onyx turned their heads away and Violet ducked down in her bed and closed her eyes. Spinney sat by the water bowl, shifting his paws like a guilty kitten. Rose sat still behind him, expressionless. Dust's fur began to rise, *they're hiding something...* he thought, *there's something they haven't told me...*

Dust stepped back out of his bed and turned to face them. He knew that there was one cat who wouldn't hide anything from him. 'Gloworm?' he mewed as he glanced around the Meeting Box, looking for the white tom.

'I'm sorry,' Briar hung his head, 'he's not here. Gloworm didn't return from scouting.'

14

The Code

THE FLAT LIGHT BATHED THE MEETING Box in a soft pinkish-blue glow. Violet got out of her bed to help Dust climb back into his, but he couldn't settle. Gloworm had vanished, Conker was still missing, and his cats were looking to him for answers. He rested his fuzzy head on the side of his bed while he listened to Briar's report.

'Rose and Gloworm scouted soon after the noise stopped,' Briar hopped up onto the full boxes and crouched next to Dust's bed, 'they went as far as the Cold Box, but the humans were still there so they turned back. Rose came back, but Gloworm vanished somewhere between the Cold Box and the flap.'

Dust lifted his head, 'Was the blue door open?'

Rose didn't say...' Briar glanced at the red she-cat.

'Not when I ran past,' Rose widened her eyes and flicked an ear to the wall behind him, 'he was behind me.'

The Blue Box... He's looking for the other cat... Should I tell them...

'Then Rose went back out to hunt with Violet and Onyx,' Briar went on, 'they say the blue door was closed, and there was no sign of Gloworm in the Cold Box or the Vast Tower Box.'

Dust realised that with Conker gone, he and Rose were the only cats who knew they'd seen inside the Blue Box. Had Gloworm asked her to cover for him?

Dust nodded to Rose and looked at Briar. 'What about the dull brown door? Could he be in the box behind it?'

Briar narrowed his eyes, 'Why would he be?'

'He could be hiding somewhere,' Violet stepped forward quickly, 'Perhaps a human spooked him.'

Violet knows... Dust let his eyes wonder around the Meeting Box as he decided what to do. If Gloworm was in the Blue Box, John would find him, and he'd be back soon. But if he hadn't returned by the time John walked past the flap, then they should start searching. For now, Dust decided to go along with Rose's cover. He sat up and nodded to the sisters. 'Did you check everywhere in the Cold Box and the Vast Tower Box?'

'I hunted with Rose and Onyx afterwards,' Violet mewed, 'We checked the Cold Box and caught three rats in the Vast Tower Box. There was no sign of Gloworm or Conker.'

'Do you think the humans are taking us away again?' Fern shuddered.

'Maybe,' Onyx mewed, 'They bought us here, they could take us away too.'

Violet closed her eyes and rested her tail lightly on Rose's back.

Dust looked at the despondent faces of his cats. He needed to reassure them without giving Gloworm away. 'I don't think the humans are taking us away. They'd put us in traps if they were.'

Spinney's eyes went wide, 'The Green Female doesn't.'

'Fiona has only taken us to the Healing Box, which is under here, not away.'

'Fiona?' mewed Rose.

'What do you mean under here?' Briar asked.

'The Healing Box is down, somewhere. I went down in a Dropping Box to get there,' Dust flicked his tail to the floor, 'The Green Female's name is Fiona. And the White Male is Craig. Fiona is kind, but Craig ... he can be cruel.'

'He's right, down ... down in a Dropping Box' Spinney nodded his agreement.

Dust went on, 'Conker and Gloworm left on their own paws, so I don't think humans took them. I'm sure they're still here.'

'We should all scout and hunt together,' Fern mewed.

'No need,' Rose flicked her tail, 'we should be more watchful.'

'Being watchful is good, Rose,' Briar growled, 'but it won't stop cats—'

'Chasing rats into boxes,' Rose hissed, 'or not telling their scouting partner they're in trouble?'

'Trouble?' Fern mewed nervously.

'Gloworm would have alerted every cat in The Boxes if he'd run into trouble,' Briar growled, 'He went somewhere.'

Dust stood and flicked his tail, 'Gloworm is smart and cautious. He could be hiding to watch something. I'm sure he'll return when it's safe. And Rose has a point, we should be more vigilant, and gather more information about The Boxes.'

Briar nodded slowly, 'I agree.'

'After we've eaten,' Onyx purred, 'I'm starving.'

Dust nodded, 'I ate in the Healing Box, so we can talk after you've all eaten.'

Every cat agreed and gathered by the water bowl to help Rose portion up the rats. Dust slumped down into his bed box, laid his head on the soft bedding, and closed his eyes. He tried to sleep but worry tore at him. *Should I tell them now....?*

'Dust, are you still awake, do want any rat flesh?' Violet leant over the side of his bed and gently touched her nose to his.

Dust blinked, 'I had dry nuggets.'

Onyx hopped up beside Violet and dropped a scrap of rat flesh into his bed. 'You need proper food, not that human stuff.'

Dust purred, 'Thank you,' he licked at the scrap. It tasted good, but he wasn't hungry. Something else was gnawing at his stomach, *I should tell them...* Dust pushed the scrap of rat flesh away and sat up, 'There's something I didn't tell you.'

Every cat exchanged confused glances as they turned to look at Dust.

When he had their attention, he began, 'When Gloworm and I scouted, before the hunt where we lost Conker, we saw behind the blue door. John, the Blue Male opened it and let us look inside. There wasn't much to see, which is why we forgot to tell you all after we heard the rats speak.'

'John? Like Fiona and Craig?' Onyx mewed, 'how do you find out their names?'

Dust purred, 'They say their names after they make the sound, "*hey*".'

'Okay, that makes sense,' Onyx nodded, 'Did you find where those scents came from?'

'Yes.'

'What was in there?' Briar hopped onto on the full box beside Dust.

'The Blue Box is full of full boxes, sweepers, and bowls,' Dust mewed, 'Gloworm found a small hole in the wall, behind a large white box with a circle. That is where the scents are coming from. But John shooed us out before we found out what was making them.'

'See, Gloworm's safe. He probably fell asleep in the Blue Box?' Spinney purred.

Briar nodded, 'Spinney could be right, but the scouts should report everything before the hunt goes out. The Blue Box didn't sound important then, but it has claimed another cat.'

'But Rose didn't see John,' Fern glanced at Rose, 'did you?'

Rose twitched her whiskers, 'No.'

'So how can he be in the Blue Box, 'Fern mewed, 'how can he be safe? Conker isn't safe ... none of us are.'

'Fern,' Violet stepped to her side, 'We will find them,'

Dust stood up, 'I was wrong to forget about the Blue Box, and Briar is right, scouts need to report everything on their return.'

'Then the scouts should say that they saw something that can be discussed later,' Violet added.

'But quickly, or we could lose the rats?' Onyx mewed.

'And what if they're wrong about what they saw?' Briar flicked his tail, 'What if they saw something that seemed unimportant, but as they discuss it later, it becomes clear that it will be a problem for the hunters.'

'We need a code,' Spinney mewed.

'Okay,' Onyx agreed, 'that sounds useful, tell us Spinney?'

Spinney nodded, and explained, 'When we were kits, the humans would take me and my brother, Esker, and my three sisters, Thistle, Moss, and Nettle to the Ratbot Boxes one at a time, and we always went to different boxes. It was before Esker and Thistle were taken away, so there were five Ratbot Boxes, and we never knew which one we would go to.'

'Go on,' Onyx shuffled closer to Spinney, flicking her ears with interest.

'Well, there wasn't much time to talk when the humans bought one of us back and took another, so we made up a code.'

'Which was?' Rose mewed.

'Very useful,' Spinney purred, 'You see, when one of us returned, we'd say, Grey Box, or Two Door Box, or Dark Box or Warm Box or Turn Box.'

'Why?' Onyx twitched her whiskers.

'Because it made it easier to guess which box the rest of us might get if we knew where the others had already been.'

Onyx flicked Spinney on his head with her tail.

'Why did it matter which box you went to?' Briar mewed.

Spinney batted Onyx's tail away, 'It didn't, it was just fun to guess right.'

'Fun?' Fern hissed, turning to Spinney, her fur rising along her spine, 'There was nothing fun about the Old Place. The humans trapped me in those Ratbot Boxes ... and they drove Ratbots into me ... and pulled me from under ledges by my tail when I hid...'

'Fern is right, this isn't a game anymore,' Briar mewed, 'The Boxes are dangerous, and we need a way to warn each other about danger.'

'Then a code *is* a good idea,' Onyx pressed against Fern's side, 'Don't you think, Dust?'

Dust considered Spinney's story. *He has a point...* 'It's a clever idea. Spinney may have been playing a game with his littermates, but the object of the game was to pass information to each other quickly. Spinney's code can help scouts report quicker *and* help us understand The Boxes better.'

'It can?' Spinney exchanged a confused glance with Onyx.

Dust nodded and went on, 'We know the humans by their names, or the colour of their covers, and we have a name for every box. We should watch which humans go to which boxes, and what colour the flat light is when they go and what noises we hear and when. Whatever we see and hear when we scout, we can report back using Spinney's code.'

'Yes!' Spinney mewed with a little bounce.

'And no cat should go anywhere alone...' Fern mewed, 'there is danger everywhere ... Listen ... I can hear it now...' she shuddered, 'terrifying ... noises...'

'You can hear your own fear, Fern,' Rose mewed, 'Calm down.'

Violet rested her tail over Fern's back and glanced at Rose, 'We won't leave you alone, Fern, and we can hunt for you until we know The Boxes better.'

Onyx licked Fern's ear, 'Of course we will, and we'll find Conker, I'm sure.'

Dust flicked his ears. He could hear something too. Faint, and on the very edge of his hearing, a cat was yowling.

One by one the cats pricked their ears as they too heard the yowls, until all ears were trained on the flap. Fern shivered and slunk down between Onyx and Violet as the yowling grew louder. Rose strode towards the flap, fur bristling, and claws extended. Briar hopped down from the full boxes to join her, followed by Spinney. Dust stepped out of his bed, raised his head and sniffed the air.

A heartbeat later the flap banged open and Gloworm stumbled through it into the Meeting Box. Barging past Rose, he slid to a halt in the middle of the floor, licked a forepaw and ran it over his head, 'Wash ... for Shadow white,' he panted, 'wash for ... Shadow White...'

'What happened?' Dust hopped down from the full boxes. Cats moved aside as he padded to the white tom. Gloworm's fur was on end, and he was shaking and struggling to catch his breath, but his fear scent was mixed with excitement.

Gloworm lowered his paw and looked at Dust, 'It's true,' he mewed. 'Everything my mother told me. It's true.'

15
Icicle

'SLOW DOWN,' VIOLET STEPPED FORWARD AND licked Gloworm's ear.

Gloworm took a deep breath, 'I'm sorry ... I'm just shocked ... thrilled! This is everything I dreamed of, but it's ... it's ... I don't know...'

'What did you see, Gloworm?' Dust asked. The white tom looked shaken, but his fear scent was fading.

'There's a hole in the wall...' Gloworm began, 'And through the hole ... there is a cat. And I spoke to him. He told me it's all true.'

'Is it a big hole?' Spinney asked, 'did you go through it?'

'No, it's too small for a cat. Maybe even too small for a rat.'

'Did you see this cat?' Onyx asked kindly.

'I didn't need to see him,' Gloworm went on, 'I just talked to him.'

'Then how do you know this cat is real, how do *we* know it's true?' Briar's voice was laced with suspicion.

'You have to believe me,' Gloworm sighed.

'Why not start at the beginning,' Dust laid his tail over Gloworm's back, 'you said that everything your mother told you is true. Why not start by telling us *what* she told you.'

'Okay, I will tell you...'

Fur flattened and ears flicked with curiosity as the cats gathered around Gloworm, eager to hear his story.

'I remember my mother well. Her name is Icicle. Me and my littermates, my brother, Grasshopper, and sisters Butterfly and Moth, were with her until our jaws were strong enough to chew our own food. She was taken away just before Butterfly died...' Gloworm took a deep breath, then went on, 'I remember ... we'd wash and curl up with Icicle after a meal and she'd tell us stories about her life before the Old Place. My favourite story was about the adventure she had in The Outside.'

Fern and Violet gasped and exchanged glances.

'In The Outside?' Onyx mewed.

'Let him talk,' Rose mewed.

Gloworm half-closed his eyes and continued, 'Icicle was born somewhere called *Farm*. She told us that Farm was a place with a vast outside. Where a twisted old tree stood high on a hill and the nearby floor was made from water and grass. She said the air moved so fast that it knocked the paws off cats, and water fell from the sky roof.

'Icicle didn't live at Farm for long. She was named Bella then, and her mother, Polly, was still teaching her to hunt when her new humans took her away. She didn't like her new humans and felt trapped in their box. So, when one day she found some moving air, she followed it through a hole, and found herself back in The Outside.

'Icicle followed the fast-moving air back to trees. They gave her shelter and calmed her with their rustling voices. She stayed at trees for a while, and she was happy.

'But, with time,' Gloworm sighed, 'Bella began to miss Polly, so she decided to try and find Farm. She climbed trees and looked around the vast outside until she saw a floor of grass and water and set off towards them.

'Bella walked through the fast-moving air and falling water until she was completely lost. She saw many human boxes, but none like Farm. She was ready to give up when she met a young tom cat called Piccolo.

'Piccolo told her he'd climbed into a truck ... like a Moving Box ...and had become trapped. When it opened again, he was lost.'

'Truck?' Rose mewed, 'the Grey Male said that.'

'A Moving Box?' Fern mewed nervously, 'Could Conker be in The Outside now?'

'We don't know, Fern.' Dust mewed kindly, 'Let's listen and find out all we can.'

Gloworm licked his shoulder as he waited for quiet, then continued, 'Piccolo told Bella much about The Outside, how the humans called their boxes *homes* and how they shared them with other creatures. But most importantly of all, Piccolo told her about Shadow White.'

Dust pricked his ears. *Wash for Shadow White...* The words Gloworm uttered to himself when facing the unknown. He couldn't recall Breeze ever saying anything like it.

'Piccolo told Bella that Shadow White is a Host. The first ghost. And when a cat dies, she appears and offers them choices, so they can return to their body or accept her invitation to the place after life. They met many other cats on their travels, some believed in Shadow White, and some didn't, but Bella found the stories comforting.

'Bella became Piccolo's mate, and when they learned she was expecting kittens, they tried even harder to find Farm. It was around then that they met a little she-cat called Sweep.

'Sweep was a Runner. She told them that cats who lived in The Outside organised their territories into wards, and a Runner's job is to carry messages between the wards. They told Sweep about Farm, and she knew a place just like it.

'Bella and Piccolo travelled with Sweep as she delivered her messages from ward to ward. Then one day, in the distance they saw a twisted old tree on a hill, near a floor of grass and water. It was the Ward of Shady Ly. But Sweep told them that getting there would not be easy.' Gloworm closed his eyes, 'Bella and Piccolo did not reach the twisted tree together.'

Violet gasped, 'What happened?'

Onyx laid her tail over Violet's back. Rose took a step closer to Gloworm, eyes wide with curiosity. Fern folded her ears and pressed closer to Briar. Spinney sat bolt upright, ears pricked and eyes wide. Dust felt his skin tingle as his fur began to rise. Something in Gloworm's words made him shiver.

Opening his eyes again, Gloworm continued, 'There was a farm ... but not her *Farm* ... a bad farm that stood between them and Shady Ly. There were no trees on this farm, only hard grey floors, huge wire trap barriers and cruel humans who lived with dogs.'

'With what?' Spinney mewed.

'Dogs' Gloworm mewed, 'Icicle told me that a dog is a bit like us, but they are unreasonable and can't think for themselves, so, they chase cats and follow humans.'

Fern hissed and shuddered.

Gloworm went on, 'The dogs on that farm were dangerous. They hunted cats as we hunt rats. Sweep told Bella and Piccolo that to get past without being scented, they needed to swim through the dangerous moving water that flowed around its edge. They agreed to try and waited for the bad farm to go dark before they set off.'

Dust glanced at the flat light. It was a dark blue now and would soon be black. *Dark, when the humans leave...* It made sense. Dust turned his attention back to Gloworm.

'They'd barely made it into the moving water when the dogs began to bark. They stayed close to the steep banks at the edge, but the water still it came up to their bellies. Then, as they were half-way past the farm, bright white eyes with swirling blue lights screeched at them from the other side of the moving water.'

'Sweep leapt out onto dry land and yowled at Bella and Piccolo to follow. Piccolo got out, but Bella got stuck. Then humans appeared. Some went to the farm, but one saw Bella. Piccolo yowled her name. but she was too heavy with kittens to scramble up the steep bank. She panicked and slipped and was dragged down below the moving water. And everything went black.'

'No!' Gasped Onyx, 'did she die? She can't have ... did she?'

Gloworm nodded, 'A bright warm light appeared and pushed the darkness away. Bella was sat on the dry bank of the moving water. Beside her sat a small white cat with bright blue eyes and a tatty blue bow around her neck. It was Shadow White, and she had come to offer Bella her choices.'

Silence fell in the Meeting Box. Whiskers twitched and tails curled, and Dust was mesmerized. He'd never heard such a story.

'Bella chose to return to her body, for her kittens. But before she returned, she asked Shadow White if they would ever find Farm ... if they were heading towards the right tree. And my mother never forgot Shadow White's answer:

'"*There are many trees, some as twisted as their tales. The one you seek is not where you want to go, but it is the one sought by cats who need direction.*"

'Bella never got to Shady Ly. And she never saw Piccolo again. She woke up in a trap, feeling better than she'd ever felt before. The White Kitten had healed her every ache, cut and scratch, and she felt strong. But the humans took her to the Old Place and called her Icicle. Soon after she arrived, she had her first litter of kittens, and when they were grown and gone, she was taken to a box where she met a tom called Glitterbug. My father.'

Fern sniffed. Violet rested her tail over her back.

'And you believe your mother's story?' Briar held Gloworm's gaze.

'Yes, I do now,' Gloworm mewed certainly.

'You didn't before?'

'Before...' Gloworm's voice quavered, 'Before ... I wasn't sure. I'd never seen or heard of any of the things she spoke of. I wanted to believe it, it gave me hope that there is a better place, but I wasn't sure it was real.'

'Why do you believe it now?' Rose mewed.

'Because of the cat I spoke to through the hole. He lives in The Outside. His is an old tom called Benny and he says he is the Warden of Warmroot Copse. He told me that

Warmroot Copse is next to Shady Ly. And there is a twisted old tree on a hill ... and...' Gloworm broke off, his voice catching in his throat. He took a deep breath and gathered his words, '...and he knows a cat called Piccolo.'

Dust jumped to his paws. He had so many questions, he couldn't speak for having too much to say. Meows of surprise, and disbelief, filled the Meeting Box.

Gloworm slumped onto his side and closed his eyes.

'Do you think he's telling the truth?' Fern mewed quietly.

'I don't think he's lying,' Violet sniffed over Gloworm's fur, 'At least, he must believe it?'

Onyx stepped forward, 'Then we must decide what *we* believe.'

Briar nodded, 'We should vote.'

'Why not?' Rose sighed.

Dust crouched down next to Gloworm and lent close to him. Violet sat on his other side and groomed his fur. Dust looked up at his cats, 'Briar's right, He mewed, 'It's fair that every cat should have their say, and if most of us believe Gloworm's story, we should then decide what we want to do about it.'

Gloworm raised his head and nodded.

Dust looked around at his cats. 'Rose? Do you believe his story?'

Rose nodded, 'Yes.'

'Thank you,' Dust mewed, surprised. Then he turned to her sister, 'Violet? How about you?'

Violet nodded, 'Yes, I do. I don't think Gloworm would invent such a story.'

Two believe... Dust dipped is head to Violet and turned to Briar, 'What about you?'

The tabby tom shook his head, 'No. I just can't imagine the things he speaks of. I have no doubt his mother told him stories, but he probably just fell asleep and dreamt about this other cat.'

Gloworm sighed and dropped his head back onto his paws.

'Spinney?' Dust asked.

'I don't think I do. It does sound like a strange dream.'

Two believe, two don't...

'Fern?'

'It sounds too good to be true, doesn't it?' Fern shook her head. 'Maybe The Outside exists ... maybe Conker's there ... but maybe not. They're right, it's just a dream.'

Two believe, three don't...

'Onyx?'

The black she-cat twitched her whiskers. 'What cat can dream about things that aren't real. And those scents floated into The Boxes from somewhere, so I believe him.'

Floated into The Boxes ... moving air... Dust had the deciding vote. And no doubts. He got to his paws and faced his cats. 'I was with Gloworm when he discovered the hole. He wasn't asleep or dreaming, and he wasn't lying. And Onyx is right. No cat dreams of untruths. And those uplifting scents float on moving in air. Air doesn't move in The Boxes, so the scents must come from The Outside.'

'So, you believe him?' Briar mewed.

'Yes. I believe Gloworm's discovery proves that The Outside is real. And we can find it through holes in The Boxes. If Benny lives in The Outside, and Icicle went there, then so could we.'

Gloworm sat up slowly, 'Thank you...' he mewed.

'The majority believe Gloworm's story,' Briar looked at Dust, 'So, what do we do now?'

'We find out more about it,' Dust laid his tail on Gloworm's back. 'If Benny is in The Outside, how did he get there?'

'He's always been there,' Gloworm mewed, 'He told me he's never been inside The Boxes.'

Dust nodded, 'Does he know how we can get there?'

'No, I don't think he does,' Gloworm mewed sadly.

'What if the humans could take us into The Outside,' Spinney flicked his tail, they bought us into The Boxes, they could take us back out.'

Onyx slapped him on the side of his head with her tail, 'They bought us here in traps, they'd take is out the same way. They're not going to take us to The Outside and let us go.'

'But the humans *do* leave The Boxes,' Violet mewed, 'so, we should watch them.'

'Yes, and then sneak out with them,' Spinney purred.

'I don't think I could ... they'd catch us...' Fern shivered.

Dust felt his mind wonder as he listened to them talk. *The humans...* If humans could get in and out of The Boxes, so could cats. Humans needed big holes ... doors, to get out but a cat only needed a small gap, not much bigger than a rat would... 'Wait!' Dust flicked his tail.

'What?' Onyx jumped.

Dust blinked apologetically, 'What about the rats? how did they get in here?'

'The humans bought them here,' Spinney mewed, 'for us to eat.'

'But why?' Dust went on, 'Why bring rats here, then bring us here to eat them?'

'Because this is their game,' Briar twitched his whiskers, 'They made us hunt Ratbots before, now rats. It's what they do.'

Onyx tipped her head to one side and stared at Dust, 'What if the humans *didn't* bring the rats here ... is that what you mean?'

Dust gathered his thoughts, 'Yes, that is what I mean. What if the rats came here themselves ... to eat the food the humans drop? And the humans bought us here to catch the rats.'

'That doesn't make any sense,' Onyx purred, 'why would they need us to catch the rats. If they stopped dropping food, the rats would go away.'

Dust thought about John, 'Maybe the humans don't know they're dropping food. Or the rats could be here for another reason, but they'd know how to get in and out.'

'They talk, so ask them,' Rose flicked her tail.

Onyx glanced at Rose, 'She's right, again. It's a clever idea.'

'But will they want to talk?' Violet mewed, 'surely we are their enemy.'

Rose sniffed, 'Catch one and make it talk.'

16

Boirey

DUST SPLIT THE LAST PIECE OF rat flesh with a claw and carried half to Gloworm's bed. The tom was still resting and hadn't eaten since he'd returned. Around the water bowl, the hunters were discussing their plan as they waited for the scouts to return.

'Violet should catch the rat,' Briar mewed.

'Why?' hissed Rose.

Briar flicked his tail, 'Because we need it alive.'

Rose's eyes widened, 'Meaning?

Dust dropped the rat flesh in Gloworm's bed, 'Wait,' he mewed, 'that's a good idea,' He hopped down and padded to the she-cats, 'Violet is patient. She *is* most likely to get it back here alive.'

Rose turned to Violet, 'Are you okay with that?'

'Yes, I'll do my best.'

'If it bites you, kill it. We can get another.'

'Should I try and talk to it first?' Violet asked.

Dust shook his head, 'No, it will run.'

Violet nodded again, 'So, Rose follows me while I catch the live rat, and Onyx kills any others that interfere?'

'Yes,' Dust mewed, 'And when you catch one alive, run straight back here. Don't hesitate. Rose will alert Onyx and help carry any catches as they follow you back. And try and catch a slow one, one that's less able to fight.'

'Got it,' Violet shifted her paws uneasily.

'All they do is fight,' Spinney's fur bristled, 'and bite.'

'So, we stop it biting,' Rose mewed.

'How?' Spinney curled his tail.

Briar shook his head, 'If we injure it, it could die before it talks.'

'They eat human food,' Rose looked at Spinney, 'So, they will eat the dry nugget you hid in your bed.'

Spinney licked his shoulder. 'I want that.'

Dust looked at Spinney and twitched his whiskers. 'If you still have one, we could use a dry nugget to entice the rats out.'

Rose shook her head, 'Attack the rat when it bites the nugget.'

Dust purred, 'Because it can't bite with its mouth full.'

'Thank you, Rose,' Violet licked her sister's ear, 'I'll do that, just stay close to me.'

'Always,' Rose mewed.

Spinney slumped onto his belly and grumbled, 'It better work, that's my last nugget.'

Rose glanced at Spinney and twitched her whiskers just as the flap banged open and Onyx bounded in, followed more calmly by Fern.

'Rats in the Cold Box and Vast Tower Box,' Onyx Panted, 'everywhere.'

Rose got to her paws, 'Let's go.'

'I'll tell you more on the way,' Onyx slid back through the flap, Violet close behind her.

Rose hopped up onto the full boxes and rummaged in Spinney's bed for the dry nugget, found it and bounded out of the flap after Violet and Onyx.

'There were lots of rats...' Fern shivered as she lay down beside the full boxes, 'they really are everywhere.'

Dust padded to her side and licked her ear, 'They will be fine. They are fast and smart.'

'But what if they get attacked ... what if there are too many of them?'

'Don't worry, you should rest now,' Dust mewed, 'you will need your strength for when they return.'

Fern signed as she got to her paws and hopped up to her bed. Spinney followed and padded his bedding straight before he got in and curled up. Gloworm shifted in his sleep.

The flat light was a shimmering black as Dust climbed into his own bed. He rested his head on his paws and stared up at the little red light above the water bowl. It never changed colour, but it was harder to see when the flat light was bright. If the colour of the flat light told them where the humans would be, and when, what could this little red light tell them? He closed his eyes and tried to recall where he's seen the other little red lights, but his thoughts were interrupted by the sound of paw steps as Briar repeatedly paced the floor.

Covers rustled beside him. Dust flicked his ears.

'Thank you for believing me.'

Dust turned to Gloworm, 'Of course I believe you,' he mewed, 'And I think Icicle wanted you to believe in The Outside. I see Breeze in my dreams now. My memories of her are still hazy, but I'm sure she's telling me how to escape.

It's a feeling I get, that she will somehow help us to find the way out.'

'Dreams are hard to understand, but anything that you see in them could be helpful, no matter how strange it seems.'

'I think she's telling me that the cats around me will help find the way out.'

'Maybe. We are smart and we are looking.'

'And asking.'

Gloworm purred, 'Do you think the rats will know how to get out?'

A cat yowled somewhere in the distance.

Dust raised his head and pricked his ears. It was one of the hunters, but the voice was too far away to tell who it was.

Briar hopped down to the floor and padded to the flap.

A rat's screech echoed in the Long Box.

Dust got to his paws and gave Gloworm's ear a lick, 'Stay there, I think were about to find out.

Dust had barely made it to the flap when Rose crashed through. The red she-cat bounded across the floor, flicked her head up and opened her jaws. Two dead rats flew across the Meeting Box and landed with a thump behind the water bowl. Then she whirled on the spot and leapt back to the flap just as Violet's pushed through a squirming shrieking rat.

Rose extended her claws, snatched the rat from Violet's jaws and slammed it into the floor. Violet slid though the flap and they stood together, panting, as they pinned it down, pressing their claws into its writhing body.

Onyx thrust her head through, dropped another dead rat, and disappeared. She returned a heartbeat later with a mouth full of rat tails and climbed clumsily through the flap, dragging another two bodies with her.

Spinney bounded over to help Onyx drag the catches to the pile. She had scratches on her flank, but they didn't look deep.

Dust turned to Briar, 'Bar the flap, don't let it escape.'

Briar sat down in front of the flap and leant against it, using his back to keep it closed.

Rose gave Dust a long expectant look.

Dust nodded, 'Let it up.'

Rose and Violet released the rat, and as Dust watched its white rump scurry away and dive behind the full boxes, he felt his skin prickle. 'It's the same rat that led Conker into the Moving Box,' he mewed. 'I chased that white rump through the Vast Tower Box, I'd recognise it anywhere.'

Fern gasped, 'It is?'

Rose nodded. 'Yes, and it's a leader.'

'What do you mean?' Briar asked.

'It was giving orders,' Violet mewed.

Briar snorted, 'A leader stupid enough to stop and eat when it's being hunted?'

'It didn't,' Violet shook her head, 'I put the nugget down and waited. The rats were swarming everywhere so it was hard to hide. The rat that picked up the nugget was facing me and would have seen me if I'd moved. Then that one...' she flicked her tail towards the sound of little heavy breaths in the shadows, 'attacked the one that had stopped to eat. It was so angry that it didn't see me, so I took it.'

'That was brave, Violet,' Dust mewed kindly.

The grey she-cat shook her head. 'It was my only choice, or we would have failed.'

'You did well,' Onyx purred as she padded to Violet's side and sat down. Then she looked at Dust, 'So, what do we do with it now?'

'Talk to it. Ask it questions,' Dust purred.

Rat claws scrabbled on the floor.

'Come out, rat. We only want to talk,' Onyx padded towards the full boxes and peered into the shadows.

'You kill eat rat. You cat, cat do that,' the rat squeaked.

'Only if you don't answer our questions,' Onyx mewed.

'If rat answer, what? what?' A little black nose appeared from behind the full boxes, twitching above sharp yellow teeth. The rat raised its front paws and flexed its claws. It shivered with fear, but the malice remained in its cruel little eyes.

'We have a question for you,' Dust took a step forward and sat down, 'We think you can help us.'

'Why rat help cat?'

'If you help us, we will leave The Boxes and not hunt you anymore,' Dust mewed.

'Rat hide from cat. Cat no find rat, why rat help?' The rat lowered its front paws to the floor and took a step towards Dust, its nose twitching rapidly as it sniffed the air around him, 'cat afraid, cat smell of fear.'

Dust flicked his tail to the pile of bodies by the water bowl, 'We are not afraid of rats.'

'Not rat. Cat fear box,' the rat took a step closer, 'cat fear rat not help.'

Fern gasped.

Dust waved his tail, telling his cats to stay calm.

Rose ignored him and got to her paws. She padded to the rat and growled, 'Rat help or Cat. Will. Kill. Rat.'

The rat flinched under the glare of Rose's brilliant green eyes, but instead of backing away, it ducked and tipped its head to one side. Dust saw it part its jaws and shuffle its hind legs, readying itself to leap up and sink its long yellow teeth into her throat.

'Rose...' Violet saw it too.

But Rose was quicker. As it hunkered down ready to leap, she lunged upwards and sideways, lifting her neck out of the reach of the rat's teeth. Then she side-swiped hard with her paw, sending it scudding across the floor and thudding into the bottom of the door.

'Rose!' Briar growled.

Rose flicked her tail, 'It's a rat.' she hissed, 'if it won't talk, we kill it and get another.' She padded towards the rat, 'This is no leader.'

'Rose, wait,' Violet mewed gently and trotted to her side, 'let me try.'

Rose stopped and looked at Violet. An unspoken conversation flickered between their eyes before they both looked at the panting rat.

Rose sat down.

Violet dipped her head to her sister, then turned to the rat. 'Hello,' she mewed kindly, 'My name is Violet, and this cat is my sister, Rose,' she pointed to the red she-cat with her tail, 'I am the cat who caught you. I was given the job of capturing you alive because I am nice. Please remember that I could easily have killed you then. And as no other cat could have carried you back here without sinking their teeth deeper into your neck, I am your best chance of survival, do you understand?'

Dust let out his breath. Rose was fast and fierce, and he wouldn't want to make an enemy of her, but Violet could be just as fierce with her intelligence and patience. They had the rat so firmly under their control, he could only hang back and watch as they worked.

The rat scrambled to its paws and looked up at Violet, 'Rat ... understand.'

'Okay, good. So, let's start at the beginning. You talk, and you seem smart, so you must have a name, please tell me your name.'

The rat stood up on its hind legs and tipped its head to one side as it looked at Violet, curiosity slowly clouding the malice in its eyes, 'Rat name Boirey, Ard Boirey.'

'Well, Ard Boirey, it's nice to meet you,' Violet dipped her head politely, 'We captured you alive so we could ask you a question. You see, we cats did not choose to be here. We were brought here by humans to catch and eat rats. You and your friends are the only food we have.

'Of course, this isn't what we want,' Violet went on, 'We've heard tales of a better place, The Outside, and we want to go there.'

Briar jumped to his paws and turned to stare at the flap, his fur bristling.

Dust flicked his ears as he watched Briar peer through the flap, shake his head and sit down again. *Did he hear something in the Long Box....?*

'We could ask the humans to let us out,' Violet continued as Boirey sat listening to her, as if enchanted by her kind voice, 'but we don't think they would. They don't seem to listen to cats.'

Boirey twitched his nose, 'So?' he peeped.

Dust heard Boirey scratch the floor as he spoke, but he didn't see the rat move. The other cats had heard it too. They were all on their paws watching Boirey closely, ears pricked and tails straight, ready to leap if the rat made a move on Violet.

'We have a question for you.'

The scratching sound came again. Dust felt his skin prickle and the fur begin to rise along his back. He was sure Boirey hadn't moved. No cat had moved a paw, but their fur was rising too. Gloworm flicked an ear to the wall behind him.

'Ask, cat, ask.'

'How did you get into The Boxes, and can you get out?'

'That two questions cat,' Boirey squeaked.

'Okay, let me ask it again,' Violet mewed, 'Can rats get in and out of The Boxes?'

'Yes. Rat can.'

Violet sighed, 'Oh good, then could you please tell us how we can get out?'

Gloworm spun around in his bed and stared at the wall.

'Rat no tell cat,' Boirey peeped.

Violet took a deep breath and went on, 'If we leave The Boxes, we will not be here to kill and eat rats. Rats will be safe.'

'Boirey answer question, now Boirey go.'

Gloworm's eyes followed something across the roof. Fern shifted in her bed; a low growl rumbled in her throat as she glanced behind her. Briar flicked his ear to the door and glancing at Spinney. Spinney shook his head and flicked an ear to the corner behind the litter boxes. Onyx was staring at the flap. Rose didn't take her eyes or ears off Boirey.

'All we want to do is get out of here,' Violet's voice sharpened as she became aware of the cats shifting behind her.

Dust looked up as the scratching sounds moved up the walls and across the roof, then down again ... through the walls ... behind the door ... beyond the flap... The sound was everywhere, but he couldn't lock his ears onto it.

Boirey flung his head back and let out a hacking screech. Every cat froze. Tails bushed and fur bristled. The rat was laughing.

'Cat need rat. Too bad. Rat no help,' Boirey peeped, before he screeched with grating laughter again.

'Why won't you help?' Violet asked, her ears flattening as her kind voice gave way to a hiss of frustration, 'It's best for —'

Violet didn't finish.

Rose bunched her quarters and leapt at the rat with her claws extended. She landed on Boirey, crushing him into the ground with a sickening crunch of bone, and as his tormenting laugh broke into terrified squeals of pain, she bit down hard on his neck. Boirey fell silent as his blood bubbled out over her paws.

No cat moved as Rose lifted her head. Blood dripped from her chin, 'Plenty more of them,' she growled as she picked up Boirey's body and dropped it on the pile with the other catches.

Dust sat down.

Rose hopped back up to her bed and began licking her paws.

Violet gave herself a quick wash before she joined her sister. One by one, the other cats followed. None spoke.

Dust felt the disappointment in the silent exchanges that passed between them, but he couldn't tell if they were disappointed with Rose, the rat, or him because the plan had failed. He was the last to return to his bed.

Gloworm shivered beside him.

'Are you okay?' Dust asked.

'They were here,' Gloworm growled softly as he licked a fore paw and ran it over his ear, 'Wash for Shadow White...' he mumbled, 'They were all here...'

17

The Bright Box

DUST SNIFFED THE COOLING BODY. NO cat wanted to eat Boirey. His scent seemed more familiar than the other dead rats, as if talking to him had made him less palatable. Even Rose had passed over him when she'd shredded the other rats on the pile. Maybe later when he'd cooled, and their hunger had returned, he would smell more like food.

The flat light was bright blue when Fiona arrived. Dust had eaten well, and he remained curled up in his bed as she cleaned the litters and refilled the water bowl. Her scent was calm, and she hummed quietly as the cats in the Meeting Box groomed and comforted each other. Rose and Violet took turns cleaning each other's ears and Fern nibbled at a knot in her tail. Briar chewed a claw sheath while Spinney snoozed upside down in his bed. Only Onyx sat up watching Fiona, her whiskers twitching.

Gloworm slept soundly beside him. The white tom was convinced that rats had been in the roof, but Dust wasn't so sure now. After Boirey had died, the scratching sounds had stopped. *Boirey must have been scratching the floor...*

Onyx caught his eye, hopped out of her bed and padded over. 'Dust, I've had an idea.'

Dust nodded, 'Okay?'

'Remember what Violet said, about just asking humans to let us out?'

'Yes, but I'm sure they won't.'

'I know they won't,' she purred, 'but we might still find the way out if we watch them more closely.'

'What do you mean?'

Onyx glanced at Fiona, 'We should scout when the flat lights are blue, like you said, so we can watch where the humans go, and if they go out.'

Fiona picked up the litter cover and opened the door, '*Seeyoualllater, begood cats.*'

'It's a good idea,' Briar mewed, 'but there are too many humans about, and it could be dangerous.'

'They won't hurt us,' Onyx looked at Briar, 'I think they'll just shoo us away like John shooed Dust and Gloworm out of the Blue Box.'

Dust knew she was right, 'She has a point, Briar.'

'If we go now,' Onyx added, 'we could try and follow Fiona.'

Every cat had stopped grooming to listen with interest. Dust looked around their curious faces and nodded, 'Okay, Onyx and I will scout the Long Box, to follow Fiona.'

*

Dust took the lead as they padded up the middle of the Long Box. Muffled human voices drifted from beyond the Bright Corner, and as they peered around, they saw the vanishing doors sliding back out of the walls. Fiona's scent hung strong in the air until the doors met in the middle.

'There are humans behind that,' Onyx flicked an ear to the bright brown door, 'I can hear them.'

Dust padded forwards and listened. 'I hear them too.'

'It's the way we came in,' Onyx mewed, 'so it must also be a way out...'

Dust remembered hearing the voices of Fiona, Craig, John, and another female, as he'd been carried into The Boxes, but his trap had been covered, hiding everything from his view. They'd stopped after a door closed, before walking on a short distance to another door. The distance between the bright brown door and the Meeting Box door was about the same.

'...And the cover slipped off my trap a little when I came in and I saw the bottom of the vanishing doors.'

Dust sniffed the air, 'Let's have a closer look.'

As they padded to the bright brown door, Dust took in the scents. Fiona's scent was the strongest, then John's, and Craig's stale scent lingered too, but all their scents stopped at the vanishing doors. Beyond them, he could only smell sour damp. He turned to Onyx, 'No humans have been through here for a while.'

'Can we open the door ourselves?'

'Maybe. The green door opens when Fiona pulls the lever down.'

'Try it.'

Dust padded closer. The lever was bigger than the one on the green door. He stood up on his hind legs and reached up, just touching it with his claws extended. He rocked back on his haunches, jumped, and grabbed the lever in both fore paws and hung on for a heartbeat, but when it didn't move, he slipped back down to the floor.

Onyx Purred, 'Let me try.'

She leapt at the lever, gripped it firmly with both paws, and hung on longer than Dust had done. But when the lever still didn't move, Onyx let go and growled, 'This doesn't work. It can't be the same. We need to watch how the humans open it?'

Dust nodded, 'We can listen for footsteps from the Meeting Box ... and follow them.'

'Good idea,' Onyx turned and padded back to the vanishing doors, 'Do these go to the Healing Box?'

'Yes,' Dust caught up with her, 'they slide back and vanish into the wall. When you go into the Dropping Box behind them, the doors come back out of the walls and close. Then the Dropping Box goes down.

'And the Healing Box is down where, exactly?'

Dust closed his eyes and tried to recall the route he'd taken on Fiona's shoulder, 'I can't remember clearly, but I remember that after we got out of the Dropping Box, Fiona carried me through a box that was same shape as the Long Box, but under it. I thought Fiona was going back to the Meeting Box at first, as the route was the same. The white door was close to where the blue door should have been. So, I think the Healing Box is under the Cold Box.'

'How did Fiona open these doors?'

'She pressed that light bump,' Dust flicked his tail to the illuminated square on the wall beside the doors.

Onyx stood up on her hind legs, reached up a paw and pressed the light bump. There was a beep, and the light bump lit up orange. She took her paw away and stared wide eyed as the vanishing doors parted and began to slide back into the wall to reveal the Dropping Box. Then she looked at Dust, 'After you, boss.'

Dust peered into the Dropping Box. He could see his own reflection in the shiny silver wall at the back, and the reflection of three more glowing light bumps. 'We said we'd only scout the Long Box, what if we get trapped.'

'I'll wait here,' Onyx purred, 'if you don't come back, I will tell the others where you went.'

Dust flicked her with his tail as he took a step forward. 'There are more light bumps inside. Fiona pressed one of those too. The middle one, I think.'

Another beep made Dust jump. The vanishing doors began to slide out of the walls. He shook his head and glanced at Onyx, 'If I get taken to the Healing Box again, I'll watch again which ones Fiona presses.'

'I'm not sure it's a good idea to *try* to get taken there when we could just come back and press it. But I want to check the other brown door now.'

Dust nodded and led Onyx back around the Bright Corner and down the Long Box. They paused by the blue door to take in the uplifting scents that flooded out from below it.

'Moving air,' Onyx mewed, 'So is this what The Outside smells like?'

Dust closed his eyes and let the scents roll over his tongue. He tried again to imagine what could make such smells, but his thoughts were disrupted by the scrinch of a door lever.

'A door! come on...' Onyx mewed.

Dust leapt after Onyx and rounded the Dark Corner just in time to see the dull brown door move. A column of light appeared as it opened, and a silhouette of a female human appeared.

'Ohhello, lookjanicethe cats havecometoseeus.'

Dust blinked up at the silhouette. She moved carefully and seemed relaxed, but her scent was sharp and acrid. 'Stay back,' he mewed, 'her scent is strange.'

'Don't judge them on their scent, Dust,' Onyx flicked him with her tail as she padded towards the human, 'They can disguise it.'

Dust watched in surprise as Onyx moved around the human, and once her face could be seen in the light, stared up into her eyes.

'They are safe,' Onyx mewed.

'How can you tell?'

'Look at their eyes. If the black circle gets bigger when they look at you, they're safe.'

Dust stepped closer until he could see the soft brown eyes of the female human. The black circle in their centre widened as she smiled down at him. 'And if it gets smaller?' he mewed.

'Run,' Onyx purred, 'they're the broken ones.'

Dust shivered as he remembered Craig's icy blue eyes.

Another female human appeared behind the first, *'Awwtheyarecute,'* she uttered as it pushed the first female aside and closed the door.

As the harsh light slid back behind the dull brown door, Dust saw that both females had smooth, bright covers. Their sharp unnatural scents were almost identical and revealed no emotions.

'When they open it again, try and run past them,' Onyx mewed. ·

'*Awwhelenlook, thefluffyonelookslikemybobby,*' The second Bright Female uttered.

'*Ohhedoesdoesnthe,*' the first Bright Female crouched down and held out a hand to Dust.

Dust stepped forward and flicked his tail to Onyx, 'Go around them, I'll keep them distracted.'

Onyx nodded and began to creep around their legs.

'*Comeheresweetie, lookatyourcurlyears,*' Onyx froze as the second Bright Female rested her hand on her head. Dust purred at her confused expression, then jumped when the first Bright Female dropped her hand onto his own head.

'*Awtheyrenotwild, theyrejustsweetkitty cats.*'

'*Theyshouldntbetrappedinaplacelikethis,*   *no   cat shouldbe aprisoner, mybobbygetsmadifilockthe flap.*'

Dust flicked his ears back to the flap.

'*Shhjanicelisten, ithinkhesback,*' the first Bright Female stood up and made a grab for the door lever.

Onyx leapt back as the second Bright Female shooed her away with her hands.

'*Letsgetback, wontbegoodifheseethemhere.*'

As the first Bright Female pulled the door open, Dust dropped his eyes to avoid the light and followed them. He padded carefully around their legs and glanced at Onyx as he slipped through the closing door.

The new box was dazzlingly bright and so cluttered with human things that he struggled to focus on any single object. Boxes of all shapes and sizes lined the walls and littered the floor. Some flickered in a dizzying haze of colourful light, others sat on ledges surrounded by stacks of scratching sheets and strewn with sticks. As Dust watched, the second Bright Female hurried to a curved ledge, sat down behind it,

149

and picked up a shiny white object. She held it to her ear and began uttering quietly. Without the echoes of the Long Box, Dust recognised her voice. She had spoken to Fiona when he was in the trap. *This is the way out...*

He took another step forward and gazed up at the soft light flooding into the Bright Box through three huge flat lights and a big grey door on the far wall. These flat lights were different to the smaller ones. He could see shapes in them, spaced out over a patchy floor of smooth grey and clumpy green, they looked like boxes. Some looked like the walls of the Vast Tower Box, others like the Metal Box that sat inside the Cold Box. On top of the nearest grey box, Dust spotted a black rat like figure, sitting up tall and fluttering a long flat ragged foreleg. Around it, flew three more dark figures, gliding and whirling, like flying rats in silhouette against the bright blue roof. His heart sank. *If this is the way into The Outside, why is it all just boxes and rats...*

A door lever creaked, then a door slammed. A male human voice frosted the air.

'*Getbacktowork,*' Craig strode across the Bright Box, a covered trap swinging in his hand.

Dust gasped and stepped back. His shoulder brushed the first Bright Female's leg.

'*Helenopenthedoor, lethimout.*' The second Bright Female hissed.

Dust hopped around her legs and as the dull brown door opened, he lunged for the gap.

'Craig's coming,' Dust meowed as he ran back to the Dark Corner, 'he has a trap.'

'A trap?' Onyx leapt off the full box and started after him.

They skidded around the Blue Corner and as they neared the flap, Craig strode around the Bright Corner, swinging and bashing the trap into full boxes as he walked.

The cat in the trap growled.

Dust and Onyx slid to a halt and watched as Craig stopped in front of the green door.

'Come on, let's see who it is,' Dust nudged Onyx through the flap.

18

The Moving Box

DUST COLLIDED WITH ONYX AS SHE slid to a halt in the middle of the Meeting Box floor. Craig stamped his foot as he raised the trap with one hand and undid the catch with the other. Cats shrunk down in their beds. Craig tipped the trap forwards and shook out a cat.

The cat hissed. Claws scraped metal and a mass of ruffled black fur fell out onto the floor.

With a grunt, Craig left the Meeting Box and slammed the door behind him.

'Conker!' Fern gasped as she leapt out of her bed to greet the black tom.

Conker raised his head and shook himself. 'Fern! It's good to see you,' he mewed, bracing himself against her fussing. After a heartbeat, he took a step back, raised his head and looked around at the other cats, 'It's good to see all of you.'

'It's good to see you too,' Dust flicked his tail for quiet as he hopped down to greet Conker.

Conker tipped his head to one side as he looked at Dust, then he glanced at Briar, confusion in his expression.

'Some things have changed since you've been away,' Dust mewed.

'Like what?'

'He's our leader now,' Onyx pointed her tail at Dust.

'Our leader?' Conker twitched his whiskers, 'Well, okay.'

Briar stepped forward, 'We had a vote.'

'A vote?' Conker looked around, 'and everyone voted for Dust?'

Onyx purred, 'Dust got three votes, Briar two, Violet, Rose and you got one vote each?'

'I got a vote?' Conker glanced at Fern.

Fern licked her shoulder and mewed, 'You can still vote ... if you want to.'

'But if you vote for Briar, he will tie with Dust and let him lead anyway,' Onyx purred.

'My vote?' Conker shook his head and looked from Briar to Dust, 'Well ... I'll vote for Dust, I'm fine with him being our leader if you all are.'

Briar nodded and turned away.

Dust studied Conker as he spoke. He was blinking fast, and his gaze darted around the Meeting Box, from one cat, to the wall, to the roof, then to another cat. It was as if he couldn't see clearly and was trying to refocus his eyes. He looked dishevelled. His long fur matted and dirty, and his scent was strange. He smelt of Conker, but of Conker from somewhere else.

Gloworm clambered awkwardly down from his bed and sniffed the black tom, 'Were you in The Outside?'

Conker sat down heavily and looked at the floor, 'Yes, I was. I got trapped in that Moving Box when I chased the rat. When it stopped and opened again, the Grey Male was there, but we were somewhere else.'

'What was it like?' Onyx mewed.

Conker slumped down onto the floor and let out an exhausted sigh as he rested his chin on his paws, 'Strange ... huge ... it looked like a box at first. A huge box with a grey box inside it ... and other things that moved ... but didn't move. At first you can't see how big it is, and after a while, it just stops looking like a box and starts looking like forever...'

Dust recalled the huge flat lights in the Bright Box as he mulled over Conker's description. *a box full of other huge boxes?* Had he seen The Outside after all? Or was it just another giant box? When Gloworm had told Icicle's story, he'd made no mention of her seeing huge grey boxes. *Just twisted trees and moving air...* 'What about the air?' Dust asked. 'Did it move?'

'The air moved all the time,' Conker shuddered, 'it was hard to walk...'

'It's true, I told you,' Gloworm meowed over the gasps of the other cats.

'He really *has* been in The Outside!' Fern purred.

Rose got to her paws and stepped forward, flicking her tail from side to side. 'Then why is he back?'

Conker dipped his head to the red she-cat, 'To help you get out.'

Fern nuzzled into Conker's neck fur, 'You came back for us?'

'Of course,' Conker licked Fern's ear as he sat up. 'We can all get out if we get into the Moving Box behind the slide-down door.'

'But ... what if the humans catch us?' Fern mewed.

Conker purred, 'The Grey Male wasn't fast enough to catch me, and he'll be slower if he's trying to catch all of us.'

Or faster now that he's expecting it... Something about Conker's plan made Dust feel uneasy. *If no human notices us all in the Moving Box... If we are quick, we could get past the Grey Male... Conker got past him...* Dust took a step towards Conker and sat down, 'If the Grey Male didn't catch you, then how did you get back?'

Conker licked his shoulder, 'I met a cat. He ... helped me find the sign.'

'Benny?' Gloworm mewed, 'Was his name Benny?'

Conker shook his head, 'No, his name was—'

'What sign?' Rose interrupted.

'A big sign, with the shape of a cat on it. The humans at the sign can understand these...' Conker scratched his ear, 'my ear marks. The marks mean where I come from.'

Dust flicked his ear. He remembered Craig painfully turning it inside out and looking closely at it. Fiona had done it too, but gently. *Do I have ear marks...?* As he looked around his cats, he wondered why he'd never noticed them before. 'We all have them,' Dust stood and padded around his cats, peering into their ears, 'the marks in our ears ... all of us.'

'We do?' Violet studied Rose's ear, 'yes, I see them.'

Onyx sniffed Spinney's ear, 'Yes, looks like we all do.'

'The humans must have put them there,' Spinney scratched his ear, 'one of the times when they made us have long sleeps ... maybe.'

'I think you're right Spinney,' Dust peered into the orange and white tom's ear. *Scratching sheet... Light Bumps... Towers... Human marks...* 'The humans make marks on everything. It must be how they remember what things are ... and where they belong.'

'Then we can't escape?' Spinney sat down heavily and hung his head.

Briar flicked his tail, 'We can if we stay away from humans.'

'And the sign,' Conker mewed, 'If we don't want to come back, we just don't go there.'

'Too risky,' Rose glanced at Violet, 'We could be caught and separated.'

Conker sighed and rested his head on his paws.

Dust padded back to the exhausted tom and sat down, 'Thank you,' he mewed, 'Not every cat would have come back to help us.' He looked around the other cats, 'I believe Conker has found a way into The Outside, but the Moving Box may not be safe. We should discuss it again after he's rested.'

'I could use some sleep,' Conker purred, 'and some food. Is that rat for sharing?' Conker flicked his tail towards the last dead rat by the water bowl.

Dust looked at Boirey's body and shifted his paws uncomfortably.

Conker looked confused, 'Did I miss something else?'

'If you're that hungry, we won't stop you eating our little friend,' Onyx purred.

'Friend?' Conker twitched his whiskers.

Dust flicked Conker's shoulder with his tail and motioned to his bed, 'You may as well get comfortable while we explain.'

Conker dragged himself to his paws, scrambled slowly up onto the full boxes and flopped down heavily into his bed, 'I'll eat later, when I know what I've missed.'

Fern followed him and began grooming his matted fur as he rested his chin on the side of the bed.

Dust glanced at the blue flat light. It was dulling and a faint glimmer of red had appeared at the bottom. It would soon be time to scout. Every cat began to climb back into their beds to rest before John returned to wash away the scents with the sour damp. Dust crouched on the full boxes beside Conker's bed and told him about the Blue Box and Benny and how they were using Spinney's code to help them understand The Boxes better. Then Gloworm retold Icicle's story.

Conker had no trouble believing it. 'Your mother's right, Gloworm, the air never stayed still, and water did fall from the roof.'

Dust felt his paws tingle. *Conker's escape and return... Benny... Icicle's story... The uplifting scents in the Blue Box... The rats can get in and out of The Boxes... Moving air...* There was no doubt in his mind now. The Outside was real. All he had to do was find the safest way to get his cats into it, without the humans discovering them.

When the flat light had darkened and John's footsteps had faded away, Rose offered to scout and took Spinney with her.

Violet waited for them to go before she explained how she'd caught Boirey to interrogate. 'He acted like an important rat, then he laughed and refused to help us,' Violet shook her head, 'So Rose killed him.'

Conker purred, and just before his eyes closed and he drifted into sleep, he mewed, 'I'll eat that white rumped rat when I wake up...'

158

Fern rested her tail lightly over Conker's shoulder and curled up as close to him as she could, purring as she too fell asleep.

Dust padded back to his own bed, but Briar stopped him with a flick of his tail.

'Dust, Let's get a drink before we sleep.'

Dust nodded and followed Briar to the water bowl.

'Do you believe him?' Briar mewed quietly.

Dust swallowed a gulp of water, 'Why would he lie. His story matches Benny's and Gloworm's.'

'Gloworm told us about Benny. No other cat has seen or smelt or heard him. He probably made him up to make us all believe his mother's made-up story. And Conker is agreeing with Gloworm, so we don't find out he just fell asleep somewhere. This is no proof that The Outside exists.'

'Why would any cat make up stories,' Dust glared at Briar, 'He's exhausted. His scent is different. And he was blinking and straining to see.'

Briar nodded. 'Trying to hide the lies in his eyes.'

'He needs to rest,' Dust growled, 'We can ask him more questions later.'

'Of course,' Briar took a step back and dipped his head, 'But *we* should find out if Benny is real. Gloworm claims this cat spoke of a place with no humans, so we need to hear that with our own ears. And if it's real we should go there. We'd be foolish to get into the Moving Box. Conker didn't come back to help us escape. He was bought back here by Craig.'

Dust sighed. Briar was right, Craig did bring Conker back. He looked at Briar and mewed, 'I will get into the Blue

Box and find Benny. And I won't plan an escape until we have investigated both ideas.'

'Thank you,' Briar dipped his head, 'I knew you would understand.'

'Should we have another vote?' Onyx mewed from her bed.

Briar fattened his ears.

Violet lifted her head and blinked kindly at Dust, 'She does have a point. If there are two possible ways to get into The Outside, then we should find out what every cat wants to do.'

'Three,' Onyx nodded to Dust, 'The Bright Box. You said Craig brought Conker in through there. It could be the way the humans get in and out.'

'Then we should investigate all possibilities.' Briar mewed.

'We will,' Dust mewed as he hopped up to his bed, and as he lay down, worry gnawed at his stomach... *Do we really have proof that The Outside exists, or just hope....?*

He had barely closed his eyes when the flap banged open and Spinney bounded into the Meeting Box, Rose following close behind.

'They're everywhere,' Spinney meowed, 'and nowhere.'

Dust sat up again, 'Who?'

'The rats.' Spinney went on, 'We went through the Cold Box to the Vast Tower Box, and there's fresh rat scent ... it's on everything ... all over the place...'

Rose slapped her tail across Spinney's nose, 'Their scent is there, they are not.'

19

The Only Way

'HOW FRESH?' DUST HOPPED OUT OF his bed and padded to Rose and Spinney.

'Very fresh,' Spinney mewed, 'it was like we were just missing them ... like they were right next to us. But we couldn't see them ... nothing even moved.'

'Did you hear them?' Dust asked, 'A squeak, scratching? Did you feel them watching?'

Rose shook her head, 'No.'

'It sounds like they marked,' Briar hopped down to join Dust, 'They left their stench everywhere, and then they hid.'

'Yes, Spinney nodded, 'that makes sense.'

Dust carefully sniffed around Rose and Spinney. He could smell rat scent on them, faint on their fur and stronger on their paws. *They are marking...* He looked around the anxious faces of his cats, and purred, 'If they're trying to mark The Boxes as their territory, they can't hide for long. They'll come back after John washes their scent away with the sour damp.'

'Perhaps we should confuse *them* by using their scent to mask our own, before it gets washed away,' Onyx stood up in her bed and stretched, 'then we can hide and wait for them.'

'Use it how?' Violet sat up in her bed.

'Roll in it,' Onyx twitched her whiskers.

'What?' Spinney gasped, 'I don't want to smell like a rat!'

'You already do,' Rose mewed.

'Change our scent to confuse them,' Dust nodded to Onyx, remembering what she'd said outside the Bright Box, 'Like the humans do.'

'That's right,' Onyx purred.

Dust nodded, 'We can't follow the rat's scent now, but we can hide and wait until we see them.'

'Which means scouting alone,' Rose twitched her whiskers as she glanced at Briar.

'Yes, it does,' Dust sighed.

'It won't be safe,' Briar growled.

'We are bigger and faster,' Dust reassured him, 'And we only need a glimpse of one rat to find their freshest scent trail. We can track them from that.'

'Couldn't we lure them with food again?' Spinney asked.

Briar sniffed, 'Do you have any more nuggets?'

Spinney shook his head.

'What about the humans?' Violet mewed, 'Didn't you say they dropped food and the rats came to take it?'

Dust glanced at the flat light above her. It was still black. 'They would've taken it by now.'

'But it's a good idea, Violet,' Briar dipped his head to the grey she-cat, 'We could follow the humans and wait for them to drop more.'

Dust shook his head, 'How do we know where the humans will drop their food? Onyx's idea is best. We disguise our scent then hide and wait for them to return.'

'I can hide in the Cold Box,' Spinney mewed, 'so when the rats go past, I can leap out and grab one.'

'You'll need two cats,' Rose twitched her whiskers.

'Yes!' Spinney hopped around her, 'You can block their escape!'

'If they go that way,' Gloworm mewed.

Dust looked at the white tom. He was sat up in his bed, his fur spiked and rippling down his back.

'What other way would they go?' Briar sniffed, 'They must go through the Cold Box to get to the Long Box...'

As Gloworm raised his eyes, his tail quivered, 'Then why is there a hole in the roof?'

Dust looked up just as a white roof square slid away. Twitching noses appeared around the edge of the hole and malevolent little eyes glinted down from the darkness.

'How did they get up there?' Violet gasped.

'Up,' Conker tipped his head as he watched the shifting shapes milling about in the roof, 'Rats always go up, because they come from down.'

With a squeal, a rat leapt from the roof and grabbed hold of the drip light. It swung wildly to and fro until it found its grip, a heartbeat before a second rat leapt onto its back. The first rat squealed again as the second dug its teeth into its flesh.

Rose growled and circled the floor under the hole.

Another rat leapt for the drip light. Then another, and another. Each one swinging from the haunches of the rat above as they began to form a chain.

Onyx leapt up and hissed as more rats scurried down the growing chain. Conker nudged Fern out of her bed and as the rats swung closer, he and Onyx pushed her off the full boxes and they ran towards the door.

Rose leapt onto the full boxes beside Violet, narrowly missing a falling rat as more and more scuttled down the chain, and as it reached the floor, a writhing sea of greasy bodies pooled outwards, filling the middle of Meeting Box.

'Get to the Long Box!' Briar yowled.

'No! Wait,' Dust glanced at Onyx, Conker, and Fern. The rats had them trapped by the door, 'We can't leave them.'

Briar hissed and turned for the flap, but he'd barely taken a paw step before it slammed open. Two large rats slid through, reared onto their hind paws, and held the flap up to let in more. Briar skidded to a halt and tried to knock the rats aside, but there were too many and he was pushed back into Dust and Spinney.

More rats slithered through the flap and scurried along the bottom of the full boxes, forcing Dust, Briar, and Spinney back into the middle of the floor, and trapping Rose, Violet and Gloworm in their beds.

Snarls and hisses rang out above maddening squeaks and squeals. Hackles raised and claws sliced the air as cats spun in circles, slashing at the rats around them. Greasy dark bodies swarmed closer, forcing the cats back as they stole their space. Dust forced himself to stand still and watch as the seething, squealing, mass of fur and tails covered the floor, and then the full boxes, leaving just three small spaces for the trapped cats. *There's too many of them...* He shook his head. *We can't fight this many rats...*

'Throats!' Rose yowled as she clawed at the nearest rat and pinned it down in her bed. She sank her claws into its flank, clamped her jaws around its neck, and bit down hard. But before she could lift her head again, the rats closed in and slipped between her and Violet.

'Get away!' Fern hissed as she reared, her back pressed against the door.

Dust looked around. A rat nipped at Fern's tail and as she turned to swipe it away, another slipped between her and Conker.

'Get away from her,' Conker lunged after Fern, but the rats swelled around him and pushed him back. Then they closed in on Onyx. She growled and clawed at them, but they avoided her blows as they forced her back towards the litters.

'No! help me!' Fern wailed as a wave of squeaking rats ran up her legs, along her back, and dragged her down to the floor.

'Fern,' Conker growled as he leapt to her aid, but the rats gripped his hind legs and pulled him down too. A heartbeat later he was overcome.

Rose hissed as a wave of rats climbed over her back and forced her down into her bed, before they flooded into Violet's. The grey she-cat didn't have a chance to fight them off, but Rose fought back frantically, refusing to let them overcome her. Onyx yowled as the rats pulled her back and forced her to the floor. Spinney screeched and leapt to her aid, but the rats rose to meet him mid leap and took him down too. Briar circled around Dust, hackles raised, and claws unsheathed, but the malign scuttling mass only edged closer.

Dust glanced at Gloworm. The white tom sat motionless in his bed. The rats ignored him.

Stay still... Dust froze. 'Listen!' he yowled, 'Stop moving!'

Rose stopped fighting and looked from Dust to Gloworm. Then keeping her body still, she hooked the closest rat with her claws, lifted it slowly and bit down hard on its neck.

Gloworm nodded and closed his eyes.

Briar stopped pacing, 'Listen to what?' he panted.

'Conker?' Dust trained his ears on the pile of rats in the corner by the water bowl. *Growling...* 'Fern?' he turned to the pile of rats by the door, 'Fern, can you hear me?' she didn't answer, but he could hear her breathless gasping. 'Onyx?'

'Get ... them ... off ... me,' Onyx growled.

They're alive...

'Onyx ... I'm ...

'No ... Spinney ... Listen ... to ...Dust.'

'Violet?' Rose hissed.

'Be quiet ... Rose,' Violet panted.

'I can hear you all,' Dust meowed, 'Don't move. They are trying to control us, not kill us.'

'How do you know?' Briar hissed.

'We're not dead,' Rose growled.

'Just stay still,' Dust repeated. 'They are—'

A terrifying guttural screech interrupted Dust as it echoed through the Long Box.

The rats fell silent.

'Wash for ... Shadow White...' Gloworm breathed.

Dust glanced at Gloworm. The white toms' eyes were following a ripple of movement that swelled through the rats on the floor. Noses twitched and black eyes glistened as they rose onto their haunches and began shuffling backwards. Dust felt the rats around him shift and slink away, leaving a clear path between him and the flap. Then a big black rat with a ripped ear, one blind white eye and a stump for a tail slid into the Meeting Box and ambled towards him.

Dust stood still and stared into the big rat's good eye.

'You Dust? You lead cat?' it peeped, twitching its nose.

Dust nodded.

'Kill rat ... rat kill cat. All cat. Yes?'

Dust struggled to take a breath as he looked around the Meeting Box. He felt the stillness, the silence broken only by the faint desperate gasps under the mounds of unctuous bodies where his cats lay trapped. *They beat us...* He knew these rats could kill every one of his cats before he could get to their leader. But his cats were strong and fast, and they would not go down without a fight. *There'd be a lot of dead rats too...* He glanced over a thousand pairs of tiny black eyes and shivered. *Would they even notice their loss....?* Dust turned back to the big rat and dipped his head, 'If you want to talk, let my cats get up.'

The big rat twitched his nose and squeaked, 'Let cat up.'

At his command, every rat glided back into the walls and watched, teeth bared and claws flicking as the cats began to rise.

Conker was first onto his paws. He hurried to help Fern get up and guide her to the empty floor behind Dust. Onyx and Spinney scrambled up and joined them. Rose licked Violet's ear as she sat up and pushed a dead rat from her bed. Briar took a step back to sit beside Spinney. Gloworm didn't move.

The big rat watched with interest as the cats tended to their wounds. Dust wondered if rats cared for each other as cats did, but from the glint of amusement in this creature's eye, he didn't think so. The scent of blood and fear was heavy in the air. Cat and rat. Briar twisted his head to inspect a deep bite on his hind leg. Onyx licked the blood from her belly fur as she sniffed at the long scratch on her side. Spinney's eyes darted nervously about the Meeting Box as he held up a bleeding fore paw. Fern crouched trembling behind Conker, who laid his tail over her back to comfort her. Rose sat upright and kept her brilliant green eyes trained on the big rat as Violet leant into her shoulder. Gloworm still didn't move.

When the big rat had every cat's attention again, he squeaked, 'Aside.' The rats beside the water bowl moved at his command, revealing the body beside the pile of remains, 'What cat killed Ard Boirey?'

'I did,' Rose growled.

The big rat turned and looked her up and down, 'Why kill Ard Boirey?'

'Are you, Skeeal?' Rose hopped down from the full boxes and padded to Dust's side.

The big rat took a step towards Rose and held her gaze with his good eye, 'I Skeeal, Ard-er Skeeal. Who red cat?'

Rose dipped her head, 'I am Rose.'

'Why kill Ard Boirey, Rose cat?' Skeeal repeated.

'He let you down, Skeeal.'

'Let me down!' Skeeal screeched and shook his head, 'Boirey good Ard rat, how let Ard-er Skeeal down?'

'Stay still...' Gloworm mewed.

Dust flicked Rose's shoulder with his tail, motioning for her to stay back.

She threw him a glance and lowered her tail, *calm down...*

Dust stayed close to Rose's side. He didn't trust her to remain calm, but he admired the way she'd duped the big rat. Skeeal was caught off guard, he'd shaken his head, losing eye contact with the cats that towered above him. He lowed himself back down onto his fore paws. Rose had taken control.

Violet hopped down from her bed and padded to Rose's side. Dust relaxed as she rested her tail over Rose's back and dipped her head to Skeeal, 'I'm sorry, but my sister is right. We bought Boirey here alive to ask him a question. I spoke kindly to him, but he refused to answer.'

Skeeal turned and looked at Boirey's body. After a heartbeat he shrugged and turned back to Violet. 'What question?'

Dust stepped forward, 'How do we get out of The Boxes?'

Skeeal sniffed, 'Why cat think there *is* out?'

'Gloworm,' Dust beckoned him with his tail, 'please tell Skeeal about the Blue Box.'

The white tom hesitantly climbed down from his bed and sat down stiffly, He looked nervously from Dust to Skeeal. His fur rippled and he shuddered as he wrapped his tail tightly around his paws. His voice trembled as he spoke, 'I was in the Blue Box, and I spoke to a cat through a hole in the wall. A cat who is in The Outside. His name is Benny.'

Tiny squeaks flittered through the swarm of rats, some sniffed, others exchanged glances.

'Old cat Benny,' Skeeal peeped, 'tell good tales.'

'You ... you know Benny?' Gloworm mewed.

'All know crazy old Benny.'

169

'Benny isn't crazy. He knows my mother's first mate, Piccolo...' Gloworm went on, 'That's how we know The Outside is real ... my mother lived in The Outside ... Benny is in The Outside.'

Skeeal listened with interest as Gloworm told Icicle's story, and when the white tom had finished speaking, Skeeal looked at Dust and peeped. 'Cat tale good. Ard-er Skeeal left tale in Rat King nest. Best place for tales. Come find me down Rat Holes. I tell cat Skeeal's tale.'

'Rat Holes?' Onyx mewed, 'is that how you get in and out?'

Skeeal snorted. 'No cat get out Rat Hole. No cat get past Rat King. If cat want out, go up, fly from roof. Only way for cat.'

Dust took a step towards Skeeal, 'What do you mean?'

Skeeal waved a paw to the two large rats by the flap, 'Ard Grouw, Ard Keoie, back, back.'

As the Ard rats lifted the flap, Skeeal began shuffling backwards towards it. He didn't take his good eye off Dust as he peeped, 'Moving Box no good. Cat come back. Benny no good. Crazy cat. Door no good, man use door, Rat Holes no good, rat only. Roof only way... Only way for cat.'

As Skeeal disappeared through the flap with his Ard rats behind him, a new rat chain formed on the drip light and descended from the roof. The cats watched in silence as the rats began to climb back up their chain and vanish into the darkness above. When the last of the rats had replaced the roof square, leaving nothing but a small hole near the door, Dust felt his skin begin to crawl again. No cat had mentioned the Moving Box. *They've been up there, listening, all along...*

20

The Only Cat

DUST FLICKED HIS EARS AND OPENED his eyes. His first breath shuddered with her scent. A dark shadow loomed above, spiralling, and spreading over the Meeting Box, smothering the sleeping cats around him. He rolled over in his bed and raised his head, listening for her paw steps, watching for the shadow to twist into her blurry outline. Not a breath. Not a rustle of fur. Not a step. Dust sat up and looked around. A cat sat in the middle of the floor, swishing her tail. He tried to catch her bright grey eyes, but she looked away and dropped her head.

'Breeze?'

'How well do you know your territory, Dust...?' She flicked her tail impatiently.

The Meeting Box darkened for a heartbeat as Dust's shadow slipped from beneath him, leapt down onto the floor and sat beside Breeze. Shadow Dust hung his head and closed his bright grey eyes.

Dust shifted uncomfortably in his bed, 'The Boxes? I know them well.'

'Show me...' Breeze mewed, 'take me on a tour of your territory...'

Dust hopped down from his bed and padded to the flap. Shadow Dust followed, his head low, his tail drooping on the floor, his eyes still closed. 'This is the Meeting Box. It's where we all met. The water and litters are here and it's where we bring our catches. And it's where we sleep'

Breeze nodded.

Dust slipped through the flap and waited as Breeze and Shadow Dust stepped through the wall behind him. 'This is the Long Box,' he told them, 'It has many doors. It's where we first met the rats.'

Breeze nodded, 'Where next…?'

'This way,' Dust stepped through the blue door, shivering at the sensation, 'This is the Blue Box. The humans keep boxes and bowls and sweepers in here. They use them to wash away scents with the sour damp. There's a hole in the wall behind the big white box with the circle. The hole leads to The Outside, and a cat called Benny.'

'Can you get out through the hole…?'

'Gloworm said it's too small.'

Shadow Dust slipped through the hole, then reappeared, shaking his head.

'Okay, next…?' Breeze flicked her tail.

Dust led them around the Dark Corner, 'The Bright Box is through here.' Dust pushed his head through the dull brown door. Breeze and Shadow Dust did the same. 'The humans sit in here. They get in through the big grey doors over there, but we can't get in here unless they open the doors as brown doors are too heavy for cats to open.'

'Is this a way out…?'

'Yes. I think so. But if we need the humans to let us in here, we can't easily escape this way.'

Breeze nodded, 'Where now…?'

'This is the Cold Box,' Dust padded past the haphazard rows of rolling cages and sat down opposite the Metal Box.

Shadow Dust padded past him and stared at himself in the mirror door.

'And ... what is this...?' Breeze curled her tail.

'I don't know. We need to watch the humans press the light bumps to find out how to open it.'

'So, could it be a way out...?'

'I don't think so. You can get behind it and see on top of it.'

'Does it go anywhere...?' Breeze asked.

Dust tipped his head to one side as Shadow Dust reached up and pressed the top light bump. As they flickered green, he pushed his paw through the floor and shook his head.

'No,' Dust shook his head too, 'it can't go down, the Healing Box is down there. And it can't go up if I can see on top of it.'

Breeze nodded, 'Where next...?'

Dust stepped through the yellow doors, 'This is the Vast Tower Box, and there is a way out at the other end, in the Moving Box behind the slide down door.'

'And you can get out that way...?'

'Only if the slide down door is up. Conker went out, but he came back. It's like the Bright Box, we can't get out without the humans being there.'

Breeze nodded, 'So, where next...?'

Shadow Dust hopped up onto a ledge.

Dust blinked in the bright light. He was standing on the ledge where Fiona had treated his wounds. Slowly he turned around to see Shadow Dust watching him from beside the nook.

'This is the Healing Box, it's down. I don't think we can get out from here, or anywhere that's down. Skeeal said

"Come find me down Rat Holes." I don't know where the Rat Holes are, but he also said, *"Rat Hole no good, for rat only."* I believe him. I don't think the rats would let any cat escape through their holes.'

'Have you explored every part of the Healing Box....?'

Shadow Dust flicked his tail and vanished into the nook. 'I couldn't ... I was injured...'

Breeze nodded, 'Is there anywhere else you want to show me....?'

'There's only the Under Box and...' Dust felt the Dropping Box lurch and rock as it went up. He turned to see the light bumps flash orange as Shadow Dust batted all three of them with his paw.

'This is the Dropping Box. It goes down to the Under Box and the Healing Box.'

'How does it go down....?'

'The light bumps. There's one outside in the Long Box and three in here.'

'So...' Breeze twitched her whiskers, 'one in the Long Box... to get into the Dropping Box... then three in here... one for the Long Box... one for the Under Box and the Healing Box, and....?'

The Dropping Box lurched to a stop.

Dust stared at the bottom light bump, 'That's all I know.'

Shadow Dust looked up at the hole in the Meeting Box roof and blinked.

Dust followed his gaze, 'Skeeal said *"go up, fly from roof. Only way for cat."*

Breeze circled him, then sat before him, 'And how well do you know your cats....?'

Movement caught Dust's eye. He turned to see the Shadow Cats flow down from the full boxes and sit in a row before him. They raised their heads as one, blinked twice and closed their eyes, then dropped their faces to the floor.

'I know them all well,' Dust mewed.

'All of them? Tell me how well you know your cats...'

Dust felt a comforting warmth surround him as Shadow Gloworm raised his head and opened his eyes. He felt compelled to curl beside him. 'Gloworm is a good cat,' he told Breeze. 'He knew his mother and her stories, and that's why he wants to find Benny. He knows things that I don't always understand, but I will always trust him.'

Breeze nodded as Shadow Gloworm closed his eyes and Shadow Rose raised her head and fixed Dust with a cold grey stare.

Dust's fur bristled at the darkness seeping from Shadow Rose, but he let her come close and circle around him. 'Rose is driven by fury for whatever hurt her so deeply. And only Violet can ever heal her pain. I don't know if I can trust her, but she's smart and keeps her mind and her eyes open.'

Shadow Rose dropped her head and closed her eyes as Shadow Violet opened hers and greeted Dust with a twinkling blink.

A warm glow surrounded Dust and shimmered faintly at the edges of his vision. 'Violet is a wonderful cat. She's suffered, just as Rose has, as we all have, but she doesn't share her sister's anger. She turns her pain into kindness.'

Shadow Violet closed her eyes and looked at the floor as Shadow Briar looked up and stared at Dust.

Dust blinked as Shadow Briar flickered between light and dark. 'Briar is strong willed, and he has good intentions.

He wants to find a safe place for himself and will welcome any cat who will follow him. But he will never truly lead them.'

Shadow Briar closed his eyes and dropped his head slowly as Shadow Spinney's eyes flicked open and glowed keenly.

Shadow Spinney cast a cool and comforting glow around Dust, and he felt safety in it. 'Spinney is a good cat. He is playful and too enthusiastic sometimes, but he is honest, and I trust him. He's very smart too, much smarter than he realises.'

Shadow Spinney glanced at Shadow Onyx before he closed his eyes and dropped his head to the floor. Shadow Onyx looked straight up at Dust.

Shadow Onyx cast a dark yet welcoming warmth around Dust. He sensed mystery, but not danger. 'Onyx is smart and observant, but she is hard to read. I'm sure I can trust her, but I'm equally sure she knows how to keep secrets.'

Shadow Onyx's eyes flickered as she closed them and hung her head. Shadow Fern raised hers but kept her eyes closed for a heartbeat. They darkened when she opened them.

Shadow Fern seemed to shrink back, and Dust glimpsed a streak of darker despair in her bright calm form. 'Fern is terrified of everything in The Boxes. She copes only because the other cats are kind enough to help her. I hope she never finds herself alone, or that fear could turn to despair.'

Shadow Fern closed her eyes quickly as Shadow Conker raised his head high and opened his own.

Dust felt the warmth ebb stubbornly from Shadow Conker, bringing with it a sense of comfort and contentment. 'Conker is kind-hearted and will protect other cats. He'd make any place a home and nothing seems to faze him. He's neither a leader nor a follower. He'd never do any harm, or truly listen, to any cat.'

Shadow Conker closed his eyes and dropped his head.

'And....?' Breeze mewed.

Dust looked along the row of Shadow Cats. 'That's all I know?'

'Is that every cat...?'

'Yes—' Movement caught Dust's eye. A creep of shadow brushed through the wall from the Blue Box. 'Except...'

'Except....?'

'Benny?'

Shadow Dust padded to the wall and dipped his head.

'Gloworm's spoken to him, and I trust Gloworm. The rats said they know him too, but they said he's crazy.'

'And you'd accept a rat's opinion before seeing for yourself....?'

'No.'

'Where is Benny....?'

'In The Outside.'

Breeze raised her head and held Dust's gaze, 'Where do you want to go....?'

Dust glanced at the wall. Soft grey eyes blinked, then vanished. 'The Outside.'

'So...'

'I need to talk to the only cat I don't know.'

21
The Engel's Tale

DUST WAITED BY THE FLAP, ONE ear trained on the sound of John's fading footsteps, the other listening to the anxious mewings around him. Fiona had cleaned the minor scratches they'd all suffered in the Meeting Box, but she'd taken Onyx, Briar, and Spinney to the Healing Box to heal their more serious wounds. The toms had suffered deep bites and the scratch on Onyx's side refused to stop bleeding. They had only just returned and were resting in their beds.

Fern and Rose had scouted, but all scent of rat had been washed away and no rat had been seen since their invasion. Dust had instructed Rose to hunt with Violet and Conker in the Vast Tower Box while he investigated the Blue Box. He'd decided to look for Benny and decide for himself if the outside cat was crazy.

As the blood red smudge faded from the deep blue flat light, Dust slipped through the flap and trotted down the Long Box towards the Blue Corner. The stench of sour damp drowned out the uplifting scents as he padded back and forth, studying the lever on the blue door. It was identical to the one on the green door. He leapt at it and curled his claws around it. The lever creaked and moved down, but his claws slipped on the shiny surface, and he slid off.

Almost... he leapt again and hooked a paw over the widest part of the lever. As it began to move, and he began to slip, he quickly curled his other paw around the back of the lever and caught his slipping paw with his claws. He winced but hung on. The lever moved down, and the blue door swung open.

The door bumped softly against a sweeper. Dust looked back at it. If the humans saw it open, they'd find him. Fiona had pushed the green door back into its gap. Dust tried the same and was relieved to find that this door also closed easily.

The flat light was almost black as Dust squeezed between the full boxes and the large white box. He could smell the uplifting scents now, flowing like spilled water from the hole in the wall. He settled as comfortably as he could in the narrow space, relaxed his jaw and closed his eyes to study the scents as he waited.

An acrid smell stirred his fear as it cut deep into the back of his throat. And when the smell strengthened, he heard a loud menacing purr. Not like a cat, but like something a cat should avoid. When the scent weakened, others took its place. He found a fresh sharp scent, laced with a fragrance that reminded him of Fiona and another that made him think of the covers in a comfortable warm bed. Occasionally he detected the scents of humans, just as he heard their faint shouts. Then the scent of another creature, neither cat nor rat, but similar, accompanied by yelping sounds that ruffled his fur. Dust began to doze, and as his eyes grew heavy, the sounds and the smells formed patterns in his mind. Soon he found that he was able to predict which scents accompanied which sounds, so when his ears detected soft paw steps, he was ready for the one scent he'd hoped to find.

Gloworm was right... Dust lifted his head. The scent of the approaching tom was calm and infused with fresh intriguing smells. Whoever this cat was, he would at least know where the uplifting scents came from.

The paw steps stopped. The tom sniffed. Dust felt his skin tingle with excitement as a shadow fell over the hole.

'Hello, Gloworm? Is that you? you smell ... calmer,' mewed a cheerful voice.

Dust caught his breath, he had so many questions to ask that his thoughts tripped over each other, 'Hello ... er,' he began, 'I'm not Gloworm. I'm ... I'm a friend of his, actually ... I am his leader.'

The shadow shifted. 'Yes, he said there were others. didn't he? Yes, he did. So, are you warden here? What is your name?' the tom's voice was pleasant, but there was authority in it.

'My name is Dust. Gloworm told us he'd spoken to a cat called Benny. Are you Benny?'

'Well, hello Dust. Yes, I am Benny. Maer'kaa Romi, Benny, Warden of Warmroot Copse.'

Dust pricked his ears. *A Mother Name...* 'Gloworm told us you're in The Outside. Is that true?'

'Well, yes, that is true,' Benny purred. 'If you are inside the Humming Place, then I suppose that I am *in* the outside of it.'

'Humming Place?'

'Ah, yes, cats out here call this a Humming Place. Because of the noise. These places are always humming.'

'Yes,' Dust agreed, 'we call it The Boxes. Because it's all just boxes inside boxes.'

'And you are Warden of The Boxes. Well, young Gloworm did tell me he was trapped in there with other cats. How many other cats are there in your ward?'

'Nine, including me,' Dust mewed, 'Conker escaped for a while. He got trapped in the Moving Box, but he came back.'

'A Moving Box?' Dust could hear the old tom licking his paws as he thought it over, 'You must mean a box that moves ... like a boat? No. How would you get trapped in a boat? The trucks maybe? Yes ... the trucks. Were there humans inside the front of it?'

Dust tried to remember, 'I didn't see him, but the Grey Male ... a male human in grey covers, he was near the slide down door when it closed.'

Benny shuffled on the other side of the hole, 'Ah yes. Grey Male, grey clothes. He moves the trucks. The Moving Boxes. He brings them here and pushes them into the walls. Then he takes them away again. So, if you get into one, you may go somewhere else.'

'So, are they a good way to escape?'

Benny sniffed, 'Definitely. Especially if you want to come back. I used to get in one quite often. It was always full of humans. It kept stopping to let them get out, and sometimes to let them get in. It moved in a circle and always ended up back where it started, up the lane from Byrgels Bold. They always come back to where they start. Oh, it was fun for a while, but, and I will not lie to you, Dust, it was often dangerous. Some human places are too dangerous for cats.

Especially cats who have never been outside. I would try to find another way.'

Dust hung his head and sighed. He didn't want to put any cat in danger. He had hoped to hear that the Moving Boxes were safe.

'But don't let a flake of truth discourage you, my young friend,' Benny purred, 'I am an old and well weathered cat. I've lived a long and wonderous life. And while I have experienced danger and fear and hardship, most of my life has been pleasant and joyful. For every hunger pang, I have devoured ten plump mice. For every injury I have lain in meadows and basked in the sun a hundred times, and for every shudder of fear, I have bowed to a thousand friendly faces...'

As Dust listened to Benny's words, he felt his heart fill with hope. He didn't know what the old cat was talking about, he had never heard of meadows or mice or sunshine, but Benny spoke in a voice filled with knowledge and confidence, and Dust was mesmerised.

'...and if young Conker has escaped already, even if he did return, then there is hope that soon you will all be free.'

Dust pricked his ears, 'Do you think so? do you really think we could escape from here.'

'Humans have immeasurable intelligence and cunning. They are the only species that can truly lie. They are at once both cruel and kind, as all they give with one hand, they take with the other. But a cat will always find a way to outsmart them, elude their cruel hands, and secure their freedom. No cat can be kept prisoner forever.'

'Do you think so?'

'Uimywim demands it so with the choices she gives us.'

'Uimywim?'

'The White Kitten, Shadow White, Pebblepaw. The Eternal Host of Warkiersu has as many names as she has choices to offer our souls when they reach Ganlengan, the border between life and death.'

Dust shivered, 'Gloworm talks about Shadow White. His mother, Icicle told him about her. Are her stories true?'

'Perfectly true,' Benny Purred, 'Young Gloworm told me his mother was once called Bella. I met the runner, Piccolo, soon after he lost her. He still talks about her. When I see him next, I will tell him about Bella's son. I hope one day you will get to meet him ... And I will never forget my little Sweep... my dear little Sweep...' Benny sniffed, then went on, 'There's no reason to fear The White Kitten. I've had the pleasure of meeting her myself ... a few times... She is the first and final kindness in this world.'

Dust shook his head, trying to make sense of Benny's words. 'I'm not sure I understand what you mean, but I see my mother, Breeze, in my dreams. She wants me to escape. And I will do anything I can to give my cats their freedom.'

'Then learn what you can about The Boxes. Watch how the humans get in and out. I will be watching from out here. And when you do escape, you and your cats would be more than welcome to join me in The Ruins, under the trees of Warmroot Copse. There are no humans there, and I do like visitors ... if you all like stories.'

Dust purred, 'Of course, and thank you, we would love to hear your stories. If all cats in The Outside are like you then we have hope.'

'Well thank you, it makes an old cat happy to hear that. Now, you are smart, Dust. I can tell. So, what have you discovered so far? Do you know why you are trapped in The Boxes?

'I'm not sure. We all grew up in the Old Place where we had to catch Ratbots. And when we did, the humans gave us food. But here, there are no Ratbots. Only rats. They are our food now.'

'Ratbots? Benny snorted, 'So you're here because of the rats?'

'We think so. We captured one called Boirey and tried to interrogate him, but when he didn't answer our question, Rose killed him. Then their leader, Skeeal, invaded with all the other rats. Skeeal said he knows you, Benny.'

'Skeeal...?' Benny mulled over the name, 'what does he look like?'

'Bigger than the other rats, he has a ripped ear, a blind white eye and half a tail.'

'Oh, yes,' Benny Purred, 'That Skeeal. A slippery rat of many tales, none of them his own. I will tell you all about him too, one day. Now, what nonsense did that irksome old disease bucket tell you.'

'He told us that the only way for cats to get out is to fly from the roof.'

Benny took a deep breath, 'Rats are untrustworthy, Dust. But old Skeeal is a seasoned storyteller, so there could be some truth in his words.'

'There could? How can a cat fly from the roof?'

'Cats can't fly. Only birds and bugs fly. Maybe that isn't what he meant. Although I have seen that raven and his crows carrying rats.'

'Birds? Raven and his crows?' Dust recalled seeing the three dark rat like creatures circling and looping around the huge flat lights in the Bright Box, 'Do they look like flying rats?'

'Exactly like flying rats,' Benny purred. 'That is a good description. But I think that even with their charming words, they'd still struggle to fly while carrying a cat.'

'Are we too big?'

'Yes ... and you'd be a fool to ask favours of them.'

Dust sighed.

'Don't give up hope, Dust. There will be a way out. Cats always find their freedom. Perhaps the humans will let you out soon, they sometimes keep cats trapped inside new places for a while.'

Dust shook his head, 'If there are rats here, I don't think they'll ever let us out. Maybe if the rats go...?'

'The promise! Of course, The promise...'

'The promise?' Dust asked, something in Benny's voice made his fur prickle.

'An ancient promise between Uimywim and the human child, Hapwyne, the Eternal Host of Halsawol.'

'I don't understand,' Dust sighed.

'Long ago, Uimywim and Hapwyne promised to help each other. And because of their promise, cats are bound to forever protect humans from rats.'

'So, the humans have trapped us here to hunt rats, because of an ancient promise?'

'I can't be sure. Many cats believe that humans have forgotten their promise and even Uimywim suspects this to be so. But as the promise has long fashioned the traditions of both cats and humans, it can be forgotten, but it will never disappear. There is a story that may help you understand. Would you like to hear it?'

'Yes, I would like to hear it.' Dust mewed, desperate for something that would help him make sense of anything that Benny had told him.

Benny coughed, and began his story:

'When I was just a kitten, my mother told me The Engel's Tale. A tale about the Engel of Shady Ly. A cat who lived here so long ago, that no cat alive recalls the colour of her fur.'

'Lived here?' Dust asked.

'Right over there, in Shady Ly,' Benny took a breath, and continued, 'Long, long ago, there was a kitten too afraid to hunt rodents. Even after she'd grown into a strong young cat and had been taken to live with her own humans, she still feared their tiny teeth and claws.

'Her humans named her Engel, and they loved her. She told them stories and they loved her stories and wrote them down, and as a reward her humans fed her well with scraps from their own table. Engel soon found she had no need to hunt.

'But the other cats of Shady Ly scolded her. They told her she was worthless and lazy, and even if her humans fed her, she should still hunt the rodents in their den.

'"But why?" Engel mewed, "I do not want to be bitten or scratched and my humans feed me well, so why should I be bothered to rid their den of rats?"

'"Because of our promise to humans," Wailed the other cats. "Because we promised that we would protect them from the Ills of Rodents."

'"I see no ills." Engel huffed. And ignoring their pleas, she returned to her den for a meal of tasty human food.

'But the cunning rats did not ignore the pleas of the other cats. News spread fast of a cat who would not hunt them. And that night, while she slept, all the rodents in the Ward of Shady Ly moved their nests into her den.

'Engel woke the next day to the glares of a thousand pairs of tiny black eyes. Too afraid to move, she was forced to stay in her bed, where she starved to death, listening to the wails of her humans as the Ills of Rodents took them too.'

Dust shivered. 'What does that mean? The Ills of Rodents?'

A loud menacing purr echoed through the hole, drowning out Benny's words.

'Benny?'

'Time for this old tom to skedaddle,' Benny mewed. 'We will speak again soon...'

A shadow shifted across the hole a heartbeat before an acrid smell stung Dust's nostrils.

Benny had gone.

22

Lullaby

A YOWL CAUGHT DUST'S EARS. HE backed out from between the full boxes and the big white box and listened. Paw steps rushed past the blue door. He leapt at the leaver, opened it on his first try and stepped into the Long Box in time to see a tortoiseshell tail disappear through the flap. As he raced after it, he tried to remember if he'd asked Fern to scout.

Rose was sat by the water bowl as Dust slid through the flap, Violet crouched at her side watching Conker and Fern as they stood panting in the middle of the Meeting Box floor. Briar padded around them, as Onyx, Spinney and Gloworm sat watching from their beds.

'There's rat scent ... in the Vast Tower Box,' Conker meowed, 'by the wall near the slide down door.'

'Dust is here now,' Rose mewed.

Briar turned and padded to Dust, 'Did you find Benny?'

'Yes, I did,' Dust nodded.

'He's real? What did he say?'

Rose stepped forward. 'We should hunt before we lose the scent.'

Briar turned to Rose and growled, 'If it's important...'

'Food is important,' Rose hissed.

'Violet stepped forward, 'Dust can tell Briar while we hunt. Who is coming with us? Conker? Fern?'

Fern shook her head as Conker leant into her side.

Dust looked at the exhausted cats, 'I will come. What Benny said was interesting, but not urgent. It can wait until we have food.'

'But a scout should always go back out with the hunters,' Briar flicked his tail to Conker.

Dust flicked Briar with his tail, 'I'm rested, and we will find the scent easily enough.'

'Then let's go,' Rose started towards the flap.

*

Dust stopped just beyond the yellow doors in the Vast Tower Box, 'We can go along the end of the towers to the far wall and the slide down door. The scent will be stale, but we should find it.'

'If we don't, Briar will overthrow you as leader.' Rose twitched her whiskers.

'Rose!' Violet scolded, 'You should stop arguing with that tom, it only makes you angry.'

'He argues with me.'

Dust blinked at Rose, 'Briar's is a strongminded cat, so he will stand his ground if he feels challenged.'

Violet let her tail rest on Rose's shoulder, 'I don't think Briar means any harm, he's a good cat. But you scare him.'

Rose sat down and sighed, 'You're right, Violet, I do get angry. I'm sorry.'

Violet leant against her sister, 'Then let it go. We're together now, and it doesn't matter what any other cat says or does.'

Rose licked Violet's ear, 'You're right, she purred.'

'I always am, little paws,' Violet purred and whispered something into Rose's ear.

Dust blinked in amazement as Rose rolled onto her side and batted Violet gently on her nose. Her brilliant green eyes soft with affection.

With a loud purr, Violet batted her back, and they began play fighting like kittens, purring and chirruping as they rolled and tussled and bounded around the open space.

It had been a long time since Dust had seen any cat play. He had no littermates, but on the rare occasions that he'd met other cats in the Old Place, he'd had fun as they chased one another around, catching each other instead of Ratbots. Loneliness tore at Dust's belly as he watched Rose and Violet frolicking merrily. He'd forgotten that cats could play.

Rose and Violet bounded back to him. Violet's head was bowed and there was a spring in her step, her fluffy grey tail streaming out behind her. Rose was glowing. Her head held high and her brilliant green eyes sparkling with delight. She was like a different cat. Her shell of rage had cracked to reveal the real Rose, elegant and beautiful, a stunning sight to behold.

'I'm starving,' Rose purred, 'let's find some rats.'

Dust got to his paws and set off down the open space, in the direction of the slide down door. He walked slowly and checked the bottom of every tower for scents. The she-cats followed playfully behind. As the end wall of the Vast Tower Box became visible through the gloom, he could see that the slide down door was closed. There was no way into the Moving Box now.

'Is this where Conker got trapped?' Violet asked as she caught up to Dust.

'Yes. When the door is up, the Moving Box is behind it.'

'There's something here,' Rose sniffed along the wall near the end of the slide down door.

'What is it?' Dust asked.

'A hole. It has bars across it, like a trap.'

Dust watched as she prodded the bars with her paw and peered into it, 'Any scents?'

Rose sat back and shook her head.

'If the Moving Box isn't here, then I suppose Conker and Fern didn't manage to scout it.' Violet mewed.

'I didn't ask them to scout it...' Dust flicked his tail, *Did I...?*

'You didn't ask us to scout anywhere, Dust. And we didn't know when you'd be back, so Conker suggested they try and find out when the slide down door is up.'

Dust nodded, 'Yes, he's right. We should scout as much as we can.' He took a step forward and sniffed at the bottom of the door. The air moved slightly, and he could taste a trace of the choking acrid stench. *Moving Boxes...* Dust thought. *The acrid smell is the Moving Box...*

Rose joined him and sniffed at the door, 'Where do the Moving Boxes go?'

'Benny told me that they go in a circle to different places, but they always come back.'

Violet gasped, 'So if we got in one, we would just come back here.'

'Conker came back, and Benny said it's what they do,' Dust mewed.

'So, it's not a way to escape,' Violet padded to Rose's side and nuzzled her neck.

Rose closed her eyes for a heartbeat, then opened them and lifted her head, 'Stay here, I'll check for rat scent.' And without giving Dust or Violet time to answer, she turned and bounded away into the shadows of the towers.

Violet crouched and tucked herself up as she watched her sister go, as if trying to contain her worries. Sadness clouded her dark green eyes, and a hint of fear tainted her warm sweet scent.

Dust wondered what she feared. At Violet's words, Rose had shaken off her anger and transformed into an enchanting playful she-cat, but that very transformation seemed to have drained Violet. *What did she say....?* Dust hadn't heard the words Violet had whispered in her sister's ear, but it was like they'd flicked a switch.

'Violet?' Dust mewed softly as he sat down beside her, 'I know I shouldn't ask, but ... when you whispered something to Rose ... she just became a different cat.'

Violet lifted her head and blinked slowly at Dust.

'I'm sorry, it's not my business ... I just—'

'It's okay,' Violet mewed, ruffling her fur, as if to shake off the shackling thoughts. 'I said her Mother Name. But I won't tell you what it is, Dust. Rose and I vowed to keep our Mother Names secret.'

Dust shifted uncomfortably, 'I heard you say little paws ... that's not a Mother Name, is it?'

'Oh, little paws,' Violet purred, 'No, it isn't. it's just a name I called her when we were kittens, Something I sang to her, to keep her strong.'

Dust nodded.

'That isn't a secret,' Violet's eyes sparkled, 'Rose will never speak of it ... but it's also my story to tell ... if you want to hear it?'

Dust gently nuzzled her ear and mewed, 'Will Rose mind?'

'Maybe. But it would make me feel better.'

Dust sat quietly as Violet shuffled herself comfortable. The Vast Tower Box was deathly silent, not a sound. Nothing moved, not even a shadow.

'We never met our mother,' Violet mewed sadly, 'but we remember her well ... and we will never, ever, forget her.'

Dust flicked his ear to show he was listening, but he remained silent.

Violet went on, 'My earliest memory was of being alone and cold in the dark. There was another cat by my side, small and wet and shivering. As I moved closer to this other cat, I began to feel warmer, but the other cat stopped moving, and grew colder. That's when the middle of my body tightened. The colder the other cat became, the tighter my body became, and the tightness didn't ease until I wrapped my body around the other cat. That's when I began to sing...

'Bring me your cold,
'Your tears,
'And your little paws.
'You have me to hold,
'You have me to hold...'

Dust's fur prickled along his spine.

'And when I sang, the tightness went away, and the other cat began to warm.'

Dust nodded and let out his breath.

'Well,' Violet went on, 'sometime later, when the darkness parted, I began to see this other cat. Bright red and glowing, and when her eyes opened, I was captivated by their brilliance. So green and clear and sharp. The humans named me Violet, and her, Rose, and that cold scrap of a cat began to grow into someone magnificent.'

Dust thought about how stunning Rose had become, right before his eyes, with just a whispered word from her sister. He understood what Violet meant.

'We grew up in the White Box,' Violet continued, 'We fed from a mound of grey fluff and slept curled up on the cold floor together. When we began to explore, we discovered that one wall of the White Box had a clear panel, and through it we could see other cats. A beautiful she-cat with long white fur and bright green eyes, and two smaller cats, almost identical to us in their colouring.

'Rose and I were drawn to those cats. All we wanted to do was watch them. The smaller cats would rest against the white she-cat, feed from her, and fall asleep in her belly fur with faces as happy as their hearts. All we had was the cold milk from the lifeless fluff which made our bellies and hearts ache. We longed to be close to that white she-cat. And it seemed that she was also drawn to us.'

Dust pricked his ears, 'She saw you?'

'She couldn't see us, but in a way, she knew we were there.'

'The white she-cat, she was your mother?'

'Yes,' Violet closed her eyes, 'but we didn't know it then.'

195

'Sorry ... I interrupted.'

'It's ok,' Violet blinked and went on, 'I think she could sense us. Rose and I would watch her sniff around the edge of the see-through panel and scratch at the bottom of it. Over time, her scratch mark grew, and she became obsessed with it.

'Rose became obsessed with the white she-cat and spent most of her time watching her. She meowed at her, demanding to know why she never looked at us. And as the scratch mark deepened, so did Rose's anger.

'The humans who attended those cats were kind to them, they took them bowls of soft food, groomed their fur, and threw soft shiny toys for them to chase. Our humans bought us cold rat flesh and stale water. And instead of toys, we had Ratbots.

'We grew like the smaller cats on the other side of the panel. But they were happy and bright and warm while we were cold and afraid and hungry. They played and wrestled with each other while we sat side by side, alone, waiting for the next Ratbot. They consoled each other, while we argued and grew apart.'

'You argued?'

Violet nodded. 'Rose believed that the white she-cat had chosen those other cats and rejected us. She became consumed by her anger and would only leave the scratch to catch Ratbots and pick at cold rat flesh. She barely slept, and when she did, it was always with her head leant against the see-through panel, her eye always close to that scratch.

'The white she-cat began to do the same. Sleeping longer with her head against the other side of the panel, her eye also to the scratch. It was as if she was trying to lean on Rose. But

Rose thought the white she-cat was taunting her. She blamed herself at first, believing she'd done wrong. Then she blamed me, then the other smaller cats. But, in the end, she always returned to blaming the white she-cat ... hating her ... wishing her away ... wishing them all away.

'Then one day the humans did take the smaller cats away. And the white she-cat was alone. All we could do was watch as she cried and paced in circles until she was so exhausted, she'd slump against the scratch and shiver with sadness. She stopped eating, then she stopped pacing and, eventually, she stopped crying.

'Rose broke...' Violets claws scraped on the cold floor, 'filled with rage, she'd rip Ratbots to shreds in a heartbeat, attack any humans who attended to us, and anything else that threatened to tear her from that scratch. She only breathed to lay against the white she-cat and growl and snarl her hatred for her through the panel. But the white she-cat just closed her eyes and slowed her breathing, as if the heat of Rose's anger warmed her. But in that warmth ... our mother gave up ... and we could only watch as the light drained forever from her beautiful green eyes.'

Dust took a deep breath and rested his tail over Violet's back. He couldn't speak, he couldn't find the words.

Violet shook herself and went on, 'What Rose saw was different to what I saw. Maybe I am more patient than my sister. Maybe Rose is too quick to react. Maybe that's why I saw a beautiful she-cat become so consumed by grief for her lost kittens, that she would lay down and die of a broken heart in the only place she'd ever felt the warmth of their presence.

'But Rose only felt rejection. She was shattered by the grief. Even when the humans removed our mother's body and the panel went dark, Rose still lay with her head against that scratch, her snarls cracking into pitiful cries. All I could do was sing the song that had saved her once before. So, I sang. Over and over and over again, until finally, Rose quietened enough to listen to my voice. And then I would sing some more...

'Bring me your cold,
'Your tears,
'And your little paws.
'You have me to hold.
'You have me to hold...

'Never get cold,
'My dear,
'In my loving paws.
'Never get cold.
'Never get cold...

'Give me to hold,
'Your fears,
'And your little paws.
'You have me to hold.
'You have me to hold...

'Never get cold,
'My dear,
'In my loving paws.
'Never get cold.

'Never get cold.
'Never get cold...'

Dust's skin tingled from the warmth in Violet's voice.

'My song eventually calmed her anger. And Rose was starting to come around when the humans took me away.'

Dust gasped, 'They took you away from her?'

Violet nodded, 'That was the next to last time I saw my sister before I came here. I was taken to the Grey Box, where I was alone, just sleeping and catching Ratbots.

'Until one day, when the humans took me to another White Box. There were two other cats already there. They didn't know me, but I recognised them as the smaller cats who'd been with the white she-cat. Their names were Aster and Daisy, our brother and sister. I told them about Rose and how we had watched them grow up with their mother. They told me that our mother's name was Wild Berry, and they told me our Mother Names. Aster and Daisy knew about us, because Berry had believed that her other daughters were trapped behind the mirror. I'd only seen our reflections up until then, but as I turned to look at that mirror, I saw it had a scratch in the bottom corner. It was the other side of the see-through panel. And when I looked closer, I saw red fur. Rose was still there ... alone ... still leaning against the other side.

'When I rested my head against the mirror, in the exact spot that our mother died, my heart broke for my sister. I never saw her again. And I never found the strength to tell Aster and Daisy that our mother was dead before the humans took me back to the Grey Box. Then it was just me and the Ratbots again, until I was grown, and they stuffed me into a trap and brought me here.'

Dust leant on Violets' side and rested his muzzle on her shoulder. He had no words for her story, only warmth for the beautiful she-cat. All his cats had suffered, but through everything, Violet had only ever given love.

Paw steps padded close by. Dust raised his head to see the dark outline of a cat slide from the shadows of the towers and pad towards them.

Rose lifted her head and fixed him with her brilliant green eyes, 'No rats here. Let's go.'

23

Watch Lights

BRIAR WAS THE FIRST CAT ON his paws as Dust pushed through the flap. On the full boxes, Onyx and Spinney paused their grooming and Fern and Conker hushed their conversation. Gloworm sat up in his bed and watched them anxiously.

Dust waited for Rose and Violet to climb through the flap, 'Cold Box and Vast Tower Box, no rats. We didn't find any scent, not even a trace.'

Briar stopped in front of Dust, 'Did you scout everywhere?'

Rose padded to Dust's side and faced Briar, 'Yes. No scent. No rats.'

Conker hopped down from the full boxes, 'We smelt them. but it was faint. They must be hiding from us?'

'Skeeal doesn't fear us,' Rose growled.

'Then why have they just ... vanished?' Onyx dipped her head to Rose.

'Because they can,' Dust shook his head, 'Rose is right. The rats are not afraid of us. And Skeeal isn't afraid of losing rats. This is revenge for Boirey. They are hiding so we will starve.'

'We won't starve, the humans have dry nuggets,' Spinney mewed.

Onyx flicked his ear with her tail, 'Nuggets are in the Healing Box, and we can't get there without being injured.'

'So, we get injured,' Spinney purred, 'Just a little ... so the humans take us there.'

Onyx shook her head, 'how will you get injured without rats, Spinney? Do you want me to bite you?'

Spinney lifted his paw and offered it to Onyx.

'Wait,' Dust mewed, 'That might not be such a bad idea.'

'I'm not biting him!' Onyx protested.

Dust twitched his whiskers, 'I think we can get into the Healing Box ... without being injured.' As his cats turned their curious expressions on him, Dust ran through the idea in his mind. *light bump opens vanishing doors ... Dropping Box middle bump ... Through Under Box... white door has a lever...* he glanced at the green door, *just like that one...* 'Yes,' he mewed, 'I think we can.'

'Let's do it!' Spinney shuffled his paws excitedly.

Dust glanced at the flat light. It was still black. 'If we go now,' he nodded to Spinney, 'we can try and get in and find the nuggets. And if we can, we can come back and send others.'

Spinney leapt to his paws, 'let's go, I'm starving!'

'We should all go,' Rose mewed.

Briar flicked his tail, 'It will take longer if we all go.'

'But she's right, Briar,' Violet insisted, 'If we go in two's what happens if the humans come back early. Who goes last? Who doesn't get to eat?'

Dust could see the hunger in the eyes of every cat. 'You're right, Violet. We don't know how long it's going to take, and it will be *quicker* if we all go together.'

Spinney bounded to the flap. 'Come on then, let's go eat!'

Dust led his cats into the Long Box and waited by the Bright Corner for them all to catch up. Then he trotted ahead and stopped in front of the vanishing doors. 'Okay,' he mewed, 'If you haven't seen these open before they can be frightening, but they are safe.' He noted the look of fear in Fern and Gloworm's eyes. Onyx, Briar, and Spinney had seen them before, Conker didn't seem worried, but Rose and Violet stepped back and exchanged nervous glances.

Spinney padded to Dust's side, 'It's safe, but it feels weird.'

'Weird?' Violet mewed, 'How do you mean?'

'It's like falling off the floor,' Spinney tipped his head to one side, 'But you're on the floor, so you're not really falling...'

'Yes, that is what it feels like...' Dust purred as he thought about Spinney's description. Then he shook the thought away. They needed to be quick if they had any chance of getting into the Healing Box. 'Okay, when I press that light bump, the vanishing doors will vanish into the wall.' He looked around the anxious faces, trying to decide which cats to send in first. He needed to stay outside until the others were in the Dropping Box in case the doors closed. He wanted Spinney to wait too, so he didn't press anything. *Who first? Who won't hesitate....?* 'Rose ... and Briar, as soon as there's a gap, leap into the Dropping Box.'

'Sure,' Briar mewed with a glance at the red she-cat.

Rose nodded.

'Then Violet and Gloworm next. Walk in as quickly as you can. When they are in, Fern and Conker, Then Onyx and Spinney. I will follow right behind you. Don't worry if the doors close, I can open them again. And don't touch the light bumps inside until we are all in.'

Every cat nodded.

'Ok, let's go,' Spinney mewed with an excited hop.

Dust stretched up the wall on his hind legs and pressed the light bump. It glowed orange. The vanishing doors hissed and slid back into the wall.

As Fern and Gloworm began to shrink back from the doors, Dust flicked his tail to Rose. She nodded and jumped over the door lines into the Dropping Box. Briar followed boldly behind her. Violet was ready, nudging Gloworm on as she hurried to join her sister. Gloworm looked straight ahead and limped in, holding his sore leg up above the lines while leaning into Violet's side. Fern closed her eyes and let Conker push her gently forward. Onyx jumped over the door lines and Spinney strode in confidently behind her. Dust slid in just as the Vanishing Doors reappeared and began to close.

As the doors met in the middle, all eyes were on Dust. He reached up with a fore paw and pressed the middle light bump. The Dropping Box jerked, then rocked as it began its descent. Dust could hear claws scraping on the cold shiny floor as fur rippled and tails bushed. Violet leant on Gloworm as he licked a paw and mumbled. Conker stood over Fern as she dropped to the ground panting.

The Dropping Box shuddered and thumped to a halt. Rose hissed as the vanishing doors began to slide back into the walls.

'Okay, let's get out,' Dust padded behind the cats, nudging them to their paws and towards the doors.

Spinney leapt out first,' It's okay, follow me.'

Onyx helped Conker guide Fern out and Violet padded out behind them with her tail over Gloworm's back. Rose and Briar walked out calmly side by side, neither cat wanting to drop behind the other. Dust followed, curling his tail over his back as the vanishing doors reappeared and slid to a close behind him.

'This way,' Spinney was at the corner, flicking his tail towards the white door at the far end of the Under Box. Every cat padded after him, gazing around as they walked.

'What's in there?' Briar nodded to the red door.

Dust shook his head, 'I don't know, we could look on the way back.'

'We should,' Briar nodded, 'It could be important.'

Dust stopped in front of the white door and waited for every cat's attention. 'Right,' he mewed, 'I'll show you how to open it.' He turned to face the door, leapt, and hooked his paws over the lever, digging his claws in to stop them slipping. The lever moved down, scrinched, and with a clack, the door opened.

Spinney purred, 'Good job, Dust. Tell me how you did it, I saw, I think, but you were so quick.'

Dust explained how to use their paws, claws, and weight to move the lever but stopped Spinney before he leapt at the door. 'Wait until I've closed it again. I'll go in and push it shut. Then you can try opening it.'

Spinney tipped his head to one side as he studied the door. 'Why? We can close it from out here,' he mewed thoughtfully, 'We will have to, or the humans will know we've been in there?'

'I left the blue door open,' Dust tipped his head and looked at the orange and white tom, *He is smart...* 'I didn't look at how to close it from outside.'

Spinney stepped forward and lowered his head to peer through the gap at the bottom of the door. Then he reached out a fore paw, turned it pads up, extended his claws, and slid them into the gap.

Dust sighed, 'Of course,' he purred as Spinney pulled the door back into its frame. It clicked shut.

'Now it's my turn to open it.' Spinney leapt up at the lever and gripped it with both paws, using the claws of the topmost paw to hold the bottom paw in place. He held fast and wriggled his hindquarters to make the lever slide down, until they heard the scrinch and clack.

Spinney landed softly on the floor and flicked his tail. Then he pushed open the door and vanished into the Healing Box.

'Follow him. He'll find the dry nuggets,' Conker mewed, 'Quickly, before he eats the lot.'

'Down here, in the box with the door.' Spinney sat in front of a small door under the ledge. He scratched at the edge of it and pulled, but it didn't open easily. Dust hurried to his side and gripped the bottom of the door with his claws. As they both pulled, the door opened enough for Dust to slide his paw into the gap while Spinney nudged it open with his nose.

Behind the small door was a small box, and it was full of packets of dry nuggets. One was open, and Dust could smell their strange stale fleshy scent. Spinney hopped inside the Small Box and nudged the packet over. The nuggets spilled out across floor.

'Careful,' Dust mewed, 'if we spill too many, we won't be able to eat them up, and the humans will know we've been here.'

Spinney looked at Dust and twitched his whiskers, 'Don't worry, I'll eat them.'

Onyx flicked Spinney on the head with her tail, 'Move aside,' she purred, 'let some other cats eat.'

Dust and Spinney were used to the nugget's strange taste, so they ate their fill quickly and went off to scout around the Healing Box. They hopped up onto the ledge and padded along it towards the nook. Spinney stopped in front of a stack of slim beige boxes and ruffled his fur. Dust caught up and sniffed the edge of the stack. Craig's damp scent was all over them, and a warm metallic breeze drifted around the holes in the back of them, but it carried no uplifting scents. They hummed, and when Dust put his nose to the side of the nearest box, it moved, like a purring cat's chest. *Humming place...* Dust recalled Benny's words. A *humming box in a humming place...*

Dust stepped around them, gasped, and jumped back, shaking away what he'd seen. At the front of the humming boxes, a stack of square flat lights flickered so brightly that they left dancing glimmers in his eyes. Blinking, Dust kept his head low and slowly looked back up at them with half closed eyes. Their light was harsh and grey and there was movement in them. Flickering images that he did not recognize at first, but slowly, as his eyes adjusted to their fierce lights, he began to decipher them.

'That ... looks like cats,' Spinney stepped to Dust's side and peered into the light.

Dust nodded. The moving images were like cats viewed from above. Dust and Spinney watched the group of cats milling around a corner at the top of the centre flat light. Then he blinked, astonished, as a fluffy head rose from the group and looked around. He glanced across the Healing Box and saw that Gloworm had raised his head.

'Spinney, look at this.'

Spinney peered at the flat light, 'What?'

'It's us.'

Spinney glanced at the cats eating the dry nuggets, then looked back at the images, and gasped, 'It ... yes...'

'Hop down and walk over to the others, then I can see if it really is.'

Spinney nodded and did as Dust asked.

Dust watched as Spinney appeared on the side of the flat light and moved towards the other cats. He could clearly make out the orange and white tom's markings, and he saw Onyx lift her head to greet him as he approached. *It's like looking down on him from up high... High up... High up on the wall...* Dust looked up at the little red light.

Spinney hopped back onto the ledge, 'Did you see me?'

Dust nodded and flicked his tail to the little red light, 'Up there, that light is like the one in the Meeting Box, and here, look,' he tapped the top middle flat light with his tail, 'what does that look like to you?'

Spinney blinked and peered at the images. 'The Meeting Box? It that our beds?'

Dust nodded.

'Found anything fun?' Onyx mewed as she hopped onto the ledge beside them.

'The Meeting Box,' Spinney meowed, 'it's in this flat light and there, that's us at the top of the middle one.'

'In a light ... what?'

Dust purred, 'look, this is ... it's like a flat light but instead of changing colours, we can see ourselves. I don't know how but look there.'

'Ouch ... what?' Onyx reeled away from the light.

'Close your eyes, then look up at it slowly,' Dust rested his tail on her back to guide her closer.

Onyx did what he said and let her eyes adjust before she looked at the flickering movements. She took her time to study them, before she mewed, 'That's Rose ... isn't it, in the middle with her head raised, and Violet sat next to her ... and ...' she tipped her head to one side, 'Gloworm, licking his paws.'

'Yes, we can watch them in this light.'

'How is it real?' Onyx blinked. 'I wish I understood how all this human stuff works.'

'I don't know how it works,' Dust mewed, 'But I'm sure it is real. It's like looking through a light to see ourselves. Look there, that's the Meeting Box.'

Onyx glanced at the Healing Box door, 'the Meeting Box is that way,' she lifted her chin, 'and up.'

'Yes, and it's also in this flat light. I think those are its eyes,' Dust nodded to the little red light high up on the wall.

Onyx stared up at the little red light, then looked at the other cats, 'It isn't a flat light. It's ... a watch light!'

Dust nodded, 'That's a good way to describe it ... and it has little red eyes all over The Boxes.'

'And look ... here comes Rose,' Onyx watched Rose in the watch light as she padded across the floor and hopped up onto the ledge beside them.

'Look,' Spinney nudged Dust's shoulder, 'That's the Cold Box, I see the rolling traps.'

'And there,' Onyx went on, 'that's the Vast Tower Box, I can see the full boxes on the towers.

'Yes, there's the slide down door,' Dust tapped the top of the bottom left watch light with his paw. Then movement caught his eye.

Rose saw it too, 'What's that?'

Dust looked closer. Something rectangular was rolling across the bottom right watch light, 'A box, a Moving Box maybe?'

'Like the one Conker got in?' Onyx mewed.

'Maybe. But where is it?' He didn't recognise the box it was in. A bright light in the top corner illuminated a dark floor marked with rows of rectangles and reflected off the surface of a large pool of water. As the Moving Box passed below the light, it circled and stopped in one of the rectangles.

A human got out of the Moving Box and walked towards the bottom of the watch light.

'That's the...' Spinney began.

'Craig,' Dust finished for him.

Spinney looked at the door nervously, 'Where is he, what box is he in?'

'I have no idea,' Dust mewed, but we need to go, now. He could be close.'

Dust jumped down from the ledge and trotted to the other cats. Briar, Gloworm, Fern and Violet had already finished eating, Conker lapped up one more nugget as Dust approached.

'We need to go,' Dust mewed, 'the humans are coming back.'

24

The Water Box

CONKER LAPPED UP ANOTHER TWO NUGGETS and Spinney grabbed the last three before they pushed the packet back into the small box and closed the door. Dust ushered the other cats out of the Healing Box and waited for them to catch up before pulling the white door closed behind them.

The cats hurried into the Dropping Box as soon as the vanishing doors slid open, eyes wide and fur rippling, but without hesitation. Dust looked around to check they were all inside before he stepped in and pressed the top light bump.

The vanishing doors hissed and slid closed, but the Dropping Box didn't move.

'Did you press the right one?' Onyx asked after a heartbeat's silence.

I'm sure I did... Dust reached up and pressed the top light bump again. The Dropping Box jerked and stopped. He shook his head. Fear scent seeped from the cats around him, and a low growl began to rumble in Gloworm's throat. Dust stared at the top light bump, then carefully reached up a paw, but before he could press it again, the Dropping Box began to shudder and fall.

'Down?' Spinney mewed quietly in Dust's ear, 'Shouldn't it be going up?'

Dust looked at the floor and extended his claws to meet it. He closed his eyes and felt the movement flow through his legs. It felt like down, but they were supposed to be going up. *'One in the Long Box... to get into the Dropping Box... then three in here... one for the Long Box... one for the Under Box and the Healing Box, and...?'* He opened his eyes and looked at the light bumps. There were two below the one he'd pressed. *The top one is up ... middle for the Healing Box ... but I didn't press the bottom one...* Dust looked at Spinney, 'It's going down, but ... I pressed the bump for up.'

'What's down?' Onyx mewed.

'Rats,' Conker mewed, 'Rats come from down. Rats and their Clooies.'

Dust shook his head, 'But what *is* down?'

The cats began to murmur and shuffle uncomfortably.

The Dropping Box juddered and stopped.

'I think we're about to find out,' Conker mewed.

As the vanishing doors slid back, Dust pricked his ears. *Footsteps...?* He stepped over the door lines and out onto a damp dark floor and listened. They were coming from beyond a nearby corner. Slowly, he padded along the sodden wall and peered around the corner, just in time to see an orange door swing closed. A human had just gone through it. He sniffed the air. *Craig...*

'What is it?' Briar asked.

'Craig. He has just left this box.'

'What is this place?' Briar followed Dust out of the Dropping Box and gazed around.

'It's not the place with the Moving Box,' Spinney mewed, 'I don't see any rectangles on the floor.'

Dust's fur began to prickle as he realised that Spinney was right. They were in a dank and dimly lit box with green tinged walls and a rough grey roof. There were no flat lights, full boxes, or little red lights. The only source of light was a large white light bump beside the orange door. Every wall was featureless except for a large domed circle that hung in the middle of the end wall. 'It's a new box,' he mewed, 'But I didn't see it in the watch lights.'

'It's empty,' Spinney mewed as he gazed around.

Briar looked back over his shoulder, 'Should we scout here, Dust, or try to get back?'

Rose stepped out of the Dropping Box and lowered her head to stare at the floor in front of her, 'We scout this.'

Dust padded to her side. The Dropping Box had opened onto a raised floor. A few strides away, the floor ended in a steep step down, about the height of two cats, and from the step, the floor sloped downwards towards the far wall, creating a deep channel. The scent of forgotten water bowls lingered in the channel, the same stale scent that Craig carried with him, but the air above was fresh and cold. The box was quiet except for a constant drip-drip-drip of water.

Dust sniffed the air again and listened. There was nothing in the box that alerted his senses to danger, but it didn't feel safe. Something was making his fur prickle. He looked back at the Dropping Box. *The doors are still open ... could I open them again if it goes somewhere else...?* 'Come out,' he mewed, 'If you stay in there, the doors could close, and you might not be able to open them again.'

'I agree,' Conker nudged Fern to her paws.

215

Violet glanced at the light bumps. 'Yes,' she shuddered, 'Let's join the others.'

'Are you sure it's safe?' Onyx asked.

'Can't be less safe than in here,' Gloworm growled, 'we should stay together.'

'Come on then,' Onyx pushed Fern forward into Conker as Violet helped Gloworm over the door line.

Dust wondered how long it would be before the humans discovered they weren't in the Meeting Box. *Would Craig notice them missing....?*

Spinney padded to the edge of the step and peered into the channel, then he hopped down and padded carefully towards the far wall.

Briar jumped down and followed, 'Any rat scent?'

Spinney sniffed along the floor, 'It's slimy and wet and smells like Craig ... But not rats.'

'What's that over there?' Onyx hopped into the channel and padded towards the far end.

Dust watched as Onyx crept towards a large, raised square on the floor at the other end of the channel. It was partly covering a hole. The square was made of bars, like a trap's door. The gaps in its bars were too small for a cat to get through, but big enough for a rat. He called to her, 'Check for rat scent, but be careful.'

'Right away, boss.' Onyx mewed as she padded closer to the hole.

As the cats sniffed around the walls and floor of the strange new box, Dust looked up at the light bump by the orange door. A tiny green light flickered just below it, about the same size as a little red light, and in its dim glow, he could just see the outlines of three more bumps below it.

Gloworm padded to his side. 'I don't like this,' he mewed, 'this place isn't like the other boxes. We shouldn't stay here.'

Dust licked his ear, 'We won't stay long, just a quick look around, that's all.'

Gloworm nodded, but went on, 'We've looked enough, we should—'

The white light bump beeped, and black human markings appeared on its face. The little green light turned red.

Every cat raised their head to look.

The beeping continued, steady, like a heartbeat. Then the light bump directly below the bright white one, lit up green and began to flash.

Briar hopped back up the step, 'What are they for?'

'I don't know,' Dust shook his head.

A heartbeat later, the green light bump went off, and the one below it lit up and flashed orange. The beeping quickened.

'We need to get out of here,' Gloworm turned and started padding towards the Dropping Box.

'I agree,' Briar meowed as he followed Gloworm.

'Wait!' Onyx mewed. 'I smell rats.'

Spinney sniffed the floor, 'Are you sure?'

'Here! Conker is right. The rats are down this hole,' Onyx flicked her tail, 'the scent is strong on the air. This must be the Rat Holes.'

Dust watched Onyx as she crouched and peered down into the hole. His fur prickled. *The Rat Holes... Is this how the rats are getting in and out...?*

The beeping quickened again. The orange light went out, and the one below it began flashing red.

Spinney took a step towards Onyx but froze as a loud grating sound filled the box.

Dust pricked his ears and look around. The noise was coming from the domed circle on the end wall. it began to move, then with a loud hiss, it slid down the wall. Water sprayed out from behind it.

'Get back to the Dropping Box.' Briar yowled above the sound of hissing water.

'Go—' Conker's mew was drowned out as the hissing gave way to a deafening roar. He grabbed Fern's scruff and pulled her into the Dropping Box.

The circle ground to a stop as a violent plume of water spewed from behind it and crashed down into the channel.

Dust pushed Rose back towards the Dropping Box, and Violet guided her inside.

Spinney hopped up the step, 'Onyx, come on.'

Dust looked back towards the far end of the channel. Onyx was getting to her paws, her eyes widening as she saw the approaching water.

The water was filling the channel, from the far wall, swelling out in waves towards the step, spraying the cats as it continued to gush into the box.

'Hurry,' Spinney yowled.

Onyx bounded over the waves and reached the step with the rising water sloshing around her legs, but before she could leap up, a wave surged back from the far wall and pulled her down below the surface.

'ONYX!' Spinney yowled as he bounded along the edge of the step and peered into the swirling torrent.

The roar was dulled by a new grating sound as the domed circle began to slide back up the wall. The jet of water slowed to a trickle. Something gurgled.

Spinney ran frantically along the step, calling to Onyx. He stopped near the hole, his fur bristled, and he dived in.

Dust raced after Spinney, looking up and down the length of the channel for any signs of the black she-cat. He spotted a flick of sodden tail near the hole, 'Over there...' he dived in after her.

The cold water took his breath away and dragged him down as it flowed through his long fur, pulling him deeper until its chill locked his muscles. Dust thrashed his legs, desperate for heat, until his paws touched the floor, and his head broke the surface. Then the waves calmed around him, and within another heartbeat, he was able to stand and stride through the water towards the hole.

Spinney's head appeared and he too began to bound towards the hole. Then his back appeared above the water, 'I see her,' he gasped, 'I see ... her,' He flicked his sodden tail towards the far corner. Dust turned to look in that direction, but he saw nothing.

The gurgling sound grew louder, and longer.

'The water's going,' Briar yowled.

Dust jumped through the receding waves that sloshed across the middle of the channel to where Spinney stood belly deep in them a few strides ahead, staring into the spiralling water that encircled the hole in the floor.

'She's gone.' Spinney shivered, 'Onyx has gone.'

25

When Your Territory Goes Bad

DUST OPENED HIS EYES. HIS FIRST breath shuddered with her scent. A dark shadow loomed above, spiralling, and spreading, plunging everything around him into darkness. Paw steps padded behind him, and he caught a glimpse of bright grey eyes as the shadow shifted into the blurry outline of a cat. He felt the aching cold and damp of the floor seep into his bones as she sat up before him, thrashed her tail and shook her head.

'Breeze...'

'You need to be more careful, Dust...'

'I know ... I didn't think...'

'You must think... Territories go bad...'

Dust hung his head. He could barely see his paws in the darkness.

'If territories go bad, you lose cats...'

'I lost Onyx...' Dust saw the darkness deepen even more. His shadow shifted, lifted its head, and slid from under him. As Shadow Dust circled Breeze, he was sure he caught a faint glimmer of Shadow Onyx behind him before she flickered and faded away. 'I lost Onyx.'

'Watch...' Breeze flicked her tail.

Shadow Dust sat down beside her and fixed him with a nervous stare. From the gloom along the walls, movement stirred and spiralled into the outlines of cats. Ebbing and flowing with the fear that lifted their fur and bushed their tails. They trembled as they stalked around him and flattened themselves to the floor, fixing him with their desperate glares.

Shadow Rose scratched a burning ear and snapped up her bright grey eyes. She growled at their reflection so clear in the glare of a thousand vicious spies.

Shadow Violet sniffed the drying blood on fragile bones and thinning fur. To the starving cat she gave all she could before it groaned and took a bite from her.

Shadow Gloworm circled the box inside and slipped through its open door, into another within, and more that hide in a never-ending nesting of more.

Shadow Spinney left the water behind and leapt from the wave to the ledge, away from a skittering danger he'd find if he'd stopped to look over the edge.

Shadow Fern lingered away all alone, far from those who'd miss her most. Stalking memories of all she's known, hunting for the closeness she'd lost.

Shadow Conker slipped into The Outside where the air beat him back to the trap, and moved the bars and safe places to hide, until he was locked back behind the flap.

Shadow Briar slipped as the next door slammed, and ran from humans blocking his way, but into the holes and doorways they rammed their boxes and bars to keep him at bay.

Shadow Dust sat and looked at the bump, if he'd pressed them wrong, he couldn't recall but the lights lit up and a jerk made him jump, and with a shudder the box began to fall.

Dust hit the floor of the Meeting Box. Shaking himself he sat up and watched in horror as Shadow Cats fell all around him, their wails and yowls fading before they dispersed into a twisting rolling mist.

Breeze flicked the remains of the Shadow Cats away with her tail as she sat before him, 'When your territory goes bad...' she mewed, 'save your cats...'

26

Chances

DUST HOPPED UP ONTO THE FULL boxes. 'We must carry on. If we don't, we could miss a sign that Onyx is okay.'

'How can she be okay?' Spinney hissed, 'She was washed away ... I've never seen so much water... and it moved so fast ... she didn't stand a chance.'

Dust sighed. The water had ripped through the channel and would have washed them all away if they'd been slower. *Moving water...*

'You went in the water, Spinney. You and Dust, and you got out,' Violet reassured the distraught tom. She stopped licking his damp fur to give his ear a gentle nuzzle.

'Icicle,' Dust glanced at Gloworm. 'You said your mother was swept under moving water, and she was ... okay?'

Gloworm shook his head, then nodded. 'She died, but then she met Shadow White. Shadow White sent her back to her body to continue her life.'

'But Icicle was okay ... after she came back?' Dust asked again.

Gloworm nodded, 'Yes, she was, but the humans took her to The Old Place.'

'So, where is Onyx now? Why haven't they brought her back here?' Spinney mewed.

Gloworm shook his head.

'Maybe she *is* in The Outside?' Conker mewed, 'Moving water is in The Outside, like moving air. You could ask Benny.'

Dust glanced at the flat light. It was bright blue. 'Good idea. Let's rest now, and when it's time to scout, I'll help Gloworm get into the Blue Box. I will scout the Vast Tower Box while he waits for Benny. We need to find the rats.'

'Alone?' Asked Briar.

Dust took a deep breath, 'The danger in The Boxes has changed, Briar,' he noted the shocked expressions on the faces of his cats as he went on, 'The humans won't harm us, nor will the rats. A bite or scratch maybe, but we know what they're capable of now. The danger is in new places we haven't explored yet. There's more to The Boxes, I'm sure of that. Above us, under us ... I don't know, but the places we know should be safe to scout alone.'

'Will we go back to the Healing Box for food? Spinney asked.

'We may have to,' Dust replied, 'The Dropping Box is dangerous and could take us anywhere, but if we can't find the rats ... we will have no choice.'

'It was the Water Box that was dangerous, Spinney growled, 'We should have stayed in the Dropping Box.'

Dust nodded. All his cats nodded with him. 'We'll stick to the places we know, while Benny looks for Onyx in The Outside.'

*

Dust awoke later to the rhythmic trudge of scuffing feet. He glanced at the flat light. It was grey. He hopped down from his bed, padded to the flap and pushed it open. John was shuffling towards the Bright Corner. He'd already swept the floor with the sour damp. The clattering sounds had faded with the quieting human voices.

'Gloworm,' Dust mewed.

The white tom raised his head and blinked.

'We should scout now. I'm sure it's the right time to find Benny.'

Gloworm frowned and looked up at the flat fight.

Dust flicked his tail, 'I don't know what grey means, but John has swept the floors and the humans have gone.'

'Okay,' Gloworm's tail bushed as he hopped out of his bed and padded over to join Dust.

'Conker?' Dust mewed.

The black tom lifted his head and yawned, 'Is it time to go?' Confused, he also looked at the flat light.'

'Gloworm and I will scout now. I'll come back once he's in the Blue Box. Find another cat and get ready to go back out to hunt when I return.'

Conker nodded and rested his head back down on the side of his bed.

Dust nodded to Gloworm, 'Come on, let's go.'

John's scent lingered in the Long Box, but it was fading fast under the stench of sour damp. If any rat had been there, there was no way of telling.

Gloworm sat down as they reached the blue door and stretched his aching leg. 'We could scout the Cold Box together first. I could do with a good walk.'

Dust nodded, 'Good idea. Benny didn't come until the flat light was black, so we have time.'

'And scouting alone is dangerous, Dust. I know I'm not much help to anyone with a bad leg. But I can sense danger, and danger doesn't just vanish because we find new places.'

'You're right,' Dust mewed, 'But there is more to The Boxes than we know, I'm sure Breeze is trying to tell me that in my dreams ... I'm sure she's trying to show me ... things.'

'Things?' Gloworm curled his tail to the side.

'She shows me shadows. Our own shadows, like Shadow Cats. And I see them go to places and find things, but it's so hard to remember.'

'Dreams are hard to understand. It can take time to find their meaning.'

'The dreams feel like a warning. The Boxes are bad, and I must save my cats. But I can't tell exactly what or where the dangers are.'

'Everywhere,' Gloworm growled, 'and everything.'

Dust gave Gloworm's ear a lick and without speaking, he turned and led the way around the Blue Corner.

The Cold Box was clear. They padded through it and climbed over the full box that held the yellow doors open. Not a sound or a scent of rat reached their senses.

'I'm not sure if they're hiding, or gone?' Dust mewed.

'If the rats leave, what will happen to us?' Gloworm asked, 'will the humans want us here if there are no rats?'

'I don't know. They could take us to another place, but Spinney wouldn't want to leave without finding Onyx.'

'And Rose and Violet will not want to be separated.'

'No,' Dust agreed, 'no, they wouldn't.'

228

'Then we must escape, together. I haven't known any other cat since my littermates, and ... I don't want to be alone again.'

'I agree. We can't risk being separated.'

'You have bought us all together, Dust. You're a good leader.'

'Thank you,' Dust dipped his head.

Gloworm licked Dust's ear and limped ahead into the open space.

Dust hesitated before he followed. He wasn't sure he'd done anything to bring his cats together. They were as happy to follow him as he was to follow his dreams of Breeze. He was sure Breeze was telling him to lead the cats out of The Boxes, but with the rats gone, they didn't have long to escape. *And how....? How can we all escape together....?*

'What do you think is up there?' Gloworm interrupted his thoughts.

Dust twitched his tail as he followed Gloworm's gaze, 'Maybe a roof somewhere, there must be a roof, or it would be The Outside.'

Gloworm purred, 'Then you believe The Outside is all around The Boxes?'

'Benny is in The Outside. We talk to him through a hole. If there was no roof up there, it would be a hole too.'

'And the rat, Skeeal, he said we should fly from the roof?'

Yes...' Dust squinted up into the gloom. He still couldn't see the tops of the towers, 'but if there's a roof up there, it is too high for a cat to fly from.'

Gloworm flicked his ear, 'Unless he didn't mean that roof.'

Dust considered Gloworm's point as they padded on through the dark deserted towers. He could be right. There were other roofs that they could see.

When they found no scent of rats, they headed back to the Cold Box.

'This,' Dust stopped and flicked his tail to the Metal Box. 'It's a box inside a box, and it has light bumps.'

'A box in a box?' Gloworm's fur ruffled along his spine, 'What do you think is in it?'

Dust padded to the mirror door and looked up at the silver lever. It looked like the levers on the other doors, but the light bumps were different to the ones in the Dropping Box. This box had nine small bumps arranged in a square. Dust reached up and pressed the top bump nearest the door. There was a beep as it lit up red. He dropped back down onto his haunches and looked expectantly at the mirror door. The light bump went out.

They are the same... 'They change colour when pressed.' He reached up again and pressed the middle top light bump. It lit up green. He waited, and it stayed green. Dust pressed the very centre bump. It beeped, turned red, and both light bumps went out.

'Gloworm padded closer, 'You need to press them in the right order. To make them stay green.'

Dust nodded, 'Yes. We should come back when the flat lights are blue and watch a human do it.'

Gloworm agreed, and they left the Cold Box and headed back to the blue door.

'What should I ask Benny?'

Dust let go of the lever as it scrinched and clicked. He landed softly on the floor, 'Ask him if he's seen Onyx, and if he knows about the Water Box.'

Gloworm dipped his head to Dust, then slipped into the Blue Box and pushed the door closed behind him.

Dust sat for a heartbeat to enjoy the uplifting scents, then he turned and headed back to the Meeting Box.

*

Conker was ready to go when Dust slipped back through the flap. Fern was crouched next to him, her fur ruffled and her eyes wide.

'Stick close to me.' Conker told her, 'If we see a rat, yowl. I'll chase it and catch it with Dust. It won't touch you.'

Fern nodded, 'Yes, but ... I just don't like this...'

It was the first time Fern had hunted. Perhaps the possibility of there being no rats to hunt was how Conker had convinced her to go. *She needs to start somewhere ... one day she may need to hunt to survive...* Dust was glad Fern had befriended Conker. The calm tom would look out for her. Gloworm was right to worry about the cats being separated. Fern needed to stay with a cat she could trust.

Conker looked up at Dust, 'Any scent?'

Dust shook his head, 'No. and if we don't find them, we'll be living on dry nuggets.'

Conker purred and licked Fern's ear, 'See, we'll be hunting in the Healing Box soon. This will be just like scouting.'

Fern flicked her tail and got to her paws, 'Okay,' she mewed, 'Let's go then.'

As Conker and Fern padded around the Blue Corner, Dust paused to listen at the blue door. He could hear Gloworm's gentle snores as he snoozed, waiting for Benny.

The Cold Box was quiet, but when they reached the big yellow doors, Dust heard human noises. He flicked his tail to tell Conker and Fern to wait, then he hopped over the full box and padded into the Vast Tower Box.

A dull clanking sound echoed around the towers. Dust flicked his ears, trying to locate it.

'I know that sound,' Conker hopped off the full box and joined him, 'it's the Moving Box.'

Dust turned his ears in the direction of the slide down door. Conker was right.

'Then ... the grey human?' Fern asked nervously.

Conker nodded, 'Yes, he could be here. Should we look, Dust?'

Dust nodded, 'Yes. He could have dropped human food. There could be rats.'

Fern took a deep breath.

Conker turned to her, 'Fern. Stay close to me. Don't worry about the rats, or the human. I won't let them come near you, just follow me.'

Fern nodded and leant into Conker's side. They exchanged a look, then together they stared ahead into the gloom.

'We should stick to the end of the towers,' Dust mewed, 'move around them when it's clear and then get back into the shadows. We should head to the last tower before the slide down door and look for any sign of the rats.'

Conker took a deep breath. 'Dust ... Fern is going to follow me. You could do the same.'

'I can lead,' Dust mewed, 'then Fern behind, and you stay close behind her...'

The clanking stopped.

'Dust,' Conker flicked Dust's shoulder with his tail, 'The slide down door is open.'

Dust shook his head, 'I don't think the rats will be in—' he stopped. He felt his stomach knot as he realised what Conker was saying.

Faint shuffling footsteps drifted from the gloom, followed by the occasional mumblings of the Grey Male.

'The Moving Box, Dust. It's there ... now.'

Dust held Conker's gaze and shook his head. 'I don't think it's a good idea to get in there again. We should wait and escape together when we know it's safe.'

'We'll take our chances.' Conker mewed.

'Come with us, Dust.' Fern mewed gently.

Dust shook his head, 'I can't just leave the others.'

'We can get them...' Fern lifted her head and looked back towards the yellow doors.

Dust shook his head, 'There's no time. Gloworm is asleep in the Blue Box ... and Onyx.' A knot of sadness gripped his stomach, and frustration tightened his chest. He couldn't leave the other cats. Spinney wouldn't go without knowing what happened to Onyx. Briar and Gloworm wanted to find Benny's Warmroot Copse. But he couldn't stop Fern and Conker from going. *Perhaps that's why he returned after all...*

'Dust?' Conker mewed.

'I'm sorry, Conker. I can't leave now.'

Conker nodded. 'We will wait for you.'

'What if the slide down door never opens again?' Dust mewed.

Fern hung her head and scratched the floor, 'I can't stay in The Boxes. Everything ... just terrifies me.'

Conker rested his tail over Fern's back and told Dust, 'I know a safe place, close to where I leapt out of the Moving Box. Just follow the outer wall of the giant grey box, then go across the broken floor and up the soft green, towards the tree.'

Dust shook his head, 'The tree?'

'Like the one Gloworm described. A tall structure with many outstretched arms. Wait there for us under it. It will shelter you all.'

Faint footsteps shuffled around in the gloom. The Grey Male grunted.

'I will tell the others,' Dust mewed. 'If they want to ... we can scout the slide down door. If they want to, we will join you.'

Conker reached forwards and licked Dust's ear, 'I hope you all can.'

Dust pressed his head against Conker's shoulder, 'If it's not safe, them come back.'

'We will,' Fern pressed against Dust's other side, 'Thank you for keeping us safe.'

Dust straightened and looked from Conker to Fern, 'Then this is goodbye.'

Conker and Fern dipped their heads to Dust, then side by side, they bounded away into the gloom.

27

Light Bumps

GLOWORM SCRAMBLED THROUGH THE FLAP A heartbeat before Fiona opened the green door. He slumped down against a full box without speaking, or taking his wide eyes off her.

Fiona cleaned the litters and dropped the shiny black cover by the door, then frowning, she stepped to the water bowl and refilled it from the bubble. When she'd finished, she looked around anxiously at the cats curled in their beds.

'*No rats, areyoueatingtheminthewarehouse.*'

'The rats have gone,' Dust told her.

Fiona turned to look at him, '*Hey Dust, youlookwell, youdontlookhungry.*'

'Hey, Fiona.' Dust sat up in his bed and blinked at her.

Fiona approached the full boxes and smiled as she went from cat to cat, stepping carefully past them, only pausing to fuss Spinney and Dust. No cat cared to get out of their bed. Despite the bright yellow rays that flooded through the flat light and warmed their backs, their mood was cold, and their worries lay with their missing friends, not the actions of the pleasant Green Female.

Fiona stopped when she got to Conker and Fern's empty beds and put her hand inside to feel the covers.

'*Stillouthuntingarethey?*' she bit her lip as she glanced at Onyx's empty bed. Then without inspecting it, she turned away and opened the door.

Wider than usual... Dust watched as she pushed the cover of litter out with her foot. He looked up; his eyes drawn to the hole the rats had left in the roof. The top of the door hovered directly below it, until Fiona stepped out of the Meeting Box and pulled it shut.

'She's got Onyx.' Gloworm blurted as he scrambled up onto the full boxes next to Dust.

Dust turned to him and shook his head, 'She's what?'

'What?' Spinney raised his head.

'Fiona. Benny said...'

'Slow down,' Dust rested his tail on Gloworm's back, 'Tell us what happened.'

Gloworm shivered as every cat turned to look at him. Rose sat upright, Violet stretched beside her, and Briar twitched his whiskers as he studied Gloworm's rippling fur.

'I asked Benny about Onyx. He told me he saw a big black she-cat with curled ears lying on the side of the Box Lake. And he saw a female human with green covers and red head fur get out of a Moving Box and pick her up.'

'Is he sure it was Fiona?' Dust asked.

Gloworm nodded, 'Yes.'

'Box Lake?' Briar asked.

'Was she okay? Was she hurt, or...?' Violet glanced at Spinney.

'I don't know, Benny was sure he saw her flick an ear when Fiona picked her up,' Gloworm took a deep breath and went on, 'And the Box Lake is a water place in The

Outside, but Benny doesn't know how Onyx got there from in here.'

'So, she *is* okay?' Spinney sat up.

'Fiona has her,' Gloworm repeated.

Dust licked Gloworm's ear, 'So, Onyx could be in the Healing Box. She could be back soon.'

'Yes!' Spinney hopped out of his bed and padded to the water bowl, 'And when she's back, we can get in the Moving Box and find Conker and Fern.'

'Where are Conker and Fern?' Gloworm glanced at their beds.

'In the Moving Box,' Spinney mewed, 'they escaped, but they're going to wait for us.'

'We still don't know where the Moving Box goes,' Briar mewed, 'Fern and Conker could also be back soon. We should keep talking to Benny. He's helping us from in The Outside ... and he has safe territory.'

'If it's real,' Rose mewed.

'Of course, it's real,' Gloworm licked his paw.

'Why wouldn't it be real?' Briar growled.

'We only have his word,' Rose hissed.

'That's more than we have from the rats,' Briar hissed.

Violet sat up and turned to Briar, 'You're right, Briar, but Skeeal and his rats are clearly getting in and out of The Boxes, and he told us how *we* can get out. Benny may be a good cat, but he doesn't seem to know much about this place.'

Dust glanced at Violet. *She has a point...* If they were ever to escape The Boxes, they needed to investigate every option. He turned to Gloworm again, 'Did Benny know anything about the Water Box?'

Gloworm shook his head. 'He doesn't know anything about it. He knows there are tunnels at the side of the Box Lake ... the rats use them, but he didn't know they led inside The Boxes. He didn't think Onyx was one of us until I described her.'

'If Fiona picked her up, then it must be Onyx. So, Onyx *was* in The Outside,' Spinney looked at the others.

'We can ask her about the Rat Holes and the Box Lake when she gets back,' Dust mewed, 'Until then, we should investigate other ways to escape. Starting with the roof. This roof.'

'This roof?' Rose twitched her whiskers and glanced up.

'Yes,' Dust mewed, 'I think we can get into it. But we need to wait until the humans have gone.'

'Dust,' Gloworm shuffled his paws, 'Fiona saw me in the Blue Box. She went in there and I ran out when the door was open.'

Dust nodded, 'Okay, we need to be careful. We should wait until Onyx has returned before we speak to Benny again.'

Gloworm sighed, 'He's watching The Boxes, but he hasn't seen any way to get out that isn't controlled by humans.'

'I'm sure he'll find something,' Dust mewed. 'You should rest now, Gloworm. We will go to the Healing Box to eat before we scout for rats again. But I want to scout the Cold Box now, while the flat light is blue. Who'd like to come with me?'

'I will,' Briar mewed.

Dust nodded, 'Good. We need to watch the humans.'

With a nod, Briar hopped down from his bed and followed Dust to the flap. As the other cats slunk back down in their beds, Violet swapped places with Rose to help Gloworm settle.

Dust and Briar kept to the shadows as they padded down the Long Box. They paused around the Dark Corner and listened to the humans in the Bright Box behind the dull brown door. When it didn't open, they carried on to the black door and ducked down behind the full box that propped it open.

Two humans in red covers, one male and one female, were pushing rolling traps through the yellow doors. They kept their heads down and their expressions blank. The female stopped in the middle of the floor and stared at the full box on her rolling trap, then she uttered something and dragged the trap back into the Vast Tower Box. The male snorted, and his eyes sparkled. Dust and Briar watched from the doorway, and when they were certain that neither human had noticed them, they hopped over the full box and slid under the rolling traps that stood against the walls.

'What are they doing?' Briar asked.

Dust didn't know, but he attempted a guess, 'Moving the full boxes around. Maybe they're heavy and the traps make it easier to move them.'

'Why do they need them—' Briar gasped, 'Dust, look.'

Dust looked up to see Craig walking through the yellow doors carrying a small black box. He stopped in front of the mirror door, sniffed, and wiped his face with his arm.

Dust crept forward, craning his neck to watch. Briar stayed close behind him.

Craig raised his hand and pressed the middle light bump at the top of the panel. It lit up green. Dust recalled pressing the same one when he scouted with Gloworm. Next, Craig pressed the middle bump at the bottom, then the middle top again and them the very centre bump.

Middle: top, bottom, top, centre...

The lights turned green, and a little ding sound accompanied a hiss. Craig grabbed the silver lever and pulled the mirror door open, then stepped inside. He came out a heartbeat later without the black box and closed the door behind him. The light bumps went out.

'What's in there?' Briar asked.

'I don't know, but I know which light bumps he pressed, so we can look later.'

'The door looks heavy. Will we be able to pull it open?'

'Only one way to find out.'

As Craig strode towards the black door. Dust and Briar shuffled back under the rolling traps.

'Let's follow him,' Dust mewed.

'Why?' Briar asked, flicking his tail.

He's not going to do anything to us. Chase us back to the Meeting Box, maybe. But that's where were going anyway. We can't try the mirror door until the humans have gone.'

Briar nodded, 'Let's go then.'

As they padded back up the Long Box, they kept their pace slow as they listened to Craig's heavy footsteps. When they stopped, Dust peered around the Dark Corner and saw him standing in front of the blue door, his hand rummaging in the folds of his white covers. With a jingling sound, Craig pulled out a bunch of shiny things, worked them around in his hand and lifted one up to his eye.

'What's he doing?' Briar peered over Dust's head.

'I don't know...'

Craig pushed the shiny thing into a hole in the blue door and twisted it.

'I've seen them before,' Briar mewed.

As Craig pulled the shiny thing out of the blue door, his face twisted into a sneer and he turned to look at Dust, '*Thatwillstopyou,*' he snorted. Then he strode away up the Long Box.

'What do they do?' Dust asked.

'They seal doors.'

'Forever?'

'Humans can use them, but ... not cats.'

Dust thrashed his tail, 'Come on, let's get back.'

*

'I'll tell them when we're sure,' Dust told Briar as they sat close to the water bowl.

'You want to check the blue door first?'

Dust nodded as he glanced at the flat light. It was still black. 'After Rose and Violet get back from the Healing Box, we can go.'

Briar nodded. 'We should check the brown doors again too,' Briar lowered his head, 'Didn't Benny say we can get out through the doors the humans use?'

'There's a big grey door in the Bright Box,' Dust lowered his voice, 'the one Craig came through when he bought Conker Back. But if we can't open the brown doors, how can we be sure we can open the grey door.'

'There must be a way.'

'The humans stay in the Bright Box,' Dust shook his head, 'If we have to ask them to open the door, they'll know we're there.'

Briar sighed, 'It's still the best way out. The Moving Box comes back. The rats can't be trusted....'

'But there may still be a way through the Rat Holes, Dust mewed, 'Benny saw Onyx in The Outside. Rose and Violet will know—'

The flap rattled, and as if summoned by his words, Violet slid through, her head low.

Rose plunged through behind her and growled, 'The white door won't open.'

28
The Roof

I WON'T LIE TO THEM... DUST got to his paws and padded across the Meeting Box to greet the returning she-cats, 'It's not the only one.'

'What?' Rose thrashed her tail.

'We saw Craig doing something to the blue door. Briar thinks he used door sealers. We don't know if we can get into the Blue Box again.'

'You don't know?'

Dust shook his head, 'We were waiting for you to return before we checked.'

Rose held Dust's gaze, then nodded and pushed passed Briar to the water bowl.

'What about Onyx?' Spinney hopped down from his bed.

'I'm sorry, Spinney,' Violet mewed, 'we called to her, but she didn't reply. She could be sleeping, but there's no way of telling if she's in there.'

'We could try following Fiona,' Dust mewed, 'maybe if we asked her, she'd let us in and give us food.'

'Maybe,' Violet sighed, 'but if Craig's in there, surely he won't allow it.'

'If we want food, we find the rats.' Rose hissed.

'There's no rat scent anywhere, Rose,' Briar turned to face the red she-cat.'

'Not where you're scouting,' Rose took a step forward and glared at Briar.

'What do you mean?' Briar's fur rippled as he held Rose's stare.

Rose flicked her tail to Gloworm, 'He was right.'

'About what?'

'The rats do not go where we go.'

Dust glanced at the roof, then sat down between Rose and Briar. 'She means that the rats are not using the same routes to get around as we are.'

Rose nodded and turned back to the water bowl.

Briar thrashed his tail, 'Then where are they going?'

'Through the roof,' Dust looked up, inviting Briar to do the same, 'The Long Box has the same roof squares, I think the rats are in them.'

'Then we need to get out of The Boxes soon,' Gloworm sat up in his bed, 'If the rats are in the roof, how can we hunt them? Three of us are gone already, and now there will be no food for the rest of us.'

'We can't leave without Onyx ... I won't go,' Spinney shook his head.

'Fiona saw me in the Blue Box, Spinney. Then Craig Sealed it,' Gloworm sighed, 'And now the white door is sealed. We will starve if we don't get out soon.'

'Are you saying that Fiona made Craig seal the blue door?' Briar growled.

Dust shook his head. 'He could have seen us in the watch lights, she might not have done anything.'

Violet looked up at the little red light, 'If they watch everything we do, and know where we go, do you think they saw Conker and Fern leave? And Onyx ... did they see what happened to her too?'

Dust shook his head. 'Possibly, there are little red eyes everywhere.'

'So how can we ever get out if the humans are watching us?' Gloworm hung his head.

Dust glanced at the flat light. It was turning from black to pale green. *We still have time...* 'We need to go where the rats go ... where the humans can't see us.'

'The roof?' Briar mewed.

'Yes,' Dust flicked his tail.

'But, how,' Spinney stared up at the hole, 'We don't have cats up there to make cat chains.'

Dust purred, 'We don't need chains, we can use the door ... let me show you.'

One by one the cats hopped down from their beds to watch as Dust leapt at the silver lever and opened the green door.

'Look,' he motioned with his tail to the top of the door, 'It opens directly under the hole. If I can get on top of the door, I can get into the roof.'

Briar nodded, 'Okay, but how?'

'Jump,' mewed Rose.

'Exactly,' Dust nodded to the red she-cat, 'but the door will move when I land on it, so I need you all to hold it steady.'

'What do you need us to do?' Briar asked.

'You, Gloworm and Spinney, sit behind the door and press your backs into it. Rose and Violet, if you do the same on this side, that should stop it moving.'

The cats hesitantly moved into position around the green door. When they'd settled, Dust backstepped towards the flap, keeping his eye on the top of the door. 'Okay ... ready?' he mewed as he straightened his tail and padded the floor with his hind paws.

Rose and Violet nodded.

'All ready,' Briar grunted from the other side of the door.

Dust focused on the lever, then bounded forward, leapt, grabbed it in his front claws and lifted his hind paws onto it. He landed squarely but the lever began to slip down, and the door rocked. He couldn't push himself upwards in time, so he twisted around and leapt back down to the floor.

'Get your front paws closer together,' Rose mewed.

Dust nodded as he circled. He'd landed too close to the end of the lever and his weight had pushed it down. 'Okay, I'm going to try again. Hold the door steady.'

He leapt again, focusing on the spot where he needed his paws to land. He landed right and slid his hind paws between his fore paws. Balancing on the lever for a heartbeat to take a breath, he lifted his head, focused on the top of the door, tucked up his fore paws and pushed himself upwards. He reached the top of the door, dug his claws into it, and hauled himself up. As he found his balance, he looked down into the wide eyes of his cats.

'Keep the door steady,' Dust manoeuvred himself until the hole was above him, 'I think I can reach it.'

The door rocked and steadied as the cats pressed closer to it. When it was still, Dust reached up and nudged the roof square. It moved easily and the hole widened as it slid away. He raised his head and sniffed the air. *Rats...* 'I'm going up,' he mewed, and without hesitation, he leapt up into the roof.

The dark cavity was large enough for Dust to stand up in. He reached up with his tail and felt another roof above, and as his eyes adjusted to the gloom, he began to make out the silver strips that edged the white roof squares. Odd shapes, the size of curled sleeping cats, crouched where the silver strips crossed at the corners of the squares. Nothing touched the white roof squares between them. Dust tested the silver strip with a paw. It was solid. Carefully, he walked along it toward the nearest odd shape, and prodded it. It was soft, and as it unravelled at his touch, he saw that it was made from fragments of boxes, all chewed and twisted together into something that looked ... comfortable. *Beds....?* He sniffed the inside of the shape. Tiny hairs loaded with the stench of rat tickled his nose. *A rat's bed...*

Reaching out with his tail, Dust felt along the wall to his side. It was in the same place as the wall below in the Meeting Box. The silver strip was wider next to it, so he stepped onto it, keeping his tail tip on the wall as he padded cautiously around more rat beds.

As he reached the corner above the water bowl something long and thin touched his leg. His fur bristled as he looked down at a red tail. He lifted a paw, ready to strike, but it didn't move. He sniffed it, but it didn't smell of rat. It was twisted around other tails ... They looked like the strings on the back of the humming boxes in the Healing Box. He looked along the tail to where it bent downwards and vanished through a hole in the silver strip. It was going to the little red light. Dust stepped over the tails and carried on, he could look at them again later, for now, he was more concerned about the rat beds. *There could be hundreds of rats sleeping up here...*

Dust inspected each bed as he passed. All the scents were stale and there were no droppings. *They don't live here...* but he couldn't see how they were getting in or out, and by the time he'd arrived back at the hole above the door, he was confused. *How do they get in...? I've missed something ... they can't get in from the Meeting Box...* Dust looked around again, and up. In the corner above the water bowl, he saw a dark patch on the wall that he'd missed while inspecting the tails. He padded towards it and reached out a paw. It was a hole, crusted with rat grease and hair where they'd slid in and out. The hole was too small for him to get through, but he could see more roof squares and another wall beyond it. *The Long Box...*

Dust had seen all he needed to see. His cats were growing restless in the Meeting Box below, so he decided to head back. Sliding out of the hole, he balanced on the top of the door as his cats steadied it. When he'd found his footing, he leapt down to the floor.

'What's up there?' Briar padded over and sniffed his fur.

Dust beckoned his cats close, 'Rats...' he mewed quietly, 'They've made beds up there. They were getting comfortable ... and watching us.'

Violet gasped.

Rose looked up and thrashed her tail.

'But how?' Briar peered up at the hole, 'Why haven't we smelt them or heard them?'

'The roof is too high up for us to pick up their scent, and they were careful not to leave too much. They *are* getting around The Boxes through the roofs. There's a hole in the walls up there ... it's too small go get through, but I could see into the roof above the Long Box.'

'We could hide up there,' Spinney mewed, 'and wait for them to come back. Our scent is all around them so they wouldn't know we're there until we'd caught enough for a good meal.'

'The first time.' Rose mewed.

Dust nodded, 'And we could be waiting a long time if they don't come back. But we could follow their tracks, find out where else they go.'

Rose nodded.

'Through the hole in the ... roof-wall?' Spinney asked.

'Could we make it bigger?' Briar mewed.

'Shhh,' Gloworm hissed, 'they could still be there ... listening...'

'Their beds were empty, and their scent is stale,' Dust glanced up. The sight of the hole made him feel uneasy. He wasn't sure they'd gone for good. 'Let's rest now and discuss this later,' he mewed, 'when the humans come back. The rats won't hear us so easily then.'

The flat light warmed as a bright yellow band crept across it. Fiona arrived soon after. Dust watched with his head resting on the side of his bed as she changed the litters and poured fresh water into the bowl. Then she walked around the cats, stopping at each bed in turn to fuss them and inspect their fur, Dust wondered if she was looking for injuries.

'*Youookfine,butwhereareyouall, three cats missing,*' She uttered as she peered into the empty beds.

Dust watched Fiona closely as she looked in Conker and Fern's beds. Her fear scent increased, and she frowned as she straightened their bedding, but as she approached Onyx's bed, her fear scent began to fade. She didn't touch the bedding, but she glanced at the little red light as she raised her voice and uttered, *'Stillnotback Onyx mustbehunting.'*

As Fiona stepped back to the door, she pulled something jangly from the folds in her green covers.

'Sorryguys,' she mumbled as she picked up the cover of litter and closed the door behind her.

Dust's heart sank as he heard the jingling of the door sealers.

Spinney raised his head and caught Dust's eye, 'She's not worried about Onyx! She knows where she is.'

Dust looked at Spinney, 'I saw that...' he mewed, 'She's afraid about Conker and Fern ... perhaps they did escape after all.'

Spinney nodded.

'But she sealed the door,' Briar mewed.

'Yes,' Dust sighed, 'She did.'

Without speaking, the cats slunk back down in their beds and hid their faces. Dust could sense their frustration in every ruffle of their fur and flick of their ears. He rested his head on his paws and closed his eyes. *No rats... No doors... No food... What do I do now...?*

29

When Your Cats Go Bad

DUST BLINKED. THE PAW STEPS STOPPED. His first breath shuddered with her scent. A dark shadow loomed above, spiralling, and spreading, plunging everything into darkness. Bright grey eyes shifted and enlarged, and he shivered as claws scraped the cold damp floor of the Meeting Box. She glared at him, flicked her tail twice and turned away.

'Breeze....?'

'Quick, Dust, this way...' Breeze walked through the wall.

Shadow Dust slipped from under his paws, leapt across the Meeting Box and ran through the wall after her. More Shadows began to lift from the beds, barely recognisable as the shifting shapes of cats as they rippled down the sides of the full boxes, flowed across the floor and washed through the wall.

Dust stood alone in the Meeting Box. Darkness closed in all around him, fluctuating temporarily as a faint echoing yowl drifted through it. He flicked his ears, trying to locate the sound, but it seemed to come from nowhere, and everywhere inside his head.

He shook the sound away and pushed through the wall after the Shadow Cats. Halting in the Long Box, he looked around for Breeze, but saw no glimpse of her. As he stared into the gloom, something shifted in the shade of the Blue

Corner. Bright grey eyes flickered as Shadow Dust dipped his head and swirled away. Then a dark form emerged from the shadows and slid toward Dust.

Shadow Briar snarled as he faced Dust and bowed. Dust evaded his wild eyes and beckoned him near, but he remained where he stood, so tall and proud before he crept aside with a flippant flick of his ear.

Dust sidestepped through the swirl of mist where Shadow Briar had been and pushed uneasily through the wall next to the blue door. Shadow Dust hovered for a heartbeat, then slid behind the rolling traps. Dust padded past him through the Cold Box, keeping his eyes wide for any sign of Breeze. Seeping warm air billowed around his paws, making him stumble and slow, and he narrowly escaped the hurtling blur that exploded from the mirror door and landed in the middle of the floor.

Shadow Rose yowled and lunged from the darkness. All around Dust, she circled, flashing tooth and claw, but her eyes were pleading as she turned with a hiss and then away through the shivering shadows of his cats, she tore.

Breeze blinked as she padded lightly through the wavering mist that ebbed reluctantly around the bottom of the yellow doors. Shadow Dust followed her, his head low. Dust hurried through the unsettling empty air, trying to keep up, but he faltered when bright grey eyes caught his and stopped him in his tracks.

Shadow Violet raised her head and without a voice she yowled and flicked her tail to Dust, inviting him to move near. But no steps could take him across the line she prowled until her shadow shifted and faded to leave his path clear.

Dust hopped up onto the full box as the shadows slithered from the walls and gathered around him. He could see Breeze and Shadow Dust padding slowly down the open space. The Towers seemed to bob on a sea of undulating darkness as Dust leapt down into the Vast Tower Box. He caught Breeze's bright grey eyes and raced after her, but his way was blocked by a falling mote that fluttered and swirled before it stood and shuffled towards him.

Shadow Gloworm lifted his leg and lowered his tail, as circling, he fell behind Dust with a wince of pain. Then he slowed even more, falling into a pace so faltering and frail, fading like his lonely wail, a voice never to be noticed again.

Breeze sat in the open space, her tail swishing away the motes as she flicked her ears. Shadow Dust stared upwards. Dust followed his gaze and saw that he was studying human markings on the end of a tower. A line and a circle. Dust felt his spirit lift as he stared at the marks, as if drawn to them, but as he moved towards them, a fast dark air swirled before him.

Shadow Spinney whirled through the towers in a race, on fast jumpy paws that wove ways he'd never go, if the designs in his head ever abandoned their chase to run him out of his mind with all he wished to know.

As Dust turned a circle to watch Shadow Spinney flicker away, Breeze rocked back on her haunches and placed a fore paw on the marked tower. Shadow Dust shifted uneasily as she lifted and placed her next paw, then began walking vertically up the end of the tower. Dust looked on as she padded lightly upwards, past the line and the circle, and on, up into the gloom. Before she vanished from sight, she flicked her tail twice for him to follow. But as Dust put a tentative paw on the tower, a grasping darkness swelled beneath him.

Shadow Dust moved too late, and the darkness dragged him down. Shadow Cats reeled, wailing with their widened eyes, clawing against the unseen, grasping, and gasping as they tried to climb. And as Dust stepped up onto the tower and started to ascend, lost grey eyes were the last thing he saw as Shadow Dust melded into the darkness, and sank below.

Dust followed Breeze, up the tower and into the gloom, up and away from the fading caterwauls below, up and over the line and the circle, and up, further than he'd ever climbed before.

Breeze stood on the top of the tower and looked down at him.

He looked up into her bright grey eyes, 'What do I do now....?'

'When your cats go bad...' she held his gaze, 'save your cats...'

30

UP

DUST SHUDDERED AS HE WOKE. HIS fur rippled along his spine as he slowly raised his head. His cats were sat up in their beds, staring at him, their eyes wide with concern.

'Were you dreaming?' Gloworm mewed.

Dust nodded, then looked up at the hole in the roof, 'It's not this roof,' he mewed, 'It's another roof and I know where it is.'

'Where?' Briar asked.

'In the Vast Tower Box,' Dust hopped down from his bed and padded to the water bowl. As he lapped at the stale water, numbing hunger clawed at his stomach.

'How do you know?' Briar padded after him.

'Breeze... I see her in my dreams...' Dust hesitated as the evasive images of the fading Shadow Cats eluded his mind, 'I followed her, and she led me up a tower. It has markings on it ... I recognised them. That's how we get to the roof. We climb the tower with those marks.'

'I don't know...' Gloworm licked his paw, 'It doesn't sound ... safe. Dreams ... they're not always what they seem. It may not mean what you think.'

'I know,' Dust sighed, 'It's risky, but it's worth a look. And what else have we got?'

'Benny,' Briar thrashed his tail, 'We know a cat in The Outside. You said yourself that he's going to help us.'

Dust faced Briar, 'The humans are watching us now and the Blue Box is sealed.'

'The Bright Box then,' Briar went on, 'we can try and get to the grey doors.'

'We can try...' Dust paced around Briar, 'And we can try the roof in the Vast Tower Box.' He turned to face his cats, 'We won't find anything if we don't look. If you want to scout the tower with me, then come, But I understand if you don't.'

Gloworm licked a paw, 'I can't climb that high ... my leg is still too weak. I can't come with you, Dust, I'm sorry.'

Briar shook his head, 'There's no point in going up there. Even if it is a way out, Gloworm couldn't escape with us.'

'I am just going to look, Briar, not escape. We are only scouting the tower.'

'I'll go,' Rose mewed.

'Rose?' Violet stared at her sister, 'Why?'

'Why not. We climb. We know what's up there.'

'But it could be dangerous,' Violet insisted.

'Yes,' Rose twitched her whiskers, 'are you coming?

Violet nodded, 'Of course.'

'You don't have to do this, Violet,' Briar mewed, 'A scout group only needs two cats, let them go if they want to waste their time.'

Violet dipped her head, 'Thank you, Briar, but I need to make sure Rose behaves. I'll be fine.'

Dust turned to Spinney, 'What about you?'

Spinney shook his head, 'Onyx may come back ... I'll stay.'

Dust nodded, 'Rose, Violet, let's go.'

*

Dust looked up into the gloom. He couldn't see the top of the tower, but the human markings were the same as he'd seen in his dream. A line and a circle.

'This one?' Rose asked.

'Yes,' Dust sniffed at the bottom ledge. He could smell traces of human scent and sour damp, but no rats.

'Oh my,' Violet rocked back to get a better look at the tower, 'I can't even see a roof, are you sure there will be one?'

'There has to be,' Dust mewed, 'The Boxes can't just go up forever.'

'Are you sure?' Rose flicked her tail.

Dust twitched is whiskers, 'No, but there's only one way to find out.'

'You say you followed your mother ... Breeze ... in your dream?' Violet mewed, 'So, did she show you how to climb it?

Dust sat down and looked from Rose to Violet, 'In my dream, Breeze just ... walked vertically up the end. That's not possible, and Gloworm's right, dreams are never what they seem... But she was telling me to climb this tower, I am sure of that.'

'So, how do we climb it?' Rose mewed.

Dust took a deep breath and looked back up at the tower. Rows of full boxes sat on each ledge, and each one had enough space on top of it for a cat to twist around and grip the full box on the ledge above. They had the lower ledges to practice on, where a fall to the floor was jumpable, but they would have to get it right on the higher ledges.

'When you're ready, Dust.'

'Rose,' Violet scolded her, 'let him work it out.'

Rose flicked Violet with her tail and purred.

'I've got it,' Dust mewed, 'Just watch what I do, it won't be too hard.'

Rose and Violet exchanged glances as Dust hopped up onto the first ledge, crawled into the gap above a full box, and rolled over onto his back. Then he stretched his forelegs out around the ledge above and dug in his claws into the next full box up. With a grunt he clawed his way up the side of next full box and slid into the gap above it.

'Got it. Come on Violet,' Rose trotted to a full box a few paces along from Dust and climbed on top of it. Violet hurried after her, and when Rose had effortlessly pulled herself up onto the top of the second full box, she padded a few paces on and began to climb.

Dust climbed steadily, hauling himself up the sides of the full boxes with his claws as he ascended into the darkness. He could see Rose, already a few ledges higher than him, and Violet further along the tower, her grey fur hard to make out in the gloom, but he could hear her voice, reassuring Rose that she was fine. There was no stopping now and he was thankful for the company of the sisters, their carefree banter kept his attention away from the growing ache in his claws as they laboured to grip the full boxes. He enjoyed hunting and scouting with them. They were intelligent and didn't need to be led, and Dust relished the opportunity to hang back and just follow. So, it came as no surprise when Rose was first to reach the top of the tower.

'I see the roof,' she meowed, 'but it's still too high.'

'Hang on,' Violet mewed, 'I'm almost there, I see something.'

'What?'

Trying not to rush, Dust hauled himself up the next full box and chanced a look up. There was no ledge above. He could just make out the dark grey lines that sloped away into the distance high above him. He pulled himself up onto the top full box and stared around at the vast roof. *Rose is right, it's too high...*

'It's not far, I'll check.'

'Violet, wait.'

Dust could see Rose's red tail a few paces ahead of him. In the distance he could see a faint silver shimmer. A cat shaped shadow flashed in front of it as Violet moved. She was well ahead of Rose, heading for the end of the tower.

'It looks like a...' Violet mewed, 'No, it's different...'

'Wait for me,' Rose hurried forwards.

Dust hopped across the full boxes to catch up.

'Rose, Dust, look at this...'

'Violet ... stop!'

'Oh ... oh, oh no ... Rose ... ROSE!'

Claws scrabbled frantically on boxes.

Dust hurried forward.

'Violet! Hang on, I'm nearly there,' Rose yowled.

'I'm falling, help me, Rose!'

'Hang on, Violet, I'm coming...'

'Rose ... help me ... HELP...'

Dust dug his claws into the top of the full box to stop himself colliding with Rose. She stood motionless, her fur fluffed, staring down to the unseen floor below. The full box in front of her was gone, and so was Violet.

Dust flinched as he heard a dull thud.

Rose screeched, 'VIOLET!'

31

Lament

'ROSE....?' A SHAKY MEW DRIFTED UP to them through the gloom.

Rose sprang into action, pacing back and forth across the top of the full box, peering over the edge, 'Violet ... VIOLET?'

'Turn around. Go down backwards,' Dust stepped towards her and rested his tail lightly on her back to calm her, 'Go steadily and we will reach her quicker.'

Rose glanced at Dust, then turned and lowered herself over the edge of the tower, reaching down with one hind leg, then another until she found the top of the full box below. 'Violet? Violet, stay there, I'm coming,' she meowed as she began to scramble down.

'Rose ... Be careful... Be careful...' came Violet's pained reply.

Rose was already out of sight as Dust lowered himself over the edge. Violet's shaking voice guided him down, and as he concentrated on placing his paws carefully, he tried not to think of what he'd find on the floor below. He felt like he'd been scrambling down full boxes and ledges forever when he heard Rose's yowl.

'Violet ... NO!'

Dust chanced a glance behind. The distance to the floor was jumpable. He stretched his hind legs down onto the next ledge, twisted his body and leapt, and landed lightly behind Rose. She was stood staring at a crumpled full box. Violet's back legs were trapped underneath it.

'My legs, Rose ... I can't feel my legs.'

Rose slumped down next to her sister and buried her muzzle in her soft grey neck fur. 'It's okay, Violet ... we'll get you out,' she looked at Dust and hissed, 'Get her out. Get her out!'

Dust sniffed around the fallen full box. It was wet and smelt of mouldy damp. It had split open, spilling scratching sheets out across the floor. Dust knew it would be too heavy for him to push away by himself, but if he could empty it, then he might be able to move it off Violet's legs. He began scratching at the sheets, pulling them out of the full box and kicking them away behind him.

'Help him!' Violet hissed at Rose, 'Get me out!'

Rose joined Dust, hastily digging more sheets out of the wet full box.

'DUST?' A cat yowled. Paw steps thudded through the Cold Box.

Dust raised his head. 'Briar?' he turned to Rose, 'I'll get him, we need his help.' He raced along the bottom of the tower and out into the Open Space just as Briar bounded over the full box between the yellow doors, followed closely by Spinney. Gloworm limped as fast as he could not far behind.

'We heard yowling—' Briar began.

'Violet...' Dust panted, 'she fell, come on we need to free her.'

Without question the toms followed Dust back to the sisters. Gloworm hesitated to lick a paw and mumble before he joined them in scratching away the sheets. Rose returned to Violet's side to comfort her. The wet box was soon emptied, and between them, the toms easily dragged it aside.

Violet didn't look injured. There was no blood. Her fur was barely ruffled, but when she tried to stand, her hind legs didn't respond.

Rose sniffed her legs, 'Try again,' she mewed gently.

Violet raised herself up on her front paws and curled her rump under her. Her hind legs shifted forwards with her hips, but they didn't fold. She thrashed her tail and winced, 'I can't feel them. They just won't move.'

'It's shock,' Spinney mewed, 'Violet, you told me that when I couldn't feel my leg after the rat bit me. Then Fiona healed me, and I was okay.'

'Just shock,' Rose mewed as she slumped down beside Violet and licked her shoulder.

'You need to stay warm,' Gloworm dipped his head to Rose as he lay down on Violet's other side, 'You told me that too when I was injured.'

'Thank you,' Violet mewed as she rested her head on Rose's shoulder.

'We need to get help,' Dust paced around his cats, 'Briar, Spinney, we need to find Fiona.'

'I'll stay,' Briar sat down beside Violet, 'If the rats come, I'll keep them away from her.'

Dust nodded. He knew that nothing would get close to Violet while Rose was with her, but Briar cared for Violet too, 'Good idea,' he mewed.

Dust glanced at the flat light as he and Spinney raced up the Long Box. A bright yellow glow was creeping across the pale green. *She's here...* He heard footsteps as he rounded the Bright Corner. Fiona was there, pressing the light bumps at the side of the vanishing door.

'Fiona, Come quickly. Violet's hurt,' Dust yowled.

'Hey Dust, whatsthematter.'

'Hurry!' Spinney meowed, flicking his tail twice, 'follow us.'

'Hey Spinney, areyouhungry.' Fiona uttered as she stepped toward them.

'Come on, quickly!' Dust yowled again.

Fiona crouched down and reached out her hand.

Dust leant forward, sniffed her hand, then stared up at her, 'Please follow us, Violet needs help.'

Fiona reached out a hand to Spinney and tried to fuss his chin, but he pulled away. 'No, we need you to follow, not that.'

Fiona stood up, '*Icantgiveyoufood, imsorry,*' She stood and walked back to the vanishing doors.

'NO!' Yowled Dust.

Fiona shook her head, *'Imsorry Craig willsackme ififeedyou.'*

Something inside Fiona's covers buzzed. Dust watched as she pulled out a small red box, tapped it, raised it to her head and uttered, *'hello ... whatwhere ... towerten, grey cat ohno, Violet, okayimonmyway.'* The colour drained from her face as she looked at Dust and Spinney. *'Isthatwhatyouresaying, Violets hurt ... letsgo.'*

Fiona ran down the Long Box with Dust and Spinney racing at her side. As they hurried into the Vast Tower Box, Dust heard another human voice, and Rose yowling. He glanced at Spinney and bounded ahead towards the tower with the line and the circle.

'Get away from her,' Rose hissed to a female in red covers.

The Red Female shuffled backwards and glanced at Dust as he slid to a halt.

'Fiona is here,' Dust panted, 'Rose, they are trying to help.'

'Fiona will help, no others!' Rose growled.

As Fiona caught up, the Red Female stood up, '*Fiona thegrey cat ishurt, butthatonewontletmenearit.*

'*Hey Steph,*' Fiona knelt in front of Violet, '*Itsok iknowthem.*'

Steph... Dust flicked an ear.

'*Theresabroken box,*' '*ithinktheywereclimbing.* Steph went on, *Ihadtocall Craig togetyournumber.*'

Fiona looked at Violet, then at Rose, '*Areyougoing toletmehelpher Wild Rose?*'

'*Isthathername.*' Steph uttered.

Fiona nodded, '*Yesandthegreyoneis Free Violet. Theothersare, Gloworm, Edge Briar, Tor Spinney andtheonesatbymeis Dream Dust. Thereareotherstoo.*'

Steph smiled as Fiona pointed to the cats in turn, saying their names, '*Wowsosweet, theyrebeautiful ... theyshouldnt betrappedinhere.*'

'*Dontlet Craig hearyousaythat.*'

Steph took a deep breath and looked at Violet. '*Issheokay.*'

Fiona looked at Rose.

Rose lowered her head and took a step back, 'Don't you hurt her,' she growled.

Violet blinked at Fiona, then turned her head and nudged her hind legs, 'I can't move them. I can't get up.'

Fiona ran her hand along Violet's spine and down her uppermost hind leg. Gently, she lifted it and slowly straightened it part way, then stopped and shook her head. Then she felt the hind leg underneath, straightening it as she did the first, stopping part way. *'Ithinkifeltabreak, nottoseverebut possiblybothlegs.'*

'Ohnowhatdoesthatmean.'

'Itmeans, ineedtogethertothevet.'

Steph nodded and stood up. '*Willshebeok.*'

'Ificangetherawayfromhersister.' Fiona looked at Rose again, *'Rose, letmetakeher, please.'*

Rose growled.

'Rose,' Dust stepped forward, 'let Fiona carry her. We can follow, she will be safe.'

Rose stood her ground for a heartbeat, then nodded.

Dust nudged Rose aside to give Fiona room to pick up Violet.

Violet winced, but before Rose could take a step towards her, she mewed, 'Rose, it's fine. Fiona will heal my legs. Stay with me but let her do what she needs to do.'

'If she hurts you...'

'She won't...'

Fiona said her farewells to Steph and carried Violet towards the yellow doors. Rose padded after her, keeping her distance, never taking her eyes off her sister.

Dust turned to the others. 'I'm going to follow them. I'm sure Violet will be fine but Rose could cause problems. You should head back to the Meeting Box and rest. I'll be back as soon as I can.'

Briar shook his head, 'Violet Shouldn't have gone with you...'

266

'She wanted to, Briar. It's just shock. She will be fine.

'Yes, shock. I had it and I was fine,' Spinney added.

'Let's hope so,' Briar glared at Dust as they waited for Gloworm to finish mumbling.

Dust nodded and hurried after Fiona. He caught her up at the vanishing doors.

'*Youcomingtoo Dust.* She uttered when she saw him. Rose stayed a pace behind her, thrashing her tail impatiently.

Dust padded to Rose's side and as the vanishing doors slid open, they jumped into the Dropping Box together. Fiona gave them space as she stepped in, secured Violet in her arms, and pressed the middle light bump. No one spoke again until they'd walked through the white door and into the Healing Box.

'*Youtwostaythere,*' Fiona spoke softly as she gently lay Violet down on the ledge. Rose hopped up beside her, and Dust followed.

'If she hurts you, Violet...' Rose growled.

Violet blinked at her, 'Rose, my tail hurts and I can't move my legs, but I feel fine.'

'Are you sure?' Dust asked.

Violet nodded, 'Yes, I landed fine after I fell ... but the full box caught my back legs when it landed behind me.'

Fiona manoeuvred Violet onto her side and began examining her uppermost hind leg. When she'd done, she gently lifted her and turned her onto her other side.

Violet winced.

Rose growled, 'She's hurting you.'

'*Sorry Violet, illtrynottohurtyou.*'

'No, Rose. My tail is hurting. Fiona isn't hurting me.'

267

When Fiona had examined Violet's other leg, she walked to the back of the Healing Box and picked up a scratching sheet and stick.

The door opened and Craig walked in. He slammed the door behind him as he glared at Fiona, then he glanced at Dust and Rose, '*Whatareallthese Ratters doinginhere Fiona.*'

'*Theyrefine Craig theyarekeeping Violet calmwhile iexamineher.*' Fiona put down the stick and walked back to Violet.

Craig stepped forward and glared at Fiona, '*Theonethatfell, whatsupwithit.*'

Fiona ran her hand over Violet's, back and sighed.

'See, Rose. It's going to be okay,' Violet purred.

'I don't want you to be hurt,' Rose mewed.

'*Fractures, shewillneedtogotothevetforxrays.*' Fiona uttered quietly.

'I will be fine, but I might not be able to hunt with you for a while,' Violet sighed, 'I'm sorry.'

Dust stepped forward and rested his tail on Rose's shoulder, 'We can hunt for her while she recovers.'

'*Why? Ratters withbrokenbonesarenousehere.*' Craig snorted.

'*Shewillheal.*' Fiona uttered.

'See, Rose, Violet purred, 'Every cat will help. And I'll be better soon. Spinney was back on his paws quick enough. You were too, weren't you, Dust?'

'She's right, Rose. We all recovered. And we'll all help.'

'*Itwillcosttoomuch ratevictwontpaythebill, that Ratter isnonviable.*'

'*Whatdoyoumean,*' Fiona gasped.

Dust watched Craig open a compartment under a ledge and take out a small green bundle. He held it out to Fiona, '*Youknowwhatimean, justdoit.*'

'*Icanpaythebill.*' Fiona waved the bundle away.

'*Ratters arenotyourproperty.*'

Rose crouched down and licked Violet's ear, 'The toms can hunt for both of us.'

Dust turned back to Violet, 'Yes ... yes, we will,' he mewed, trying to be more reassuring, but he couldn't drag his attention away from the arguing humans.

'*Icouldbewrong Craig itmightnotbebroken, thevet—*'

'*Itrustyourassessment, ifyoudontdoit, iwill.*' Craig pushed Fiona aside. '*Getthemother Ratters outofhere.*'

'*No, donttouchher, illdoit,*' Fiona sobbed and held out a shaking hand.

Craig dropped the bundle into her hand and sneered, '*Getonwithitthen.*'

Dust shivered as he watched Craig stride away and slide into the nook behind the watch lights.

'*Imsosorry,*' tears welled in Fiona's eyes. Her fear scent was stronger that it had ever been.

Rose growled and buried her muzzle in Violet's neck fur, 'I won't let him near you.'

'Nor will Fiona,' Dust growled, 'Don't worry, Rose.'

Fiona turned away, rustled the bundle in her hand and turned back to Violet. Wiping the tears from her eyes as she uttered, '*Imsosorry, imsosorry,*' then she gently gripped the fur on Violet's neck.

Dust looked up at Fiona's face. *What did Craig do...* Her weeping eyes were so full of sorrow and her scent so full of fear.

Violet purred gently, 'And when I'm better, I will show you what I found.'

'Was it worth the fall?' Rose purred back.

Violet winced as Fiona rubbed her neck, then mewed slowly, 'I think so ... Rose ... you were... right ... you—'

Fiona turned away and walked to the other side of the Healing Box.

'About what?' Rose mewed.

Dust looked down at Violet. Her jaws parted, but no words came. Her eyes glazed and clouded ... their sparkle lost as the light drained away, 'Violet?'

'Right about what?' Rose shifted and nudged Violet's shoulder with her muzzle.

'Rose,' Dust's voice shook as he laid his tail over her back, 'Rose, I...'

Violet shuddered as her head collapsed to the side. Her mouth fell open and her tongue lolled. Her blank eyes stared up at them, lifeless.

'Violet?' Rose lifted her head, 'What's wrong?'

'Rose, I don't think...'

Rose hissed and leapt back. She reached out a paw and pushed her sister's shoulder, 'Wake up,' she growled, 'Violet, wake up.'

'Getthem Ratters outofhere,' Craig shouted from the nook.

'Berry's eyes...?' Rose's mew trembled.

'Rose,' Dust nudged her, but she stood firm, staring at her sister's lifeless body.

'Leavethemalone Craig,' Fiona crossed the Healing Box and reached out to Rose, *'Comeaway imsosorry, comeaway Wild Rose.'*

'Berry's eyes!' Rose growled. Her claws scraped on the ledge and as Fiona laid a hand on her back, she screeched and leapt at her. 'WHAT HAVE YOU DONE TO VIOLET?'

Fiona cried out and tried to push Rose away, but the red-she cat had her claws dug deep into her head fur.

'Rose,' Dust backed away. *What do I do....?* He shook his head. *Violet. She's dead...* He didn't know how she was dead. *Rose ... she's in danger...* 'Rose ...STOP!'

Craig strode across the Healing Box and pushed Fiona to the floor. Then he grabbed Rose around her neck and yanked her from Fiona's head fur. With the red she-cat hissing and writhing in his grip, he marched to the door, opened it, and threw her out. Dust watched in horror as Rose hurtled through the Under Box and hit the far wall. Then Craig turned on him.

'Get away from me,' Dust hissed.

Craig tried to grab him, but he was quicker. Leaping down from the ledge, he ducked between Craig's legs and bolted through the half open door. He didn't stop until he reached Rose's side. Craig slammed the Healing Box door behind him.

Panting, Dust slumped down against Rose. He could feel her shivering. She was breathing, but he didn't know if she'd been injured. Would Fiona help Rose? how could she? Fiona had killed Violet...

A long time passed before Rose raised her head. A low rumbling growl burst from her chest as she dragged herself to her paws, took two paces forward, sat down again and stared at the white door.

'Rose ... Rose are you hurt? Let me help you ...' Dust mewed. But she ignored him. Her growl grew into a yowl, and she wailed...

'I gave you my cold,
'My tears,
'And my little paws...'

Dust shook himself as Rose's voice broke, cracking as it trembled with sorrow. He took a step towards her, but not too close. He didn't dare get too close.

Rose wailed on...

'I had you to hold.
'I had you to hold...'

'Rose,' Dust mewed, 'Rose I'm so sorry...'

Rose hung her head for a heartbeat. Then she shuddered. Her fur bristled along her back and fluffed out her tail as she lifted her chin and began to sing. Dust caught his breath as her voice, even more beautiful than Violet's, froze him to the spot.

'I never got cold,
'My dear,
'In your loving paws.
'I never got cold.
'I never got cold.'

'I gave you to hold,

'My fears,
'And my little paws.
'I had you to hold.
'I had you to hold.'

Dust slumped to the floor. His heart crushed.

Rose raised her voice and sang on in a beautiful, agonising wail...

'Now you are cold,
'My dear,
'In my empty paws.
'And you'll never grow old.
'You will never grow old...
'YOU ... WILL ... NEVER ... GROW ... OLD...'

32

Holes

'WASH FOR SHADOW WHITE ... WASH FOR Shadow White...'

Dust waited until Gloworm had both paws back on the floor before he went on, 'She didn't stop singing. Even after Craig came back out of the Healing Box ... and grabbed her around the neck and carried her into the Dropping Box. She still didn't stop, or even resist ... she just closed her eyes and ... kept on singing...'

'Where did he take her?' Briar mewed.

Dust shook his head, 'I don't know.'

'Not up here,' Spinney padded to Dust's side, 'we didn't hear anything until Fiona bought you back. Do you think he took her to the Water Box?'

'Why would he do that?' Briar shook his head, 'More likely we didn't hear her because he *stopped* her singing.'

'Stopped her singing ... you mean?' Gloworm shivered.

Dust glanced at Gloworm, 'We don't know that.'

'They wouldn't hurt her, would they?' Spinney flicked his ears, 'she wasn't injured. Violet was ... but...'

Briar turned on Spinney, 'Fiona *killed* Violet,' he growled, 'how kind do you think they'll be to the cat who *attacked* Fiona?'

'She's in danger ... we need to find her,' Dust slumped against the full boxes, too exhausted to return to his bed.

Fiona had returned him to the Meeting Box just after Craig had taken Rose. Dust had smelt her fear and felt her tears soaking into his fur. He was sure Craig had forced her to kill Violet, but why hadn't she refused?

'How?' Spinney mewed, 'we haven't even found Onyx.'

Briar hopped up into his bed, 'We can't even find the rats...'

'And the doors are sealed,' Gloworm sighed as he crouched next to Dust, 'so we can't ask Benny if—'

A bone chilling wail interrupted Gloworm.

Rose....? Dust lifted his head, 'That's her ... that was Rose.'

'But where?' Spinney padded in a circle, 'where is she?' he stopped in the middle of the Meeting Box and looked down, 'The Healing Box?'

'No' Briar turned to look at the wall behind him, 'Through there.'

'No,' Gloworm raised his head, 'That's the same way as the hole in the Blue Box. That would mean she's in The Outside?'

'I can't tell where she is,' Dust got to his paws and leapt up onto the full box beside Briar, 'But we need to find her. We don't know what the humans will do if they catch her.'

Briar turned to face him. 'Are you sure you want to find her? She'll blame you for Violet's death. It was your idea to climb the tower, and it was your idea to take her to Fiona.'

'Rose asked Violet to come,' Dust growled. 'Because Rose wanted to check the roof. They both believed it was worth investigating.'

'We had better options to escape. Violet should not have died.'

276

Dust thrashed his tail. 'What options did we have, Briar? Craig sealed all the doors we could open. And *they* killed Violet. Not the tower. Not the fall. Not any cat.'

Briar hissed and turned away.

'Was I wrong?' Gloworm sat up, 'Was I wrong to believe that The Outside exists?'

'No,' Dust hopped back down to Gloworm, 'No, don't say that. We've both spoken to Benny, and he is in The Outside. And Conker and Fern ... they escaped...'

'To where?' Briar asked.

'I ... I don't know ... but Conker was sure...'

'And Onyx?' Spinney stopped pacing, 'did she really get out? You say Benny saw her with Fiona, but how do we really know that's true? What if the rat was right about Benny too ... what if he's crazy and only thinks he's in The Outside?'

Rose's next wail was quieter, but it echoed. Dust searched with his ears. *The Cold Box....? The Vast Tower Box maybe....?*

'She's inside,' Briar padded to the flap, 'she's near where ... where we heard Violet when she fell...'

Dust stopped in the middle of the Meeting Box and closed his eyes. He tried to keep his ears alert for Rose's next wail, but the tension growing around him tore at his senses. His remaining cats were surrendering to their doubts. Since Violet's death, they'd questioned the existence of The Outside, their ability to escape, and his worth as a leader. They had no food, and they'd barely slept. Their coats had dulled, and so had their eyes ... like Violet's eyes. *Berry's eyes...* Dust caught his breath as Breeze's bright grey

277

eyes blinked in his mind. *If my cats are feeling bad... I must save my cats...*

'I was so sure he was real...' Gloworm muttered, 'Maybe I'm the crazy cat...'

Dust opened his eyes and rested his tail over Gloworm's back, 'Benny is real! And no cat is crazy!' he turned to Spinney and Briar, 'Benny is a real cat in The Outside. Conker and Fern escaped into The Outside in the Moving Box. Onyx was seen alive in The Outside.' he dipped his head to Spinney, 'Fiona took her, but Fiona never wanted to hurt us—'

'Until she killed Violet.' Briar growled.

Dust held the tabby tom's gaze. 'What if Craig made her do it? What if Fiona is hiding Onyx in The Outside to keep her safe from Craig?'

Spinney twitched his whiskers, 'You think so?'

'I do—' Dust paused to listen to Rose's faint, faraway wail, then went on, 'We need to find Rose before the humans do. Then we find food. Then we find The Outside.'

Spinney shook his head, then nodded, 'Okay, I won't give up on Onyx. We need to do something.'

Gloworm nodded. 'We can't give up now. We can still find Benny.'

'Briar?' Dust asked.

Briar hesitated, then nodded reluctantly, 'Okay, we find food and The Outside ... and maybe Rose.'

Dust looked at the flat light. It was almost black. The last trace of red was fading fast from its edges.

*

Rose's scent was everywhere in the Vast Tower Box, and as Dust parted his jaws to find her freshest trail, her voice echoed around the towers.

'LISTEN!'

He felt his skin tingle. She was close, but he saw no movement. He padded forward, flicking his tail twice for Briar, Gloworm and Spinney to follow. *Line and Circle...* If Rose was anywhere, it was likely that she's returned to the tower where Violet fell.

A rat screeched.

Dust stopped. His fur rippled along his spine.

'Rats,' hissed Spinney. 'She's caught a rat.'

'Yes.' Relief flooded over Dust as he turned to the others, 'She's hunting, she's found them...'

Spinney twitched his whisker's and purred. Gloworm licked a paw and ran it over his ear.

'Why didn't she tell—' Briar began.

The rat's next screech interrupted him. A tortured, echoing scream. Then Rose yowled, 'COME SAVE ARD-ER SKEEAL, OR RED CAT KILL RAT ... FOR HIS LIES!'

Dust's stomach knotted. *She's not hunting for food...*

Briar growled, 'What's she doing?'

Dust shook his head, 'I don't know,' but if she has Skeeal, the other rats must be close.'

'Listen...' Spinney padded a few steps forward.

Dust flicked his ears and caught the sound of faint, distant squeaks, 'I hear them...' the squeaking grew louder. Dust could hear their claws on the floor and the hiss of their greasy bodies sliding over one another.

'Where are they...?' Gloworm shivered.

Briar growled, 'What is she doing? We can't hunt them all. We need food ... not a fight.'

'You're right,' Dust turned to the others, 'we can't get injured. We'll hide until we see them and take the slow ones for food.'

Dust led his cats to the wall opposite the towers and padded through the shadows towards the slide down door. It was closed. The rats were not getting in from the Moving Box. The sound of approaching rats grew louder and their scent hit him before he spotted their movement under the towers. He flicked his tail towards a gap behind a stack of full boxes just ahead, and they slid into it a heartbeat before a wave of rats spilled out from below the towers and began scampering towards the yellow doors.

'They didn't see us,' Spinney panted.

'Let's hope they—' Briar began, but Rose's yowl silenced him, bone chilling but distant. She was no longer in the Vast Tower Box.

'She's going to get hurt,' Gloworm mewed.

Dust shook his head. 'She must have a plan...' *She must have...?* She'd found the rats and bought them back into The Boxes, but was it a plan that would feed every cat, or one that would only satisfy her vengeance?

'Look,' Spinney nudged Dust's shoulder, 'That's the last of them.'

Dust looked over the full box. Fewer rats scurried under the towers now. *The slow ones...* 'This is our chance to eat. Briar, Spinney, kill one rat and get back to the wall. Gloworm, stay with me. I'll take a rat, then I'll follow you back here.' The toms agreed. Dust flicked his tail twice, the signal to go.

Briar and Spinney padded along the wall, bounded across the open space, and vanished behind the last tower. Gloworm followed Dust to the next tower along and they climbed up between the fullboxes on the bottom ledge. A heartbeat later, two rats scurried out from under the ledge, crossed the floor and disappeared under the next tower. Then three more. Dust rested his tail on Gloworm's back, *Wait...*

A lone rat shuffled out from beneath them and limped after the others. It was injured, but well fed and plump. Dust lifted his tail, dropped down on top of it and sunk his teeth into its neck before it could squeeze out a squeak. Gloworm climbed down slowly beside him. Dust picked up the rat and trotted back to the full boxes, Gloworm limping along beside him.

Briar and Spinney joined them a heartbeat later, carrying a rat each.

'They're getting in through a hole in the floor,' Spinney panted as he dropped his rat, 'near the slide down door.'

'A hole?' *The one Rose found...*

'Yes, and it looks big enough for a cat,' Briar added as he began clawing the flesh from the rat's bones, 'We should look when we've eaten.'

'What about Rose?' Gloworm mewed.

'We will check out the hole,' Dust mewed, 'and if it's a way out, we go back and find her.'

'Even if—'

'Even if she doesn't want to come,' Dust glared at Briar. 'Even if she blames me for Violet's death, I will still tell her how to get out. I won't just leave her. If the humans catch her—'

'Before the rats do?' Briar growled.

Spinney sighed, 'Dust's right. We should tell her ... then run.'

After Dust had shared his rat with Gloworm, letting the white tom take first pickings before finishing off the generous leftovers himself, he led them quickly to the slide down door. The hole was easy to find, and its cover had been removed. Dust sniffed around its edge before lowering his head to look inside. It was just big enough for a cat to crawl through. Beneath the stench of rat, he could detect an acrid smell, and behind that, the faint uplifting scents of The Outside. He pulled his head out of the hole. 'It's big enough, and it goes to The Outside.'

Rose wailed from somewhere in the distance.

A rat screeched.

'So ... what do we do?' Gloworm shivered.

'We go,' Briar mewed, 'You can come back if you want to.'

Dust up looked at the toms, 'You three go. Find Benny. I'll join you after I find Rose.'

'You're being foolish, Dust.' Briar growled.

'Maybe ... but she still grieves for Violet. And as her leader, I will help her.'

'You think she needs, or want's any cat's help,' Briar twitched his whiskers.

I will save my cats... Dust took a deep breath and shook his head, 'Who wants to go first?'

Spinney twitched his tail, 'I will, Onyx could be out there.'

'Then go carefully,' Dust mewed, 'and tell us what you find down there.'

Spinney nodded and slipped into the hole.

Dust watched eagerly as Spinney's orange tail disappeared into the tunnel as he padded out of sight. A few paces in, the tom's paw steps stopped, and he gasped. 'Dust, this is ... strange.'

'Strange?' Dust mewed.

'Red fur ... Rose's scent. It's her fur, but it's on this side, as if she was going back into The Boxes ... She must have been in The Outside...'

'Wait here.' Dust glanced at Briar and Gloworm before he slid into the hole. As he padded forwards in the tight round tunnel, his spine brushed the top and he was forced to bend his knees and lower is head to move more easily. He found Rose's scent and saw her fur caught on a ridge at the top of the tunnel. Spinney was right. She had been going the opposite way to them.

Spinney's tail curled with curiosity a few paces ahead, where he stood in a pool of silvery light. His head was raised through another hole further along the tunnel.

'Spinney?'

'It's ... The Outside, Dust! It really is The Outside. I can see so much ... so much of ... I don't know...' Spinney swished his tail excitedly, lifted his front paws and hopped up out of the tunnel.

'I'm right behind you Spinney, wait ... don't go too far.'

'Dust, it's fine. I'm in The Outside. I really am.'

Dust hurried forwards as fast as he could in the cramped tunnel.

'Dust, I can smell rats, and ... Rose's scent, and ... oh...'

'Spinney?'

'Dust ... oh no, get back.'

'Spinney? What's wrong?'

'Amos, getyourcoatoverhim, iwilldistracthim,'

Dust froze as he recognised the voice. *Steph...* 'Spinney, get back in here.'

'It's the Red Female. Is she safe?'

'Who's she talking too?'

'What?

'Hey, Spinney, whatyoudoingouthere letsgetyouto Fiona,'

'Spinney, get in the hole.'

'I can't ... she's in the way.'

'I'm coming up. I'll distract her.' Dust rushed forward, but as he reached the hole, a human foot slid across it, barring his way out.

'Dust?' Spinney mewed.

There was a dull thump. Spinney hissed, and the tunnel went dark.

33

Doors

'WE GO BACK.' DUST SCRAMBLED BACKWARDS out of the hole, 'Back to the Meeting Box.'

'Why? Where is Spinney?' Briar peered into the hole.

'He got out, but the humans caught him. We will have to try again later, but now we should go to the Meeting Box in case they bring him back.'

'If they do,' Briar meowed, 'Onyx isn't back, Fern and Conker are not back. And Violet ... Violet can never come back.' Briar turned to Gloworm and growled, 'You were wrong. Your mother's stories are nonsense. Violet didn't return. Your Shadow White doesn't exist.'

'Briar...' Dust gave a warning growl.

Gloworm backed away shaking his head, 'Shadow White ... she ... she does...'

'Gloworm, wait.' Dust glanced him and then looked at Briar, 'We shouldn't argue. They could all be fine. Violet died ... but that doesn't mean Gloworm is wrong...'

'You were wrong to trust a human,' Briar growled.

'We all trusted Fiona,' Dust held the tabby tom's gaze, 'Now, let's go back to the Meeting Box.'

Rose's wail echoed from the top of a distant tower, and in its wake came the faint eerie sound of little scuffling bodies.

'Dust...' Gloworm hissed, 'They're coming back!'

Dust flicked his ears as the towers filled once more with squeaks and squeals and the scrapping of claws. He stared onto the gloom. Something moved. Then everything moved, 'Get to the doors ... Run.'

Briar bounded towards the yellow doors. Dust stayed close to Gloworm and leant into his side, supporting him as he urged him to move faster. He glanced back as a sea of rats sloshed from under the ledges. More Greasy bodies tumbled down from the towers and out of full boxes and washed like a wave across the Open Space. Dust nudged Gloworm forward. The yellow doors were close, and still propped open by a full box.

'Quick, Briar, Gloworm, the full box,' Dust mewed, 'help me move it.'

'Move it?' Gloworm panted as he slowed and turned his head to watch the approaching rats. His eyes went wide.

'To close the doors. To stop the rats,' Dust mewed.

Briar hopped onto the full box as Gloworm scrabbled up and over it, Dust close behind them. Together they pressed their forepaws onto the side of it and pushed. It was heavy, and at first it didn't seem to move. But as the squealing mass of rats neared, they found their strength and the full box slid into the Vast Tower Box, and the yellow doors swung closed.

Claws and tails flitted through the gap at the bottom of the yellow doors as rats screeched and scratched at the other side, but they couldn't get through.

'Let's go,' Dust mewed, 'we should close the black door too.'

The next full box was easier to push aside, and as the black door closed gently behind them, Gloworm flopped down on the floor of the Long Box and dropped his chin onto his paws, panting and mumbling to himself.

Dust sat next to him and licked his ear, 'Just a little further, and we'll be safe.'

'Then what?' Briar mewed.

'We rest ... and wait.'

Briar turned to face Dust, 'Wait for what?'

Dust shook his head, 'I don't know, Briar. Rose has found the rats ... we have food again. Now we need to rest, especially Gloworm, and I'm sure Rose will come back and rest too...'

'If she comes back?' Briar hissed, 'If the rats don't get her, the humans will.'

'Don't say that...' Dust shook his head, 'Rose ... she—' As if in answer, Rose's wail sliced through the air. 'She's close...' Dust looked around.

Gloworm raised his head, 'she's here ... in the Long Box ... but, how?'

Dust flicked his tail twice for Briar and Gloworm to follow. They hung back and stayed close to the wall as he padded forwards and peered around the Dark Corner. *Nothing...* He parted his jaws and found Rose's scent. *Fading...* His ears caught no sounds, and his eyes caught no movement, but they must have passed over the body two or three times before he picked up the scent of rat. 'She's gone,' he sat down and stared at the dead rat, 'but she was here. She's hunted.'

Briar flicked his tail for Gloworm to follow. Slowly they padded to Dust's side and looked down at the rat.

'She could be in the Meeting Box,' Gloworm mewed, 'she could be taking her catches there.'

287

'Then we help her,' Dust sniffed at the dead rat. It was big. He turned it around with a paw. Its head was missing, and so was its tail.

Briar prodded the dead rat's rump, 'Where's the rest of it?'

Dust turned the rat over, 'This is fresh. She's bitten its head off, but the tail ... this rat lost its tail long ago. This is Skeeal...'

Shuffling footsteps approached the Blue Corner.

'Human...' Gloworm stepped back from Skeeal's body.

Dust sniffed the air, 'It's John,' he mewed, 'but ... why is he here now?'

'Benny,' Gloworm mewed, 'if we can get into the Blue Box—'

'I will speak to Benny this time,' Briar nudged Gloworm back. 'Hide behind these full boxes. Dust, keep John distracted until he opens the blue door.'

Reluctantly, Dust nodded, and as soon as Briar and Gloworm were out of sight, he stepped over Skeeal's body and mewed, 'Hey, John. Why are you here now?

John smiled as he walked around the Blue Corner, *'Hellolad, whatareyou cats upto, wheresyourfriend, Wild Rose, shescausingtrouble.'*

Dust purred and rubbed around John's leg as he mewed, 'He's looking for Rose. Stay hidden until he opens the blue door.'

Muffled meows and human voices came from behind the dull brown door. *Spinney...?* Dust strained his ears, *Fiona...*

'Goodlad, thatsameanlooking rat thatis.' John bent down to look at Skeeal's headless body. Then in one swift movement, he threw it aside, grabbed Dust around his

middle and lifted him up over his shoulder. *'Keepstilllad, ineedtokeepholdofyou, dontwantyougettingouttoo.'* John stood up slowly, and holding Dust tight, he opened the dull brown door.

Dust clung to John's shoulder as he walked into the Bright Box. It was dark. Globes of orange light flickered in the huge flat lights, casting a weak yellowish glow over the three human figures stood before them. Fiona, Steph, and the Grey Male all looked around when John entered.

Fiona gasped, *'Ohnois Dust okay John.'*

'Ayehesfine Fiona justdontwanthimrunningoffnowwhats happening.'

'Spinney wasoutsidehesfine, Steph hasjustputhiminmycarilltake himtothevet, haveyouseen Rose anywhere,'

'I heardherwailing buticantfindher, shestooquick.'

'Weneedtofindherbefore Craig does.' Fiona walked over and lightly ran her had down Dust's back. He tensed at her touch, then looked back at the dull brown door. Briar and Gloworm were peering through the gap. The humans hadn't seen them. Dust dug his claws into John's shoulder.

'Ouchladcarefull.'

Fiona smiled sadly, *'Idontthinkhetrustsme, notafter Violet.'*

Dust looked up at Fiona. Her fear scent was sharp and her voice heavy with sorrow, but the dark circles in her eyes widened as she looked at him. *She's not broken...*

'Whatwill Craig dowhenhefinds Rose.' Steph uttered as she joined Fiona and held her hand out to Dust.

Fiona took a deep breath. *'Hesgoingtoputherdown, shestoo agressive, Rose isnonviablenow.'*

Dust rested his head back on John's shoulder. Gloworm blinked up at him with wide eyes, then flicked his ear to the far wall. Dust looked over and saw Briar stalking towards the far end of the Bright Box. 'Where are you going?' he mewed.

Briar paused, blinked at Dust, then slipped under a ledge.

'*Maybeshegotouttoo.*' The Grey Male walked to the big grey door, '*Illhavealookaround.*'

'*Ihopeshehas.*' John uttered.

'*Justfindherbefore Craig does,*' Steph added.

The Grey Male pulled the big grey door open, and turned back to Fiona, '*Whatdoidoifiseeher.*'

'*Callmefirst not Craig. Illbeinthebasement.*'

A brown blur slipped past the Grey Male's legs.

Gloworm growled.

'*John behindyou*' Steph uttered.

John turned.

The Grey Male pulled the door shut.

'*Ohnoyoudont Gloworm,*' Fiona uttered as she stepped towards him, waving her arms.

Gloworm hissed and ducked back out into the Long Box.

'*Illshutit,*' John pulled Dust from his shoulder and dropped him gently onto the floor of the Long Box beside Gloworm. Then he closed the dull brown door.

'Did Briar get out?' Gloworm mewed.

Dust nodded. 'He went through the big grey door.'

'Is he in The Outside?'

'He could be,' Dust shook his head, 'but they have Spinney, and they are all looking for Rose.'

290

Gloworm shivered and licked a paw, 'She's stopped yowling. Maybe she's hiding.'

'I hope so—' Dust pricked his ears. *More footsteps...* The black door opened, and a full box slid into the Long Box. he tasted the air, *Stale water...*

'Human,' Gloworm mewed.

'It's Craig, let's go.'

As they rounded the Dark Corner, Craig strode through the black door. Dust nudged Gloworm forwards, hurrying him along as fast as he could go around the Blue Corner, up the Long Box, and through the flap.

'Get into the beds,' Dust mewed.

Gloworm nodded and complied.

Dust shivered as he hopped up onto the full boxes beside Gloworm. Something felt wrong. The flat light was black, but the humans were still there. The Meeting Box felt cold and lonely now only he and Gloworm remained. But as he stepped into his bed, he shook his head, *that's not it...* There was something else, something that made his skin crawl.

'I smell rats,' Gloworm mewed.

Footsteps thudded past the flap and full boxes scraped the floor as Craig strode up the Long Box, kicking them aside.

Dust felt his fur rise along his spine.

Gloworm looked up, raised his paw, and licked it.

Scratching sounds trickled down the walls, from the roof to the floor. With a faint squeak, and a scrape of claw, a roof square moved. Then something stirred in the full boxes beneath them.

'The flap. Go!' Dust nudged Gloworm out of his bed and they slid through the flap just as the first rat chain began to descend from the roof.

As they ran towards the Blue Corner, Dust looked back to see a stream of rats was pouring through the flap. Screeching filled the air behind them as they ran on, around the Dark Corner and on towards the black door. It had been propped open again with the full box. *Craig...* Dust slowed to a halt. *Craig has opened the doors again...*

'The...rats...' panted Gloworm.

Dust helped Gloworm scramble over the full box and into the Cold Box. 'We need to hide,' he flicked his ears and circled, listening. The rats in the Long Box were gaining on them, but without Briar to help, they wouldn't be able to move the full box and close the black door.

The yellow doors were open too. And from the gloom beyond them, he could hear the scuffling of rats as they scurried around under the towers.

'Hide where?' Gloworm backed into Dust as the first rat reached the black door.

Dust glanced around. The rolling traps offered no cover, and the full boxes were not rat proof. His eyes fell on the light bumps beside the mirror door. 'In there.'

'We don't know what's in there?' Gloworm mewed in alarm.

'There's nowhere else to hide,' Dust padded to the Light Bumps. *Middle; top, bottom, top, centre.* He pressed them in order. They lit up green, dinged, and the door hissed. Dust took a step back, leapt for the lever and curled his paws around it. When the lever slid down, he leapt away. The mirror door had moved enough for him to slide his paw into the gap and pull it open. 'Go on,' he mewed.

'Dust ... it's too cold...'

Dust felt the freezing grip his throat as he nudged Gloworm into the misty box behind the mirror door. He could hear the chatter of the approaching rats, but he could see nothing through the white cloud of breath that escaped his nostrils. They were trapped. It was too late to escape the sticky piercing cold that slithered into his lungs as he tried to take another breath. Dust pressed against Gloworm's side, and they shivered together as the rats reached the mirror door and it slammed shut behind them.

34

The Ice Box

DUST BOUNDED ACROSS THE BONE CHILLING
floor and leapt at the door. It didn't move. All he could see
through his billowing breath was the flickering of a little red
light high on the wall. And he heard nothing in the still
frozen air except Gloworm's raspy breathing beside him.

'It's stuck, there's no lever to open it.' Dust ran frantically
back and forth in front of the door.

'Dust, where ... are ... we?' Gloworm panted. His breath
hung in the air above him.

'I don't know. There must be something ... something in
here.'

'It's so cold ... It's all ice...'

'Gloworm ... keep moving ... keep warm. I'm looking.'

'I can't move as well as you. My leg hurts from running,
and this cold... just makes it worse. This box is ... ice. like
the food ... in the Old Place.'

Dust returned to Gloworm's side and licked the tom's
cooling ear. Then he closed his eyes and listened to his
senses. *Something... there must be something...* He felt the
floor with his paws. It didn't move. The Dropping Box
swayed and juddered as it moved up and down, but there
was no movement in the floor of the Ice Box. He held his
breath as he opened his eyes, so he could look around. He

glanced at the little red light, then looked back at the door to where it reflected along edge of a raised bump. 'There!'

'What ... where?'

'By the door, there's a light bump.' Dust padded to the wall and rose onto his hind legs. With an outstretched paw, he felt along the frozen wall. When he found the bump, he pressed it. It lit up green, but nothing happened.

Dust sank back to the floor and looked around. In the faint green glow, he could make out a tower of thin ledges at the back of the box. On the bottom ledge were four small black boxes, like the one Craig had been carrying. He was surprised to see they had light bumps on them.

The green light bump went out.

Dust felt the skin of his hind paws sticking to the frozen floor as he twisted around, leapt at the light bump, and pressed it again.

'There ... behind you,' Dust padded to Gloworm.

'What?'

'Gloworm, move,' Dust nudged the white tom to his paws. His fur was cold, he was shivering uncontrollably, and his eyes were wide with fear.

Reluctantly, Gloworm staggered to his paws. Dust leant into his side and guided him towards a space on the ledge. 'Get on the ledge, stay off the cold floor while I find a way out of here.'

Gloworm nodded stiffly and clambered up, curled himself into a ball and rested his head on his paws.

'Stay warm ... we'll get out of here,' Dust nuzzled Gloworm's shoulder as he looked at the black boxes on the ledge.

Gloworm shivered.

The green light bump went out.

Dust ran a paw across the top of the nearest black box. when he found the small light bumps, he pressed them. There was a hiss and the light bump lit up red. Then the top of the black box split open, its two sides parting to reveal a blue glow from within. Dust peered inside.

'What ... is ... it?' Gloworm shivered.

'It's a small box. It opens and it has lights inside it. A light box...? There's something in it. It looks like a tiny rat covered in shiny covers, like the covers Fiona takes the litter in, but I can see through it. And it's cold, even colder than this Ice Box.'

The light box hissed and closed.

'Don't ... touch ... it...' Gloworm's voice quivered.

The green light bump went out.

Exhausted, Dust sat down in the dark. The sticky cold of the floor froze his paws to the spot as his breath clouded around him. He could hear Gloworm's shallow rasps and feel his little puffs of warm breath in the freezing air behind him. *We need to stay warm...* Dust turned and eased his paws off the floor. There was space for him beside Gloworm, so he stepped up onto the ledge and pushed in beside the white tom and crouched down. Gloworm raised his head a little and blinked, then dropped it back down to his paws. If they kept close, they could keep each other warm, but he could feel the cold seeping into his own bones as he pressed close to Gloworm. The cold had settled into his fur too. Sleepily, Dust closed his heavy eyes. *How long can we wait...?*

'No!' Dust called out to stop himself falling. He forced himself awake. *Don't sleep... We need to get out...* He opened his eyes. The little red light flickered. *Watch light eyes...* He stared at it. *We need to keep moving...* Suddenly he knew what to do.

Dust leapt across the Ice box and hit the light bump. Then he bounded back to the ledge and nudged Gloworm's shoulder as he hopped up onto it and padded across the light boxes, stamping on their light bumps as he went. All four boxes hissed and opened, bathing the Ice Box in a soft blue glow. Dust peered inside each of them. There were tiny frozen rats inside them all.

Gloworm shifted, but he didn't look up.

'Stay awake, Gloworm,' Dust mewed as he looked at the ledges above him, 'The humans will see us if we move.'

Above him, the ledges were stacked with small boxes that looked like beds. He reached up and sunk his claws into the nearest one and pulled. It slid forward and fell off the ledge, narrowly missing his head. Its contents spilled across the frozen floor.

The green light bump went out.

The light boxes hissed and closed.

Dust hopped off the ledge and hit the light bump again. Then he ran back over the light boxes.

Gloworm took a short breath. A little cloud of white air seeped from his mouth.

Dust looked at the frozen objects spilled across the floor, then up at the red light. *They must be there... They must be watching...* Shaking himself he took a deep breath and yowled. 'Here. Craig. Fiona. Here.'

Move... he needed to keep moving. Gloworm needed to keep moving. When they'd first discovered the watch lights, Dust's eyes had been drawn by movement. He circled the

Ice Box, yowling and bounding around the spilled objects until it went dark. Then he hit the light bump and opened the light boxes again.

Gloworm didn't move.

'Here! We are in here! Dust yowled. He leapt at the ledges again and pulled down another box, spilling more objects across the floor. As he hopped down, his paw nudged one aside and it spun away and unrolled across the floor.

The green light bump went out.

The light boxes hissed and closed.

'Gloworm?'

Dust stepped carefully across the floor and around the spilled objects. When his whiskers touched the door, he leapt up at the light bump. In the green glow he looked around to see tatty rolled up scratching sheets uncurling slowly across the floor.

'Gloworm?'

The green light bump went out.

Dust hit the light bump again. Then hopped over the frozen objects, stopping for a heartbeat to sniff at the edge of one. *Human marks...* His shuddered as he hopped up onto the ledge and opened the light boxes.

He nudged Gloworm's side, but the tom didn't move. 'Gloworm, you need to keep warm,' Dust pushed the tom's shoulder with his paw, but he didn't respond.

The green light bump went out.

The light boxes hissed and closed.

Dust felt along Gloworm's flank. No movement. If he were breathing, Dust couldn't feel it. There was no sound in is chest, and no billowing cloud of white breath came from his mouth. 'Gloworm! Wake up!' Dust wailed, 'You need to move ... you have to get warm...'

With a loud clunk and a hiss, the door moved, and harsh white light flooded the Ice Box. Dust backed away and blinked, stepping protectively in front of Gloworm.

'Morenonviables,' Craig growled as he pulled the door open.

Dust stood over Gloworm and licked the tom's ear, 'Wake up, please wake up.'

Craig crouched and picked up a rolled-up scratching sheet. He turned it over in is hands, twisted it tight and put it back in the fallen box. Then he carefully collected and rolled up the others, putting them back in the box before he replaced the box on the ledge. Then he looked up at Dust.

'*Timetogetsomenew Ratters,*' Craig grabbed Dust by the scruff and dragged him away from the ledge.

'Glo—worm...?' Dust meowed, the skin on his neck stinging in Craigs tight grasp. He couldn't move his head enough to bite him, or his legs enough to scratch. He was helpless as Craig leant forward again and picked Gloworm up by his tail. The white tom didn't resist, he didn't move, he just dangled in Craig's grasp, lifeless and limp. Craig carried them out of the Ice Box, through the Cold Box and up the Long Box towards the flap.

'Glo—worm ... wake ... up...' Dust hissed as he writhed, but Craig just tightened his grip even more. Dust's scruff was numb by the time Craig stopped to kick a full box up against the flap, blocking it. Then he opened the green door with his elbow, carried Dust and Gloworm into the Meeting Box, and dropped them on the floor.

Dust got to his paws as Craig slammed the door and sealed it. And as his heavy footsteps faded, Dust felt the cold of the Ice Box melting in the heat of his rage.

The Meeting Box was silent. A warm yellow glow was beginning to creep along the bottom of the flat light. Dust paced a circle around Gloworm, then another, and another before he finally slumped down onto his belly. He rested his chin on the floor and pressed his cheek into the frozen fur of his last cat.

'Gloworm ... wake up ... I'm sorry. Please wake up.'

No breath... No movement... No life... Dust closed his eyes and let the creeping cold of his friends' body encircle him like a bone chilling breeze.

Breeze...

He tried to picture his mother's eyes in his mind. He tried to see her face but couldn't find her. His mind was dark, and her haunting voice was all he could hear, *Save your cats...*

'Breeze ... I'm sorry. I couldn't save them. They're all gone. I couldn't save my cats.'

35

Shadow White

COOL AIR FLUTTERED ACROSS DUST'S CHEEK, ruffling his whiskers. 'I'm sorry. All of you...' he felt the cold of the floor seep into his heart, 'My cats ... You wanted me to lead you. You believed I could get you out of The Boxes. But now you're all gone ... and I am still here ... I couldn't even get out myself.'

Another cold breath stroked Dust's face.

'Breeze?' Dust lifted his head.

'Dust?' Gloworm opened his eyes.

Dust shuffled backwards and stared in amazement as Gloworm lifted his head and blinked. His blue eyes were bright and clear and full of warmth. He lifted his chin and sniffed the air around him, 'We got out of the Ice Box?'

'Craig ... Craig carried us out. But ... you were...'

Gloworm nodded, 'Dead. I know.'

'But...'

Gloworm's blue eyes sparkled as he purred, 'Shadow White.'

Dust sat up and watched in amazement as Gloworm sprang lightly to his paws and trotted nimbly around him, raising, and curling his tail as gracefully as he lifted his knees.

'I met her, Dust,' Gloworm hopped effortlessly up onto the full boxes, 'She's real. She gave me my choices and I chose to come back,' he leapt off again and landed lightly

303

beside Dust. Then he raised a paw, licked it, and ran it over his ears. 'Thank you, Shadow White.'

'Your leg?' Dust mewed, edging forward to sniff the tom. His scent was strong and bold and there was no trace of fear.

'No pain. It moves as well as it did when I was a kitten,' Gloworm sat and shook out his thick gleaming fur.

'She did this?' Dust purred, 'Shadow White, she healed your leg? Took away your fear?'

Gloworm nodded and licked Dust's ear. 'She is The White Kitten. Her real name is Uimywim and everything Icicle said about her is true. She's small, and fluffy with magnificent blue eyes full of tiny lights, and she has a tatty blue bow around her neck. She met me in a bright warm place. She knew my name and how I died. She knew everything about ... me...'

'She knows about every cat?' Dust asked as he padded closer.

Gloworm's eyes clouded, and he looked away, 'She asked me why I wanted to return to The Boxes?'

'Why did you?' Dust held Gloworm's warm gaze.

'For you. I told her I couldn't leave you alone in the Ice Box ... but...'

'But?'

'My answer confused her. She asked me your name twice. Then asked how many cats were here in The Boxes. I told her and she shook her head, sadly. So, I asked about Violet...' Gloworm paused and glanced around. Dust saw the white tom's fur ripple along his spine. 'Violet accepted Shadow White's invitation. She chose not to return.'

Dust felt the fur rise on the back of his neck. He glanced over his shoulder.

Gloworm went on, 'I asked her about Fiona. Why she ... killed Violet.'

'Dust looked back into Gloworm's bright eyes, 'Did she know?'

'I'm not sure, she said something about humans forgetting a promise.'

'Promise?' something stirred in Dust's mind, 'Benny! Gloworm, I forgot! Benny told me a story. It was a about a cat who refused to hunt rats. It mentioned a promise.'

Gloworm held Dust's gaze, 'Tell me.'

Dust dipped his head and told Gloworm the Engel's Tale, exactly how Benny had told it to him.

When Dust had finished telling Benny's story, Gloworm twitched his whiskers, 'The Ills of Rodents? What does *that* mean?'

Dust shook his head. 'I don't know, I didn't have chance to ask before he left,' Dust sighed, 'Benny's words are as confusing as Breeze's.'

'Breeze...' Gloworm hung his head, 'Dust, there is something you should know. Your mother ... your dreams ... it's not—'

A rustling, scratching sound interrupted Gloworm. Dust snapped his head around to see a full box heave and tear. Red fur flashed across the hole, and a brilliant green eye appeared, blinked, and widened as a red she-cat slid gracefully out of the torn full box.

'Rose!' Dust gasped.

Gloworm stood tall and raised his tail.

Rose dipped her head and padded across the floor toward them. She was carrying something. As she neared them, she let it drop from her mouth. It bounced across the floor, rolling to a stop by Dust's paw.

Dust looked down into the blind white eye of Skeeal's severed head.

'The Ills of Rodents,' Rose sat before him and licked her jaws, 'What *does* that mean?'

'Rose...' Dust dipped his head and stepped back, carefully lifting his paws over the severed head, 'I thought Craig had... How did you catch Skeeal?'

Rose purred, 'Craig threw me down the hole in the Water Box.'

'He what?' Gloworm thrashed his tail.

'Onyx was right, it's the Rat Holes.'

Dust sat down, 'Was she there? Onyx?'

'No. But there are tunnels. She got out.'

'So, you ... you got into The Outside?'

'Not at first. I heard the rats, so I stayed still,' she nodded to Gloworm, 'Played dead.'

'Dead?' Gloworm tipped his head, 'you mean, stop moving?'

'Yes. The rats dragged me to Skeeal.'

'And you killed him?' Dust asked, 'as easy as that?'

'No. As he bent to take his first mouthful of my flesh, I captured him alive.'

'Then you took him and his rats into The Outside?' Dust supposed, 'And back into The Boxes through the tunnel in the Vast Tower Box? We found your fur.'

Rose nodded.

'Why did you come back?'

'To see what Violet found.'

Gloworm glanced at Dust, then mewed gently to Rose, 'Rose ... I am glad you're safe. And Violet ... she's safe too, safe with Shadow White.'

Rose glanced at Gloworm, then looked at Dust, 'The rats are no longer our enemy,' She nudged Skeeal's head with her paw.

Dust watched the head rock twice, and fall still again, 'I never thought of them as an enemy, Rose,' he mewed, 'they're mean, but they are food ... we *have* to kill them to eat.'

'The Boxes are the enemy,' Rose purred, '...and humans.'

'Humans?' Dust felt a knot form in his stomach. He wasn't sure what Rose meant, but her tone filled him with dread.

'The Boxes first,' Rose held Dust's gaze, 'Then the humans.'

'I don't—' Dust began.

Rose turned to Gloworm, 'Where is Violet?'

Gloworm shuffled his paws uncomfortably, 'She is with Shadow White. Violet accepted her invitation. She chose not to return ... but to rest with the Eternal Host instead. She's at peace now ... with Berry ... your mother.'

Rose stared at Gloworm. Her expression unreadable. After a few heartbeats she flicked her tail dismissively, 'Why not?'

Gloworm slumped to the floor and sighed.

Rose tapped Skeeal's head with her paw as she looked up at Dust, 'The Ills of Rodents? Benny spoke of this...? What did he mean?'

'Yes, he told me a tale—'

'I heard. The Engel's Tale...' Rose rocked the head back and forth under her paw. 'I will need Benny.' She flicked the head, and it spun around on the floor, coming to a rest with Skeeal's blind white eye staring upwards. Then she hopped up onto the full boxes and stepped into her bed. As she padded down the covers, she looked back at Dust and Gloworm and purred, 'I found it. I leave when I'm rested. You should follow.'

'Found ... what?' Dust mewed.

Rose flicked an ear to Violet's bed, 'What she found.'

Dust waited until Rose had sunk down into her bed, then he leant into Gloworm's shoulder, 'What do you think is in there?' he mewed quietly.

'I'm not sure I want to know...'

'If Violet found it, it can't be bad...' Dust padded forward slowly, keeping his ears trained on Rose. The she-cat's breathing slowed as she slipped into a heavy sleep.

Dust hopped lightly onto the full boxes. He held his breath. He didn't want to disturb her. Rose was acting calmer than he'd ever seen her. She seemed to be unconcerned about anything Dust and Gloworm did or said, and this worried him ... it was not the Rose he knew. And he could see his worry reflected in Gloworm's eyes as the white tom hopped nimbly up beside him. It was like part of Rose had died with Violet. The part he understood.

It can't be bad... Dust told himself as he peered into Violet's bed. *Nothing...?* Blinking, he searched again, but as his eyes were expecting a gruesome discovery, he failed to see what was there.

'What is it?' Gloworm stretched his neck over the side of Violet's bed and sniffed at something...

Dust let his eyes follow Gloworm's nose. There *was* something, propped up against the side of the bed, barely visible against the covers. Dust tipped his head and saw a small flat shard, no longer than a rat's body. It had no scent of its own. It was familiar, yet he'd never seen anything like it before.

The Meeting Box lightened as the smudge of yellow crept across the bottom of the flat light and reflected onto the surface of the shard.

Flat light....?

Dust snapped his head up to look at the brightening flat light on the wall above him. Raising himself onto his hind legs, he reached up a paw and touched it. Gloworm sat back and watched as Dust stretched up further to sniff and then carefully lick its surface before dropping down to do the same to the shard. 'It's a shard of flat light.'

'Why would Violet want us to find a shard of flat light?' Gloworm prodded the shard with his paw, 'It's warm!'

Dust shook his head. None of this made sense. Nudging Gloworm with his tail he hopped down from the full boxes and began pacing the floor, circling around Skeeal's lifeless head. *Why did Rose have Skeeal's head....? Why did she have a shard of flat light....?*

Gloworm hopped down and padded to his side, 'What do we do? We can't follow Rose, the tunnel in the Vast Tower Box will be blocked. And the Humans are still here, watching us, waiting to catch us if we escape. They have Spinney. They probably have Briar too...'

Dust shook his head. The Meeting Box felt cold and empty. *Will my cats return....? Will Fiona come soon to clean the litters....? Or John....?* He began to pace, keeping time

309

with his growing shadow as he tried to outpace his hurtling thoughts. *Where are the rats....? Will Rose hunt them now....? How can we hunt if the flap is blocked with a full box....?*

'Dust?'

Dust stopped pacing and sat down. He closed his eyes, and, in his mind, he watched Shadow Dust carry on walking, as if his dream of escaping The Boxes had got to its paws and padded away. With a sigh of despair, he looked at Gloworm and shook his head, 'We ... wait.'

The warm yellow rays brightened along the flat light.

Gloworm took a deep breath and nodded.

Dust closed his eyes again, and trained his ears on air so silent, it was as if The Boxes held their breath.

36

What She Found

DUST OPENED HIS EYES. A CHOKING stench filled his nostrils. He raised his head and parted his jaws. Gloworm shifted beside him and tensed as the golden glare of the flat light illuminated a twisting hazy mist that hung in the air around them.

'What is that?' Dust got to his paws and hopped up onto the full boxes. A swirling white wisp curled upwards out of Violets bed and fluttered into the hazy mist above. As Dust reached out a paw to grasp it, it swirled away. As he sniffed it, it stole his breath.

'My eyes...' Gloworm hissed, it's getting in my eyes.

Dust shook his head, 'I've never seen anything like it.'

'How did it get in here?'

'It's coming from Violet's bed.'

Gloworm hopped up beside Dust and peered at the shard of flat light, 'It's what she found... What is it doing?'

Rose stirred and lifted her head. Her eyes widened when she saw the drifting haze above her and she sat up, letting her gaze follow it back to its source in her sister's empty bed. Her red fur ruffled along her spine as she craned her neck towards the wisp, took a deep breath, and closed her eyes.

Dust felt his skin prickle uneasily.

Violet's bed burst into a flash of intense yellow light, illuminating Rose's face.

Rose didn't move.

The yellow light flourished and danced around the edge of the bed, expanding as it formed new twisted tails, each with their own blackened wisps at the top, where their colour deepened into the same searing red as Rose's fur.

Rose opened her eyes again and stared into the dancing lights as they crackled and popped and waltzed around Violet's bed, turning everything in their path into soft grey falling motes, like the gentle soft grey of her fur. 'Thank you, Violet,' Rose purred as she watched the blackened wisps ascended into the hazy mist above.

Dust nudged Gloworm off the full boxes. The heat of the dancing lights curled his fur. He turned to Rose, 'Rose...? I think...'

Rose blinked and shook herself. Then she hopped down to the floor and padded to the flap, 'Let's go,' she mewed.

Dust hopped down behind her, 'We can't get out. Craig sealed the green door and barred the flap with a full box.'

Rose looked at the door, then the flap, and then the roof.

Gloworm coughed and shook his head. 'We can't push the full box, not from in here, the flap is too small for all of us...'

Dust pressed against Gloworm's side and watched the dancing lights leap from Violet's bed to Rose's, crackling and spitting out sparks onto the full boxes below. His eyes were growing sore. The Meeting Box was getting hot. *We need to get out...*

Rose flicked her tail twice, then reached out a paw to Skeeal's head, lifted it up in her claws, and yowled, 'TO ME!'

Scratching sounds joined the hissing and popping of the dancing lights.

'Rats.' Gloworm hissed.

Dust looked up. Through the hazy mist, he saw roof squares slide away, and a heartbeat later the first rat leapt onto the drip light to start the chain.

Rose rolled Skeeal's head under her paw and watched the rats descend into the Meeting Box.

'Water bowl ... we need to drink,' Dust nudged Gloworm's shoulder. He didn't argue, and they leapt into the corner, away from the descending rats and the dancing lights. The stale water was a relief and cooled their throats as they drank.

The rat chains hit the floor, and as one long skittering wave, hundreds of greasy bodies flowed towards the flap.

'Keoie, Grouw,' Rose meowed.

The two large rats slid out of the wave and pushed the flap up, holding it aloft as their smaller companions began clawing frantically at the full box on the other side. Shredded chunks of box and scratching sheet flew back and scattered across the floor as the rats ripped through them.

The dancing lights devoured Gloworm's bed, then Dust's. Gloworm hissed as he watched his own bed fold and fall into a pile of grey powder. Dust pressed close to him and laid his tail over his back, keeping him close as the rats worked.

As soon as the flap was clear, the rats began to retreat up their chain. Hissing, popping motes of light landed around them, illuminating their malevolent little eyes with a blood red glow, and igniting the scattered remains of the full box. Fewer than half the rats made it up the chain before the sparks found them. Leaping onto their backs and burrowing into their greasy black fur, the dancing lights followed them into the roof.

'LET'S GO!'

Dust glanced at Rose, then at the flap. He kept is head low, below the mist, and his eyes on the red she-cat as he nudged Gloworm to follow.

Rose picked up Skeeal's head and slipped out into the Long Box.

Rats screeched. The dancing lights engulfed their fur as they raced upwards, crackling, and popping and showering even more rats with their sparks. Before the last rat had reached the top of the chain, a hot red glow had filled the roof.

'Don't let the sparks hit you,' Dust hissed, 'Go, follow her.'

A spark tried to catch Gloworm's tail as he bounded forward and slid through the flap. Dust batted it away, and without looking back, he dived through after him.

Gloworm stood in the Long Box, his tail tucked into his side as he watched Rose padding steadily around the Blue Corner. Dust nudged his shoulder as he caught up, and together they trotted after her, keeping their heads below the hazy mist. Squealing sounds came from above, and as Dust and Gloworm neared the blue door, the roof opened above them, and a screeching glowing rat fell into the full boxes below. Sparks exploded from its twitching body and grew into new dancing lights that rippled across the full box.

Gloworm paused by the blue door, his paws submerged in the hazy mist that flowed out from under it. 'The dancing lights are in there too?' he hissed.

Dust shook his head, 'Come on, we need to keep up with Rose.'

'Is that wise? we don't know what she's going to do.'

'We can't stay here,' Dust nudged Gloworm forward as another glowing rat screeched and fell from the roof.

'Okay,' Gloworm growled as he turned and headed for the Dark Corner, 'But I don't trust her...'

Dust flicked his tail and followed.

As they rounded the Dark Corner, a human female screamed from behind the dull brown door, *'Rats, intheroof.'*

Dust stopped to listen. *Steph...*

'FIRE, FIRE getoutgetout, w*hereare Fiona and Craig, and John.'*

Dust padded closer to the door. *The Grey Male...*

'Basementone illcallher,'

'Dust, come on, she's getting ahead,' Gloworm meowed.

Dancing lights snaked along the sides of a full box and up around the blue door. The hazy mist circled in the air above, shrouding the screeching, flailing rats as they fell from the roof.

'Dust?' Gloworm meowed as he stepped back.

'Noanswer,' Steph wailed, '*whataboutthecats.'*

'DUST!'

'Leavethe cats weneedtogetout,'

A sizzling rat screeched around the Blue Corner. Dust leapt out of its way and turned and bounded after Gloworm, pushing him forward as he leapt for the full box by the black door. Gloworm leapt after him, a heartbeat before the rat hit it, twitched, and fell still. They hopped down into the Cold

Box as the dancing lights leapt from the rat and devoured the full box behind them.

'Where is she?' Gloworm hissed, 'I can't find her scent in this...'

Dust glanced at the Ice Box. The cold inside would be a relief from the intensifying heat of the dancing lights, but would they take that too, and reduce it to a scattering of soft grey powder with them inside it?

'Dust?'

He shook his head, 'Vast Tower Box ... I think she's going back to that tower.'

'I don't like this, Dust,' Gloworm flicked his tail and bounded towards the yellow doors.

Dust glanced back at the black door as he followed. It was quickly turning grey beneath the orange glow of the dancing lights that smothered it.

Rose was padding calmly down the Open Space, her tail high as Skeeal's severed head swung in her jaws. She stopped by the tower with the line and the circle, and looked up, paying no attention to terrified squeals of the rats that crept from beneath the ledges and gathered around her.

'The tower that Violet fell from,' Dust panted, coughing out the chocking air.

'Wait,' Gloworm held him back with his tail, 'Do you think she really can get out?'

Dust looked up at the tower, 'What choice do we have?'

Gloworm coughed. His tail drooped, 'I don't like this, Dust. What if she's trying to follow Violet? What if all this is to be reunited with her sister?'

'I don't know what this is, but we can't go back.' Dust flicked his tail to the dancing lights that crept over the full box by the yellow doors, 'Nothing is back.'

Gloworm raised a paw and licked it, 'Wash for Shadow White...' he mumbled as he ran it over his ears.

Dust watched Rose as she began to climb the tower. A writhing mass of rats followed her, weaving in and out of ledges and full boxes behind her as she climbed higher. Then they overtook and scurried ahead of her, up into the thickening hazy mist. Dust blinked. 'Gloworm, the rats, look...'

Gloworm followed Dust's gaze and shook his head, 'Look at what?'

'The rats know how to get in and out. Rose *was* right about Skeeal and now she's controlling his rats. They are leading her out. We *need* to follow her.'

'Is that why you wanted to investigate the towers?' Gloworm mewed, 'Because Rose believed the rat was telling the truth?'

Dust shook his head, 'It was Breeze who showed me this tower in a dream. I was following my mother ... my dreams...'

'Are you sure?' Gloworm mewed gently.

A glowing rat screeched past them and hit the bottom of the tower. Gloworm jumped sideways, narrowly escaping a cascade of sparks as the dancing lights reached out for the first ledge.

Dust nudged Gloworm on, 'Breeze led me to this tower... We have nowhere else to go.'

'Dust...' Gloworm ducked away from a burst of floating sparks, 'there's something I need to tell you.'

'Go,' Dust pushed him toward the first ledge, 'we can talk in The Outside.'

Dust clawed his way up the side of the first full box and ducked into the space above it. Gloworm caught up quickly, and with a speed and agility he'd never possessed before his death, overtook Dust, and reached the top of the tower a heartbeat before him.

Rose stood waiting in a swirl of hazy mist. Her brilliant green eyes twinkling as she watched Dust and Gloworm haul themselves up onto the top full boxes. She nodded and tightened her grip on Skeeal's head before she turned and followed the wave of rats towards a soft blue glow at the end of the tower.

Dust followed, keeping his distance, and testing every full box before he stepped onto it. Gloworm stayed close behind, treading carefully in his paw prints. Rose stopped when she reached a gap where a full box had been. *The one that caused Violet's fall...* The soft blue glow was all that filled the gap now.

And the air moved.

Not the stinking hazy mists that swirled around above the dancing lights. This air really moved. And on it, drifted faint traces of the same uplifting scents that had flowed into the Blue Box from The Outside.

Gloworm raised his head and sniffed the air.

Rose raised her head and yowled, 'OPEN IT.'

Bathed in a blue glow, the wave of skittering bodies scrabbled into the gap and began to form a pillar. Rose stepped back as more rats joined, and the pillar grew higher and higher, swaying back and forth until the rats at the top reached up and gripped the roof.

Dust looked up.

Gloworm followed his gaze.

Rose flicked her tail, and more rats ran up the pillar.

There was a crack. A shard shimmered and toppled down, bounced off the ledge and spiralled on downwards, smashing onto the floor below. Then another shard, and another.

'Flat light...' Dust leant on Gloworm's shoulder, 'it's a flat light in the roof...'

'That's what Violet found...' Gloworm leant back.

A gust of fast-moving air washed over them.

Another shard plummeted to the floor and shattered.

Skeeal's head swung in Rose's jaws as she looked back and dipped her head. Then she blinked her brilliant green eyes, clambered up the pillar of rats and leapt up out of the broken flat light.

37

A Twisted Tree

FIERCE FAST AIR HIT DUST IN the face as he pulled himself over the rats, up through the broken flat fight and out onto a grey sloping floor. He shivered as he got to his paws and raised his head. And as his senses began to adjust to The Outside, he marvelled in the sensation of the moving air, running through his fur like dry cold water. He took a step forward. *No, not a floor, this is the top of the roof...*

Gloworm hauled himself up behind Dust, gasped, and raised his head. his eyes widened and his fur ruffled as he gazed around.

Rose stood a few paces away, staring up at the swirls of hazy mist rising from beyond the highest point of the sloping roof. Dust wondered if the writhing mass of rats that swarmed around her, followed her, or the head of their leader in her jaws.

Chattering melodies floated on the moving air, dragging Dust's ears from the squealing and scrabbling of rats. He could see more grey sloping roofs nearby, and above them, a dark blue expanse full of soft pale mounds, and illuminated by a distant golden glow, went on forever. And all around the mounds, dark figures swooped and swirled like little flying rats as they chattered and chirped.

'This is The Outside...' Gloworm mewed softly.

'Yes ... it's...' Dust saw tall, twisted towers, like giant contorted human bodies reaching out with their many arms and infinite twisted fingers into the golden blue expanse. Their feet stuck in an undulating green floor, some stood alone and proud, others huddled together, shy and drooping.

'Trees ... those must be trees,' Gloworm waved his tail towards the twisted towers, 'and up, the golden bright ... that must be sky. The air ... it's moving ... and its strong enough to knock the paws off a cat.'

Beyond the grey roofs, blue lights flashed, illuminating the trees and the drab grey walls of the surrounding boxes. Excited human voices were drowned out by a distant solum wailing.

Rose raised her head, stood tall and let the bracing air flow through her fur as she took a deep breath, then she turned and padded away from her rats, back to Dust and Gloworm.

The wailing grew louder as the blue flashes quickened.

Dust glanced at Gloworm and blinked.

'Trees?' Rose nodded to where a large group of shadowy figures huddled together beyond the roofs of the other boxes.

The rats rippled and regrouped behind her.

'Yes ... and look there,' Gloworm flicked his tail, pointing into the distance, 'the floor is made of water, just as Icicle said.'

Rose followed Gloworm's gaze. Her eyes widened as they saw the shimmering surface of water and the dark undulating floor rising beyond it.

Without taking his eyes off the water, Gloworm stepped cautiously to Rose's side, 'Where will you go?' he asked.

Rose dropped Skeeal's head and held it still with a paw. She didn't answer.

The wailing grew louder, and the blue lights bounced closer to the surrounding grey boxes. A male human shouted. There was a bang below the roof and the hazy mist thickened and darkened as it billowed up through the broken flat light and soared into the bright golden sky.

Dust padded towards Rose and Gloworm, 'We need to get off this roof, find somewhere safe.'

Rose flicked an ear as Dust spoke, 'Where? The Outside is big.'

Dust nodded, 'And The Boxes are bad. Breeze ... it's what she said, when your territory goes bad...' he shook his head, trying to recall his dream, 'She wanted me to save you, lead you into The Outside.'

Gloworm turned to face him, 'Dust, I'm sorry, I tried to tell you. Those were not Breeze's words. Dreams are not what they seem. It wasn't your mother in your dreams.'

'What? ... what do you mean?' Dust stared at Gloworm.

'"We need to know our territory, that's the most important thing",' Gloworm mewed, 'you said that, just after we first met the Rats. But they were not Breeze's words. When I told Shadow White about you, and how you led us and how I wanted to return to help you, I told her those words. She recognised them, and she told me that Breeze could never have spoken to you.'

'Why?' Dust shook his head, 'I don't understand.'

'Because Breeze doesn't know you exist. She died when you were born, along with your littermates. I'm sorry, Dust, but Breeze couldn't have known that one of her kittens survived.'

'She isn't dead. She can't be, I... I spoke to her...'

'Gloworm rested his chin on Dust's head, 'I'm sorry.'

Dust pulled away from Gloworm and shook his head. The rising blackening mist swirled around them, stinging his eyes, seeping into his throat. He could barely breathe.

'Dust,' Gloworm mewed, 'when I told Shadow White how many cats there were in The Boxes, she was confused. I told her our names, but she only knew Violet, Rose, Briar, and me.'

'How?' Rose mewed.

'Because our mothers named us. We have Mother Names. That's how Shadow White can find our souls. Through our bond to our mothers.'

Rose's eyes went wide, and she shifted uneasily from paw to paw.

Gloworm went on, 'I asked her about our mothers. Berry is in Warkiersu, and Violet is with her. And I'm sorry, Dust ... I tried to tell you ... Breeze is there too, with your two littermates.'

Dust felt a cold shudder run down his spine. An emptiness began to twist and grow in his stomach. 'But ... I have no littermates ... I was alone ... how? ... I dreamt of her...'

'It was a dream, Dust. They were your own words.'

A dull thump below the roof sent sparks flying up out of the broken flat light. Plumes of black mist swirled out around them. Dust tried to think. *Shadow White recognised her words...? How...?* It was too much to take in. *I had littermates...?* He didn't remember them. *Who are they?*

324

Do they have names...? Names... 'Her name,' he raised his head, 'but I know her name.'

Gloworm nodded, 'You're good at deciphering names from human speech. Perhaps that's how you learned your mother's. You could have heard the humans utter her name.'

Dust shook his head. 'I saw Breeze in my dreams, she showed me things, and I found the things she wanted me to find.'

'What *you* wanted to find,' Rose looked at Dust, curiosity glimmering in her eyes.

Gloworm licked Dust's ear. 'Rose is right. You must have been terrified as a newborn kitten, so you grew up wanting to escape your fear. When I spoke of my mother and The Outside, you wanted them to exist. You believed it was a place you could escape to, and in your dreams, the mother you lost helped you escape by becoming the voice of your own thoughts.'

Dust hung his head, 'I saw her... The dreams were real ... I'm sure they were...'

Rose bowed her head, 'They weren't. But you were right. The Outside *is* real, and every cat got out of The Boxes. You led us well, Dust.'

Dust raised his head and looked into the red she-cat's brilliant green eyes. He couldn't read her expression, and she held his gaze only a heartbeat longer before she picked up Skeeal's head and padded back into the swarm of rats that milled around the edge of the roof.

'Where will you go?' Dust shuddered as he repeated Gloworm's question.

Rose dropped the head again and rolled it back and forth under her paw as she mewed, 'I will find my own way.'

'Benny?' Gloworm mewed, 'Will you look for him in the trees, in a place without humans?'

Rose gave a curt nod, 'And you? Both of you?'

'We will also look for Benny,' Gloworm curled his tail, 'Or another place, a safe place for cats.'

Dust nodded, 'Even if there are humans there. Some humans are kind, some ... And I've never known a place without humans.'

'What will you do when the humans have gone?' Rose purred.

Dust twitched his whiskers, 'What do you mean?'

Rose held Dust's gaze for one long last heartbeat, then with a glance at Gloworm she snatched up Skeeal's head, padded to the edge of the roof, and meowed, 'TO ME!'

Dust watched in awe as the rats circled around Rose and began to cluster at the edge of the roof to form their chains. The two Ard rats leant over, allowing the next ones to clamber onto their backs, twist around and sink their teeth and claws into their scruffs. More rats joined the chain, scurrying into one long wavering rope as the black choking mist thickened and swirled above them.

The wailing drew closer, and humans began shouting louder. Rose extended her claws, hopped lightly onto the backs of her rats, and bounded down their twisting chain to the unseen floor below.

Dust watched as the last rats let go of the roof and disappeared. Gloworm nudged his shoulder and mewed, but Dust didn't hear what he said. *Breeze...*

A shattering explosion shook the roof. Dust swayed. His fur rippled along his spine. He couldn't move. Gloworm mewed again, but he couldn't hear his words. *Breeze is dead....* Dust dug deep into his mind, closing his eyes to shut out the new world of The Outside, desperate to find her, an image of her, a memory of a heartbeat he'd been close to her, but nothing surfaced. All he could find was the lonely darkness he'd escaped once before.

'Dust!'

Dust shook his head and coughed away the mist that stung his eyes and nose. He opened his eyes and gazed into the distance. Near the huddled trees, he thought he saw a flash of red fur. *Rose...*

'DUST!' Gloworm yowled, pushing his shoulder with a paw, 'We have to go.'

The roof was hot, and he could barely see Gloworm through the swirling mist. The wailing was close. Dust looked around and tried to make out anything to give them direction, 'Where?'

'Up,' Gloworm flicked his tail towards the highest point of the roof, 'We go up and over, we can't stay here. But you must stay close to me.'

Dust didn't argue. he leapt after Gloworm, keeping his face close to the tom's tail as they plunged into the black mist. His eyes stung, and his throat burned. If he lost sight of Gloworm he'd be alone. But Gloworm kept his pace steady and let his tail brush Dust's face.

As they reached the highest point of the roof. Gloworm stopped. Dust halted close to his side. The wailing was close. The humans were shouting. Through the breaks in the mist, he could see them, crowded against the wall of another huge grey box. *Can we get to them...? would they help us...?*

He stepped onto the apex and padded towards them, 'Let's call them,' he mewed, but as he took another step, a large patch of roof began to darken and contort. Then it blackened and fell away into the hot orange glow below. A new mist rose, thick, black, and deadly. They backed away, losing sight of the humans as they turned and bounded down to the edge on the other side of the roof. Their paws searched for cooler spots but found few. The roof was heating up fast and collapsing into blackness behind them.

They ran on towards the edge, and as the mist thinned Dust lifted his head and gazed beyond the end of the roof.

In the distance, on a mound, stood a solitary twisted tree.

Gloworm scrambled to a halt and stared at it, then mewed, '"Where a twisted old tree stood high on a hill and the nearby floor was made from water and grass".'

'Icicle's farm...' Dust mewed.

Gloworm nodded, 'Shady Ly... And look ... down there.'

As the stinging hazy mist swirled and parted, Dust saw another roof below them. And beyond that, a floor marked with rows of rectangles next to a glistening square of water. 'The floor in the watch lights ... and there, that must be the Box Lake?'

Gloworm followed his gaze and nodded. 'Benny must be close ... Come on.'

Dust followed Gloworm down to the edge and looked over. It wasn't too far down to the roof below. 'We can jump onto that,' he purred, 'It's high, but ... we can fly from the roof!'

Gloworm purred, then caught Dust's eye, 'Stay close to me. If anything happens ... I need you to stay close to me.'

Dust nodded, and as Gloworm padded his hind paws on the edge, he reached down the wall with his fore paws. Gloworm pushed off. Dust jumped with him, and they landed side by side on the lower roof.

Huge red Moving Boxes with spinning blue lights roared onto the rectangle patterned floor and screeched to a stop. humans leapt out of them and ran about, shouting and waving their arms. slide down doors opened in the Moving Boxes. and more humans began pulling giant tails out of them.

Gloworm pushed Dust back against the wall, out of their sight, 'We need to jump again ... quick before those humans see us.'

Dust panted as he looked over the edge of the lower roof, 'There, between the rectangle floor and the Box Lake. The green ... it looks soft. Jump for the green.'

Dust pushed off, Gloworm at his side. And as he became weightless, a swirl of mist rolled across the green, and melted away to reveal two bright grey eyes.

Breeze....? Who are you....?

As he fell, Dust watched the little silver tabby she-cat extend her foreleg and bow. Shadows split from her own and padded around her. Shadows of his cats, Conker, Fern, Onyx, Spinney, Briar, Violet, Rose, Gloworm, and finally his own. They paused to dip their heads to him before they faded away into the swirling mist. Then she too turned and drifted away towards the twisted tree and vanished into the golden blue expanse.

Dust landed heavily and rolled onto his shoulder, coughing as he fought to get the fresh moving air into his lungs. The roof had been higher than he'd expected.

Gloworm crashed down beside him with a grunt.

Panting, Dust raised his spinning head and looked around. His gaze fell onto the golden glistening water of the Box Lake. He saw movement. Deep below the surface, the faces of Fiona, John, and Craig bobbed before his eyes. *The Water Box...* 'They got out too,' Dust panted, 'We all got out.'

Gloworm leant into Dust's side and still shaking they stood up together.

'Where now?' Dust purred.

Gloworm licked a paw, ran it over his ear and mewed, 'There are many trees, some as twisted as their tales. The one you seek is not where you want to go, but it is the one sought by cats who need direction.'

Dust dug his claws into tufts of the coolest, softest floor he'd ever felt, and as Gloworm led him away from the remains of The Boxes, it was all he could do to stay on his paws.

* * *

www.ghostsofshadyly.com

Onyx

ONYX FLICKED HER EARS. THE DOOR closed and Fiona's footsteps faded away. A heartbeat later she heard the growl of the Moving Box. When that too had faded, she raised her head and looked around.

The box she was in looked so much like the Old House that for a heartbeat she looked for Fleck, even though she knew her brother wouldn't be there. Sorrow gripped her chest as she wondered if he had kept their secret too, but she shook the thought away. She knew that he would, wherever he was.

She stepped out of the bed. The floor was a thick fluffy cover, like tufts of ungroomed fur that held Fiona scent. Scattered around the floor were soft boxes that Fiona had sat on while treating her injuries. *This is the box where she lives... Fiona's House... I am in her Rest Box...*

Onyx didn't know how long she'd been asleep in the bed in the corner, but her fur was still damp from being swept through the water tunnels, and her stomach ached with hunger. She sniffed the air. She could smell food.

There was an open door at the other side of the Rest Box, and through it she could see a bowl of dry nuggets and another of fresh water. She padded towards the door and looked around the next box. The floor was smooth and smelt of sour damp. The walls were lined with small doors below ledges and there were fresh litters in the far corner. *The Eating Box...* She approached the litters and sniffed around the door behind them. It smelt strongly of sour damp. Onyx gripped the bottom of the door and pulled it open. Inside was a tall bubble, like the one Fiona had used to fill the water bowl in the Meeting Box, only this one was white, and stank foul. She reached out a paw and gingerly touched the yellowing drips that had crusted around the top. She sniffed her paw, unsurprised to find that the sour damp had removed all trace of her own scent.

Backing away from the litters, Onyx looked up and along the ledges. Above them, on one wall, long white covers hung from the roof, glowing a warm blue as they gently fluttered. She hopped onto the ledge and padded towards them. She reached out a paw and hooked the hanging covers with her claw and pulled them aside. Behind it was a flat light, leaning at an angle away from the wall. Uplifting scents flooded through a gap at the bottom of it and found her senses. The Outside...

Conker

'WHEN THE DOOR GOES UP LEVEL with our ears, we go.'

'I can hear humans...'

Conker turned to Fern and laid his tail over her back, 'Don't worry, we can get past him. Remember to jump down. The floor will feel strange, but don't think about it. Just stay close to me.'

'Okay ... I'm ready.'

Conker pressed against Fern's side. He could feel her shaking but she was quick, and he knew she'd follow him. The light was flooding in from under the slide down door now and creeping steadily towards his paws. *Almost time...*

'Iseethem.'

Fern tensed.

Conker twitched his ears. He recognised the voice of the Grey Male.

'Letthemcomeout, theycantgoanywhere.'

'Craig!' Fern gasped, 'That was Craig.'

Conker took a step forward and lowered his head to peer under the slide down door, but the light flooding into the Moving Box was too bright and he couldn't see anything clearly, 'Don't worry, we can get past him too.'

'Areyoutakingthembacktopmd, whatiftheydoitagain,' the Grey Male uttered.

'Wait,' Conker flicked his tail, telling Fern to get back. His eyes were adjusting to the light now, and he could see the floor. A dark damp floor.

'Theyrenotgoingbackandtheywontescapefromwherethey aregoing,' Craig sneered.

Conker felt his stomach knot as the slide down door reached the height of his ears. He stepped back, pushing Fern away from the approaching humans. *This isn't The Outside...*

Fern

FERN PUSHED HER CHEEK UP AGAINST the clear door. She could just see Conker in a trap at the other side of the box. On a ledge above him, in an identical trap, was another cat she recognised. *Bracken...*

Fern tried to call out to her sister, but the anxious mewings of the other cats, and their frantic pacing, pawing, and clawing drowned out her voice. Bracken remained still, curled up with her tail laid over her eyes.

'Wait until they calm down. When it's dark and the humans go, she'll wake up then.'

Fern turned to the voice. Through a line of small holes in the side of her trap, she could see the brown nose of a she-cat, 'Who are you?'

'I'm Bolete.'

'I'm Fern...' Fern leant against the side of the trap and took a deep breath, thankful for the friendly voice, 'is this the Old Place?'

'If you went to a new place, then yes, I suppose it is.'

'I went to The Boxes,' Fern mewed, 'We escaped, Conker and I.'

'Conker?'

'The black tom, asleep in the trap over there.'

'I see him,' Bolete purred, 'So, you escaped from your new place? What did you call it? The Boxes?'

'Yes.'

'But the humans caught you?'

'Yes,' Fern felt her fur rise along her back as she looked at the long row of traps, stacked five high against the other side of the box. 'What is this place, it smells familiar, but I don't remember seeing anything like it?'

'The Box of Traps.' Bolete growled, 'It's new. Some of us tried to escape from the Ratbot Boxes, and now the humans keep us in these traps. There are so many cats here now...'

Fern heard a cat hiss from below her. She flicked her ears and heard the faint scrape of claws above. She shuddered as she realised that there were traps above and below her as well as to either side.

'When it's dark, we'll talk to the others,' Bolete mewed. 'What other cats do you remember?'

'My brother, Fescue, and my mother, Flurry.'

'Fescue is below us. You can't see him from here. I don't know Flurry, but if she's a Breeder, she'll be in the Soft Boxes.'

'Breeder? Soft Boxes?'

'Don't' worry, my mother, Dewfrost, recently came back from there. She's the brown she-cat down there with the four kittens.'

'Dewfrost?' Fern recognised the name, 'Briar! He said his mother's name was Dewfrost.'

Bolete snorted, 'So, you know my brother? Tell me, Fern, did he lead you well?'

'No, Fern purred, 'We voted for Dust.'

'Dust...' Bolete let the name linger in the air, 'Well, as annoying as he is, Briar was right about one thing.'

'What?'

'There's only one way to get out of here now, and that's to catch *all* the Ratbots.'

Violet

'I THINK SO ... ROSE ... YOU WERE... right ... you... were right about the roof.' A white glow surrounded Violet. She blinked and looked around, 'Rose?'

'Sik'rika Rora, Violet. I am sorry, there is no one here but us.'

Violet peered into the soft white glow. At its centre, sat a little fluffy cat, no bigger than a kitten. Her white fur gleamed around her big, bright blue eyes and fell delicately over the tatty blue bow around her neck. 'Oh,' Violet mewed, 'Oh ... who are you?'

'I am Uimywim,' the kitten blinked kindly, 'Also known as The White Kitten, or Shadow White.'

'Shadow White...? Then I'm ... dead?'

'Yes.'

'Gloworm talked about you. He said you gave his mother choices. Do I have choices?'

'Yes, but fewer than some.'

'Fewer?'

'A human healer ended your life. And in doing so, they limited the choices for your soul.'

'How?'

'The poison they used stays in your body. So, if you return, it will just end your life again. But fear not, you can choose to linger for ... a time, and wait for reincarnation. A new body and a new life.'

'But I need to help my sister now. I know what she's capable of and I'm afraid of what she might do ... because of what the humans have done to me. I'm afraid she will—'

'Nothing she does will have any consequence. In the end, we are, all of us, destined only to serve our souls to the forces of nature.'

Violet shook her head, 'No! you don't know Rose like I do. I must help her...'

Uimywim looked down at her little fluffy paws and sighed. She thrashed her tail once before she raised her head again and mewed, 'Then be sat by my side as she considers her *own* choices. I fear she will not be long in joining you.'

Spinney

'IPUTHIMIN FIONA'S CAR, buticouldntfinda cat box.

Spinney ducked back under the heavy cover as the voice of the Red Female drew near. He'd been in the Moving Box for a long time. Long enough to have seen the rectangles on the floor through its unusual flat lights. Long enough to see The Outside change from black to a deep blue.

'Isheokay.' The Red Female tapped on the other side of the flat light.

'Icantsee, hesundermycoat,' uttered the Grey Male.

Spinney heard a jangle of door sealers and a clunk. He raised his head just enough to see out from below the cover. The humans had opened the Moving Box door. Fresh moving air flooded in, and he took a deep breath of the uplifting scents.

'Amoslook, 'Smoke.' The Red Female gasped.

She moved away from the door just enough for Spinney to see white lines of the rectangles.

'Theresafire,' The Grey Male uttered as he followed her.

'Fiona Craig and John arestillinthere.' The Red Female hurried away, and the door opened a little more. *'Weneedtotellthem.'*

Spinney saw his chance. In one swift movement, he slid from under the cover, pushed his way through the gap in the door and leapt out of the Moving Box. As the Red Female and the Grey Male stared up at a wispy grey mist that billowed out of The Boxes, Spinney bounded away along the rectangular lines towards a tall, dark, tangle of shadows.

Briar

DAMP TENDRILS BRUSHED AGAINST HIS FUR as he ran, some snapped, others tightened around his legs, pulling him down into the dark unsettling shadows. He had no choice but to stop running. With a grunt he collapsed into the wet ground and closed his eyes tight. He didn't dare look at anything. Panting, he parted his jaws, and concentrated on deciphering the scents around him.

'You should curl yourself up, to retain your warmth.'

Briar tensed. He sniffed the air again. The voice belonged to a cat, but there was no cat scent in the air.

'You have nothing to fear from me, my friend.'

A tom cat... His voice was jaded, but friendly, and there was no trace of a threat in his words. Slowly, Briar opened his eyes.

'Good morning,' A tall ginger tom with one eye and a ragged ear sat before him, twitching his whiskers. White fur flecked his handsome muzzle. He was old and thin. Thin to the bone. But he exuded a lofty elegance as he dipped his head and asked, 'Do you have a name, my friend?'

'Briar, I am Briar.'

'And you escaped from that humming place?'

Briar nodded.

'Just you?'

'I don't know.'

'I see. Well, my fortunate young friend, welcome to the Ward of Softgrass Woods. You could be just the cat I am looking for.'

Gloworm

WASH FOR SHADOW WHITE... HIS THROAT was too sore to speak, but Gloworm held the words in his head. They'd not walked far from the remains of The Boxes, and they were not out of danger yet.

'Rest ... let me ... rest,' Dust stumbled in the soft green floor beside him.

Gloworm slowed and helped Dust lay down on the ground. The tabby tom was hurt. His long fur singed from the heat of the dancing lights, his paws sore from the hot roof and his eyes closed and stinging from the mist. But Gloworm knew that Dust's aching heart was a greater pain than all his injuries.

'Gloworm...?' Dust panted, 'You said ... you said Shadow White ... recognised Breeze's words...'

'Shhh, don't talk, rest your throat,' Gloworm licked his ear.

'But then you said ... they weren't her words ... they were mine. But how could Shadow White recognise my words ... if she can't see me?'

Gloworm felt his stomach tighten.

'If they were not Breeze's words, whose were they? Who *did* I see in my dreams?'

Gloworm's skin tingled as he rested his tail over Dust's back. And the air faltered as a touch shifted through it and padded around them like a slight, unseen shade. *He's right... There's something Shadow White didn't tell me...*

Rose

ROSE STRETCHED OUT A PAW AND dug her extended claws into Skeeal's severed head. Then she licked her lips and rocked it back and forth, making the big brazen bird hop back a step. 'Hill Cats and Runners?' she purred as she studied the bird's sleek black body, shifty rat like eyes and ragged wing, 'Very interesting. And why do you think I need their help?'

'Koselhe an spyrys, foul!' the Raven cawed as he fluttered his good wing, 'They are the cats who understand your intents. *They*, share your feelings.'

'And why should I trust you?'

'Because you can't do this alone. You don't even know how to live outside.'

Rose twitched her whiskers, 'And you want me to do *what* while I await your return?'

'Find the Ills of Rodents.'

'The Engel's Tale?' she sniffed, 'I already know that story.'

'Not the story. The truth. The unspoken, hidden truth. Find out what really happened to the Engel of Shady Ly.'

The **Ghosts of Shady Ly** Series

The Glaring
RATTERS (Book One)
CONKER'S SIGN (Novella)

Printed in Great Britain
by Amazon